THE MINUTE BOYS OF
THE MOHAWK VALLEY

JAMES OTIS

1st WORLD
LIBRARY
Literary Society

The Minute Boys of the Mohawk Valley

James Otis

© 1st World Library – Literary Society, 2004
PO Box 2211
Fairfield, IA 52556
www.1stworldlibrary.org
First Edition

LCCN: 2004195328

Softcover ISBN: 1-4218-0159-0
Hardcover ISBN: 1-4218-0059-4
eBook ISBN: 1-4218-0259-7

Purchase *"The Minute Boys of the Mohawk Valley"*
as a traditional bound book at:
www.1stWorldLibrary.org/purchase.asp?ISBN=1-4218-0159-0

1st World Library Literary Society is a nonprofit
organization dedicated to promoting literacy by:

- Creating a free internet library accessible from any computer worldwide.
- Hosting writing competitions and offering book publishing scholarships.

**Readers interested in supporting literacy
through sponsorship, donations or
membership please contact:
literacy@1stworldlibrary.org
Check us out at: www.1stworldlibrary.ORG
and start downloading free ebooks today.**

The Minute Boys of the Mohawk Valley
contributed by Tim, Ed & Rodney
in support of
1st World Library Literary Society

CONTENTS

Foreword

It seems not only proper, but necessary, that I should explain how the material for this story was obtained, and why it happens that I can thus set down exactly what Noel Campbell thought and did, during certain times while he was serving the patriot cause in the Mohawk Valley as few other boys could have done.

At some time in Noel's life - most likely after he was grown to be a man with children, and, perhaps, grandchildren of his own - he wrote many letters to relatives of his in Portsmouth, New Hampshire, wherein he told with considerable of detail that which he did during the War of the Revolution, and more particularly while he and his friends were fighting against that wily Indian sachem, Thayendanega. These letters, together with many others concerning the struggles of our people for independence, came into my keeping a long while ago, and from the lines written by Noel Campbell I have put together the following story after much the same fashion as he himself set it down.

When the work was begun I doubted if Thayendanega could have been frightened by a party of boys who were playing at being soldiers, and refused to make such statement until, quite by chance, I found the following in Lossing's "Field-Book of the Revolution":

"It was a sunny morning toward the close of May, when Brant and his warriors cautiously moved up to the brow of the lofty hill on the east side of the town (Cherry Valley) to reconnoitre the settlement at their feet. He was astonished and chagrined on seeing a fortification where he supposed all was weak and defenceless, and greater was his disappointment when quite a large and well-armed garrison appeared upon the esplanade in front of Colonel Campbell's house.

"These soldiers were not as formidable as the sachem supposed, for they were only half-grown boys, who, full of the martial spirit of the times, had formed themselves into companies, and, armed with wooden guns and swords, held regular drills each day.... He mistook the boys for full-grown soldiers, and, considering an attack dangerous, moved his party to a hiding-place in a deep ravine north of the village."

Then again I questioned if General Herkimer would have sent two boys as messengers, even though an old and experienced soldier went with them, when he must have had under his command many men grown who were thoroughly familiar with Indian warfare. As if to combat this doubt, I found the following statement by one who has written much concerning the struggles of the colonists for freedom:

"As soon as St. Leger's approach up Oneida Lake was known to General Herkimer, he summoned the militia of Tryon County to the succor of the garrison at Fort Schuyler. They rendezvoused at Fort Dayton, on the German Flats, and, on the day when the Indians encircled the fort, Herkimer was near Oriskany with more than eight hundred men, eager to face the enemy. He sent as messengers to Gansevoort two boys and a man, informing him of his approach, and requesting him to apprise him of the arrival of the couriers by discharging three guns in rapid succession, which he knew would be heard at Oriskany."

Having thus proven, at least to my own satisfaction, that so much of Noel's story was true, I set about verifying the other portions, and in no single instance did I find that he had drawn upon his imagination, therefore I resolved to write it down as the lad himself would have spoken, being able, because of the letters, to put myself very nearly in his place.

I would it had been possible to say more concerning Thayendanega and Sir John Johnson, for they played important parts in the making of Mohawk Valley history; but Noel's own account was of such length that I did not feel warranted in adding to it.

To the best of my knowledge and belief, the tale of the "Minute Boys of the Mohawk Valley" is no more than a narration of facts, as can be verified by reference to any of our standard histories of the beginnings of this nation.

If the reader can find in the reading one-half the pleasure I have had in interpreting Noel Campbell's odd speech, and smoothing down his too vigorous language, then will he be richly repaid for the perusal.

James Otis.

Chapter I.

Young Soldiers

It sounds like an unreasonable tale, or something after the style of a fairy-story, to say that a party of lads, drilling with wooden guns, were able, without being conscious of the fact, to frighten from his bloody work such a murderous, powerful sachem as Thayendanega, or Joseph Brant, to use his English name, but such is the undisputed fact.

It was the month of May in the year of our Lord 1777, when we of Cherry Valley, in the Province of New York, learned that this same Thayendanega, a pure-blooded Mohawk Indian, whose father was chief of the Onondaga nation, had come into the Mohawk Valley from Canada with a large force of Indians, who, under the wicked tutoring of Sir John Johnson, were ripe for mischief.

Col. Samuel Campbell, my uncle, was one of the leading patriots in that section of the province, and it was well known that the Johnsons, - Sir John and Guy, - the Butlers, Daniel Claus, and, in fact, all the Tories nearabout, would direct that the first blow be struck at Cherry Valley, in order that my uncle might be killed or made prisoner; therefore, at the time when we lads frightened Joseph Brant without our own knowledge, we were in daily fear of being set upon by our enemies.

Among the boys of the settlement I, Noel Campbell, was looked upon as a leader simply because my uncle was the most influential Whig in the vicinity, and my particular friend and comrade was Jacob Sitz, son of Peter, a lad who could easily best us all in trials of strength or of woodcraft.

We had heard of the Minute Men of Lexington and of the Green Mountains, and when the day came that all the able-bodied men of our valley banded themselves together for the protection of their homes against our neighbors, the Tories, who thirsted for patriot blood, we lads decided that we were old enough to do our share in whatsoever might be afoot.

Therefore it was that two score of us formed a league to help defend the settlements, and gave ourselves the name of "Minute Boys of the Mohawk Valley."

There was then living in Cherry Valley an old Prussian soldier by name Cornelius Braun, who, in his native land, had won the rank of sergeant; but, having grown too old for very active military duty, came to this country with the idea of making a home for himself. Sergeant Corney, as nearly every one called him, was not so old, however, but that he could strike a blow, and a heavy one, in his own defence, and when he learned what we lads proposed to do, he offered to drill us in the manual of arms.

We were not overly well equipped in the way of weapons, although it is safe to say that each of us had a firearm of some sort; but it seemed to give Sergeant

Corney the fidgets to see us carrying such a motley collection of guns, and he insisted on making a quantity of wooden muskets to be used in the drill, to the end that we might present a more soldierly appearance when lined up before him.

Therefore it was that, when we came each day on the green in front of my uncle's house to go through such manoeuvres as our instructor thought necessary, we had in our hands only those harmless wooden guns.

I was the captain of the company; Jacob Sitz acted as lieutenant, and all the others were privates. Sergeant Corney, as a matter of course, was the commander-in-chief.

On a certain day during the last week in May - the exact date I have forgotten - we were drilling as usual, with Sergeant Corney finding more fault than ever, when we frightened the famous Thayendanega away from an attack on the settlement, although, as I have said, we knew nothing about it until many months afterward.

It seems, as we learned later, that the villainous Brant had made all his plans for an attack upon Cherry Valley, and had secretly gained a position on the hill to the eastward of the place, counting on waiting there until nightfall, when he might surprise us; but, much to his astonishment, he saw what appeared from the distance to be a large body of well-equipped soldiers evidently making ready for serious work.

The scoundrelly redskin was not so brave that he was willing to make an attack where it seemed that the Whigs were prepared to receive him, and, like the cur that he was, he marched his force to a hiding-place in a deep ravine north of the settlement, near the road leading to the Mohawk River, about a mile and a half from where we were drilling.

Now hardly more than an hour before it is probable that the Indians got their first glimpse of us Minute Boys, Lieutenant Wormwood had arrived from Fort Plain with information to my uncle that a force of patriot soldiers was on the way to check Sir John's plans for killing all who did not quite agree with him in politics, and to request that arrangements be made to care for the men during such time as they might remain in that vicinity.

When, late in the afternoon, the lieutenant was ready to return to Fort Plain, Jacob's father, Peter Sitz, was ordered to accompany him as bearer of a message from my uncle to the leader of the patriot force, and the two men set off on horseback, we lads envying them because it seemed a fine thing to ride to and fro over the country summoning this man or that to his duty.

It was the last time Jacob saw his father until after many days had passed, and what happened to the two horsemen we could only guess when the lieutenant's lifeless body was found next day; but we learned the particulars later.

It seems that when the messengers arrived near Brant's hiding-place, being forced to pass by where the Indians were concealed in order to get to Fort Plain, they were hailed by some one in the thicket; but instead of replying, the men put spurs to their horses.

The savages in ambush fired a volley; Lieutenant

Wormwood was killed instantly, while Jacob's father was so seriously wounded that he fell from his horse, and, a few seconds later, found himself a prisoner among Brant's wolves.

When the tidings of this tragedy was brought into the settlement, Jacob was overwhelmed with grief, as might have been expected, and even my uncle had great difficulty in preventing the distressed lad from rushing into the wilderness with the poor hope that he might be able, single-handed, to effect his father's rescue.

He was only sixteen years of age - two months older than I; but within an hour after we knew beyond a peradventure that Peter Sitz was a prisoner, it seemed as if the lad had grown to be a man.

It was this first blow against the settlement of Cherry Valley by the murderous Brant, which brought us Minute Boys of the Mohawk Valley into active service, for from that day we saw as much of warfare as did our elders, and I am proud to be able to set down the fact that we performed good work, although we failed, as did the men of the settlement, in preventing it from being destroyed a year and a half later, while the fighting force of the population was absent.

The murder of Lieutenant Wormwood was sufficient evidence that the Tories and their savage allies were prepared to harry us, and within a very few minutes after the body of the officer had been brought in, the men made ready to defend their homes.

A council of war was immediately called, and while it was in session Sergeant Corney made a proposition which was like to take away the breath from those who looked upon us of the Minute Boys as mere children, for he said in the tone of one who knows whereof he speaks:

"I've been drillin' a force that can do good work in what's before us, if they're given a show, an' I'll answer for half a dozen of 'em, guaranteein' they'll show themselves to be men."

"Are you speaking of the lads?" my uncle asked in surprise, and the old man replied promptly;

"Ay, that I am, sir, an', unless all signs fail, there's never one of 'em who'll bring reproach upon the settlement."

"What is your plan, Sergeant Braun?" Master Dunlap, the preacher, asked, for so great did all believe the danger which threatened, that every man, whether able-bodied or crippled, had been summoned to the council.

"It ain't what you might rightly call a plan, sir," Sergeant Corney replied. "It's only an idee, brought out by the fact that from this time we've got to keep a close watch on what's happenin' in this 'ere valley, unless we're willin' to be murdered in our beds. There are boys enough in the settlement to do the scoutin', leavin' the elders to stand by for defence, an' I see no good reason why they shouldn't perform full share of military duty."

"Think you a lad like my nephew Noel could render any valuable assistance at such a time as this?" my uncle asked, with a smile, as if believing he had put an end to the old man's proposition, and my cheeks reddened with excitement and fear lest Sergeant Corney should allow himself to be backed down, as I listened intently for the answer.

It was not long in coming, and I could have kissed the old soldier for speaking as he did.

"Give me him an' Jacob Sitz, sir, an' I'll guarantee to follow Thayendanega an' his precious scoundrels till we know what deviltry they've got in mind."

"You shall have full charge of all the boys in the settlement, and we will see if you can make good your boast," my uncle, who held command of our fighting force, said after a brief pause, and in a twinkling Sergeant Corney left the building, beckoning us lads to follow, for our company had gathered with the men to learn what was to be done.

The old soldier did not need very much time in which to lay his plans; in fact, I believe he had mapped out the whole course before having spoken.

He divided our company into squads of six, not reckoning in either Jacob or me, and these he gave stations at different points within a mile of the settlement, cautioning every one to be on the alert, for now had come the time when it was possible for them to prove the value of the Minute Boys as soldiers. It was to be their duty, by night as well as by day, to keep careful watch lest the Indians creep up unawares, and I could well understand that never one would shirk his duty, since upon their vigilance depended the lives or liberty of all the dwellers nearabout.

Then, when some one asked why neither Jacob nor I had been assigned to sentinel duty, Sergeant Corney replied, gravely:

"I promised that with two lads I would follow Thayendanega's gang until we found out what the villains were about, as all of you well know, an' within the hour we three will set off."

Several of the more venturesome lads pleaded their right to take part in the dangerous service, claiming that they should not be left at home when it was possible to make names for themselves among men; but to all these entreaties Sergeant Corney made but one reply.

"It was Colonel Campbell himself who mentioned Noel's name, an' of a surety he has the right to say who shall go or stay. As for Jacob, have any of you a better claim than he to follow the murderers?"

This silenced the eager ones; but I would have been glad indeed had any member of the company shown that he had a better right to accompany the old soldier than I, for of a verity I was not itching to hug the heels of those savages who were doing the bidding of the Tories. However faint-hearted I might have been, however, I would have bitten the end of my tongue off before saying that which should show to my comrades that I was more than willing to remain behind, for if the captain of the Minute Boys showed the white feather, what might not have been excused in the rank and file?

Never one of all that company raised his voice against my right to follow Sergeant Corney, however, and I did my best at making it appear that the work in hand was exactly to my liking.

Even the dullest among us understood that we three might be absent from the settlement many days, and yet our preparations for the dangerous journey were most simple.

I ran home to acquaint my mother with what was afoot, and while she was trying to keep back her tears lest I might be unnerved for the duty to which I had been assigned, I armed myself with rifle and hunting-knife, making certain each weapon was in proper order.

From my father's store of powder and balls I took as much as could be conveniently carried, and this, with such small supply of corn bread and salt pork as filled my hunting-bag, made up an outfit for a journey from which it was reasonable to believe I might never return.

Mother did no more than kiss me again and again in silence, when I was ready to set off, and I now understand that she did not dare trust herself to speak, which, I venture to say, saved me from much sorrow.

On arriving at the green in front of my uncle's house, where we three had agreed to meet, I found that Jacob's outfit was even less than mine. In his grief because of his father's fate, he had thought only of his weapons and ammunition, and by the expression on his face I knew full well he would use them manfully if we came within striking distance of Lieutenant Wormwood's murderers.

Sergeant Corney was equipped in much the same

fashion as was I, and immediately after my arrival he said, impatiently:

"There is no reason why we should remain here many minutes, as if tryin' to show ourselves. It stands us in hand to strike the trail while it is yet warm, an' by dallyin' the people will come to believe our only idee is to look bigger'n we really are."

"It is for you to say when we shall set out," I replied, envying those of my comrades who stood near at hand to witness the departure, and the words had hardly more than been spoken before the old man started off at a smart pace in the direction of the thicket where Lieutenant Wormwood's body had so lately been found.

As a matter of course we two lads followed, I making every effort to keep pace with him, lest those who were watching should suspect I was not as brave as I looked, and in a few moments we had shut out from view the houses of the settlement.

We were not long in traversing the short distance which led us to the tree at the foot of which the officer came to his death; it can well be understood that we did not linger many seconds in that gruesome locality.

Jacob was eager to push on, hoping even against hope that it might be possible for him to rescue his father. Sergeant Corney had no desire to delay, lest we find it difficult to follow the trail later in the day, and there was no reason why I should care to remain in that place where were such evidences as might soon be found of our own fate.

Thayendanega had apparently given no heed as to whether his movements were known, for never an effort had been made to cover the trail, and we followed it as readily as if it had been blazed.

When we had travelled rapidly in silence for two full hours, Sergeant Corney called a halt, saying as he did so:

"There's no reason why we should push on so fast, an' much need to husband our strength, for no one can tell how soon we may be forced to take part in a hand-to-hand scrimmage. We'll have a bite to eat, for I didn't overload my stomach this mornin', an' be all the better for a breathin'-spell."

"We didn't come out to spend our time in eatin'," Jacob said, moodily, and I understood full well what was in his mind. "We can loiter when we have come up with the savages."

"It ain't in the plan that we shall get too close at their heels," Sergeant Corney replied, as he drew from his hunting-bag a generous supply of corn bread, and laid a good half of it in front of my comrade.

"It may not be in your plan, but it is in mine," Jacob said, sharply, giving no heed to the food. "We shall be doin' our duty by those we have left behind if we hug as close to the villains as is possible, while there's no chance I can serve my father by hangin' back at a coward's distance."

"An' it's in your mind, lad, that we might do him a good turn?" Sergeant Corney said, as if talking to himself.

"Why not? It wouldn't be the first time the murderin' redskins had lost a prisoner."

"True for you, lad, an' I know full well how you're feelin'; but the question is whether we can hope for anythin' while there's sich a crowd of 'em?"

"I'm not expectin' you an' Noel will run your heads into too much danger," Jacob said, passionately. "I know you would help father if the chance came your way; but it's my duty to take every risk, an' I count on doin' so even though we part company within the hour! Do you suppose I can loiter at a safe distance from the painted devils when my father is expectin' to see some sign that I'm doin' all I may to help him?"

"I question if Peter Sitz expects that any one from Cherry Valley will follow Thayendanega's snakes. He knows their strength, an' is man enough to understand what might be the price of an attempt to rescue him."

Although Sergeant Corney spoke calmly, as if he had no vital interest in the matter, I knew him well enough to feel certain he was even then trying to settle in his own mind how a rescue might be effected; but Jacob was so blinded by his grief that at the moment I believe he really thought we would let him push ahead alone, therefore I said in as hearty a tone as was possible:

"You should know, Jacob, that both of us stand ready to do all men may to aid your father, an' you may be certain we'll not let you go on alone; but just now Sergeant Corney must be our leader, since he knows better than you an' I put together what ought to be done."

"But will he do his best?" Jacob cried, in a passion. "Will he help me, or does he think the work is done when we have learned where Joseph Brant has gone on his work of bloodshed?"

I waited for the old soldier to make reply to this demand, and he hesitated so long that I began to fear I had been mistaken as to that which I had supposed was in his mind. At last, when it seemed as if Jacob could no longer restrain his impatience, Sergeant Corney said, speaking slowly, as if weighing well each word:

"I will do my best, heedin' not my own safety, givin' no thought to the labor or difficulties, if it so be you lads are minded to do as I shall say, without questionin' when it seems as if I might be goin' wrong - "

I would have interrupted him with an assurance that we were willing to
serve him faithfully; but he checked me with a gesture, and added:

"As Peter Sitz would were he in my place, so will I. He was my friend; I know if it was a question of savin' the lives of those at Cherry Valley, or turnin' his back on me, what he would do, an' even so shall I."

"Meanin' what?" Jacob demanded, fiercely.

"Meanin' that while we can do our duty by those who sent us, we will strain every nerve in his behalf; but if it should so chance that their safety depended upon us, we would give service to the greatest number."

Jacob stared as if not understanding what the old man had said, and I made haste to add:

"He means that if, while followin' Brant with the hope of aidin' your father, we found out that danger threatened the settlement, it would be our duty to warn them rather than hold on for him."

The old soldier nodded in token that I had but given different words to his idea, and Jacob replied in a tone of satisfaction:

"I can ask for nothin' more. If it so happens that you must turn back, I can keep on, for two would aid the settlement as much as three."

"Ay, lad, you shall then do as seems best to you," Sergeant Corney said, solemnly, and thus it was settled that, while it did not interfere with our duty as Minute Boys of the Mohawk Valley, all our efforts should be for the relief of the unfortunate prisoner, although at the time I had little hope the savages would allow him to live many days.

Having thus pledged himself to Jacob, Sergeant Corney showed no further disposition to "husband his strength," but led us on the march once more, and this time at a pace which we lads found difficult to maintain without actually running.

Now it is not my purpose to set down all we did and said during this long chase. It would be of no interest to a stranger, since one hour was much like another until we were come near to the Indian town of Oghkwaga, where Brant usually made his headquarters while bent on such cruel work as that of harrying the settlers who favored the rebellion against the king, and it is not necessary I should write down here the well-known fact that Thayendanega was in the pay of the British.

It seemed much as if the Indians had no care as to whether they were being followed, for, instead of sending back scouts along the trail, as Brant almost always did, the party remained in a body, and even when we were so close on them as to lie down within view of their camp-fires at night, we never saw one of the painted villains who appeared curious to know if any person was in the rear.

We were within a day's march of the Indian town, and had lain down in a thicket of spruce bushes after having looked in vain for some signs of a prisoner, as we had done during each of the four days while we were directly behind the band and at no time more than two miles distant.

Jacob's face was wrinkled, or so it seemed to me, with lines drawn by sorrow because we had not succeeded in getting a glimpse of his father, and it was evident that the lad was beginning to fear, as did I, that the savages, finding a prisoner too troublesome, had tortured him to death; for if Master Sitz was yet alive and in the keeping of Brant's followers, why had we not got a glimpse of him?

"There is no reason why you should grieve so deeply, lad," Sergeant Corney said, as if he could read the boy's thoughts. "I'll answer for it that your father is as much alive as we are."

"How can you be certain of that?" Jacob asked, moodily.

"We have seen every one of their camps, eh?"

"Of course," Jacob replied, impatiently.

"An' have you noted any sign of a prisoner's havin' been tortured - meanin' a half-burned tree, a pile of rocks near the fire, or sich other like thing?"

Jacob shook his head; he could not bring himself to speak calmly of such a possibility.

"No, you haven't, an' we know without bein' told that when sich devils as follow Joe Brant get a prisoner in their clutches, they never kill him without torture. Now, 'cordin' to my way of thinkin', we can count to a certainty that he's alive."

"Then why haven't we come across him?" Jacob demanded, fiercely. "This is the fourth time we've had their camp in full view, an' if he was with 'em we ought to have seen somethin' of him."

"I allow you're right, lad, an' that's why I've come to believe that he's been sent on ahead to the village."

"Then I must be movin'!" Jacob cried, springing suddenly to his feet. "I should have had sense enough to guess that before!" And he made as if he would leave us; but Sergeant Corney pulled him back by the coat-sleeve.

"Wait a bit. It was on my tongue's end to propose somethin' of the same kind; but we can't afford to take the chances of makin' a move till yonder nest of snakes has settled down for the night. An hour from now, an' we'll all pull out."

Jacob could not well have made complaint after this,

and he settled down with his back against a tree to wait with so much of patience as he could summon, until the old soldier should give the word.

It surprised me that Jacob was not utterly cast down by the possibility that his father had already been carried to the Indian village, for once there we could not hope to effect a rescue; but since this thought had, apparently, never come into his mind, it was not for me to add to his distress by suggesting it.

Well, we remained in the thicket until the red villains had quieted down for the night, and then Sergeant Corney led us toward the south, that we might make a long circle around the encampment, when would come the most dangerous portion of our task.

Thus far we had done as Jacob would have us, and at the same time performed our full duty as Minute Boys, for our task was to learn what Brant counted on doing, and as to that we could not be certain until he was in the village.

But now that the old soldier was leading us around the encampment to the end that we might gain a position between Brant's force and those at Oghkwaga, I said to myself, with many an inward shudder, that we were like to join Jacob's father after a different fashion than we had counted on.

It was as if Sergeant Corney had no fear as to what might happen, for he plunged into the gloom of the forest like a man who walks among friends, and Jacob followed carelessly, all his thoughts on the possible whereabouts of the prisoner he was so eager to see.

Apparently I was the only member of the party who gave heed to his steps, and so timid had I become through looking into the future for danger, that it was only with difficulty I repressed a cry of alarm when Sergeant Corney came to a sudden halt, as if he had stumbled upon an enemy.

Jacob, wrapped in his own gloomy thoughts, halted without showing signs of curiosity or surprise; but I pressed forward eagerly until standing close behind the old soldier, and then I understood full well why he had stopped.

Not thirty paces from where we remained hidden in the thicket, it was possible to see the gleam of a camp-fire, and to hear the faint hum of voices, as if a large party was near at hand.

After vainly trying to peer through the foliage, Sergeant Corney moved cautiously forward two or three paces, and, as a matter of course, I followed close at his heels, far enough to see the reflection of four or five other fires, as if those around them had no fear of being discovered.

"They must be Britishers!" I whispered, and Sergeant Corney gripped my hand as if to say that he was of the same idea.

It was our duty, however, to know exactly who it was encamped so near Brant's village, and, after telling Jacob in a whisper of what we had seen, the old soldier made his way swiftly through the thicket, my comrade and I copying his every movement.

Then, when I had decided that we were dangerously

near a large force of the king's soldiers who had come to join Thayendanega in his murderous work, Sergeant Corney called out in a loud tone:

"In the camp! Here come friends who were like to have run over you!"

In a twinkling the command was aroused, and before I had fully gathered my wits, which had been scattered by the old soldier's hail, I found myself in the midst of a large body of men, many of whom I had seen in my uncle's home at Cherry Valley.

And now, that I may not dwell too long on a commonplace story when I have so much of adventure to relate, let me say that we had stumbled on upwards of three hundred men belonging to the patriot army, who, under command of General Herkimer, were bent on paying a friendly visit to the Indian village.

As we soon learned, General Herkimer, having been intimately acquainted with Brant, hoped by an interview to persuade the sachem to join the patriots, or at least to remain neutral, and to such end had invited the chief to meet him at Unadilla for a powwow. At the same time that General Herkimer had set out to find Brant, Colonel Van Schaick, with one hundred and fifty men, went to Cherry Valley, even as poor Lieutenant Wormwood had announced, and the remainder of the American force in the vicinity was encamped at the proposed rendezvous lest the treacherous chief accept the invitation simply in order to work mischief.

"We'll march with this company," Sergeant Corney said, in a tone of satisfaction, "an' it will be possible to have a look at the village without runnin' too many chances of losin' our hair."

And thus it seemed to me that all our troubles were over, for I doubted not but that General Herkimer could induce the savages to give up their prisoner, and we would soon be on our way home with Peter Sitz as a companion; but, instead, we were just at the beginning of our difficulties.

James Otis

Chapter II.

The Powwow

When we had learned all that our acquaintances among the command could tell us, Jacob insisted that Sergeant Corney see General Herkimer without delay, in order to learn if that officer would so far interest himself in the fate of Peter Sitz as to make inquiries of Thayendanega regarding him, in case the opportunity offered.

At first the old soldier was not inclined to ask for an interview with the commander, claiming that his own rank was not sufficiently high to warrant his making such a request; but those of the force who were listening to our conversation insisted that the general was not a stickler for rank, and would receive a private soldier with as much consideration as the commander of a brigade.

Therefore it was that, after being alternately urged and entreated for half an hour, Sergeant Corney agreed to do as Jacob desired, and straightway set about seeking the leader, which was no difficult task, since his camp was a lean-to of fir boughs standing hardly more than fifty feet from where we were sitting.

After the old man had left us, one of the soldiers asked if we had seen any Tories with Thayendanega's band,

and I told him that, so far as I had been able to learn, the only white man among them was Peter Sitz, although we had not been so fortunate as to see him.

"Why did you want to know?" Jacob asked, with mild curiosity, and the man replied:

"It struck me that if any of the Mohawk Valley Tories were with Brant, General Herkimer would stand little chance of doing anything to aid the prisoner."

"Why do you say that the general would hardly be able to do anythin' of the kind?" I asked. "Surely to one so high in command Brant would listen, when he might refuse even to speak with one of less rank."

"The thought was not in my mind that Thayendanega himself would be opposed to our commander; but if you know what was done last year, it is easy to understand my meaning."

To me the soldier was speaking in riddles, and I asked for an explanation, whereupon he told us that more than a year ago, when the Johnsons had collected a large force of men nearabout Johnson Hall, and among them fully three hundred well-drilled Scotch soldiers, General Schuyler marched with nearly three thousand militia to within four miles of the settlement, demanding that Sir John surrender all arms, ammunition, and warlike stores in his possession, together with the weapons and military accoutrements then held by the Tories and Indians under his command. In addition to which, the baronet was required to give his parole of honor that he would not attempt any act against the patriot cause.

Sir John was at first furious because such a demand had been made; but, badly frightened by General Schuyler's display of force, he finally consented, since he could do nothing better, and the colonists marched to Johnson Hall, where the surrender was made.

Then it was that General Herkimer was detailed to disarm the Tories in the valley, and while carrying out such orders quite naturally made enemies of the majority of them.

Therefore it was, according to the belief of the soldier, that General Herkimer would have little or no weight with Brant so far as rescuing Peter Sitz was concerned, if there chanced at the moment to be Tories near at hand to whisper in his ear.

Just now it seems necessary for me to set down that which happened after Sir John Johnson's surrender, if so it could be called, to General Schuyler, and I can best do it by copying that which I have seen in a printed sheet concerning our troubles in the Mohawk Valley:

"It soon afterward became evident that what Sir John had promised, when constrained by fear, would not be performed when the cause of that fear was removed. He violated his parole of honor, and the Highlanders began to be as bold as ever in their oppressions of the Whigs. Congress thought it dangerous to allow Johnson his liberty, and directed Schuyler to seize his person, and to proceed vigorously against the Highlanders in his vicinity. Colonel Dayton was entrusted with the command of the expedition for the purpose, and in May (1776) he proceeded to Johnstown. The baronet had friends among the Loyalists in Albany, by whom he was timely informed of the intentions of Congress. Hastily collecting a large number of Scotchmen and other Tories, he fled to the woods by the way of the Sacandaga, where it is supposed they were met by Indians sent from Canada to escort them thither, for a certain time afterward, in one of his speeches, Thayendanega said: 'We went in a body to the town then in possession of the enemy, and rescued Sir John Johnson, bringing him fearlessly through the streets.'

"Amid perils and hardships of every kind the baronet and his companions traversed the wilderness between the headwaters of the Hudson and the St. Lawrence, and after nineteen days' wanderings arrived at Montreal. Sir John was immediately commissioned a colonel in the British service; he raised two battalions of Loyalists called the Johnson Greens, and declared himself the bitterest and most implacable enemy of the Americans."

Now it must be borne in mind that from information which we had received, there was every reason to believe Brant had come to place himself and his following under Sir John's command, and that before many days were passed we might expect the Mohawk Valley would be overflowed by all the Tories who had previously fled to Canada. Thus it can be understood that there would be such bloodshed and deeds of violence as had never before been known in the Province of New York.

With this in mind, one can better understand why Sergeant Corney made the reservation which he did when promising Jacob he would do all within his power, up to a certain point, to aid in the rescue of his father.

The old soldier returned from his interview with General Herkimer at about the same time our newly made friend finished his recital of what had been done in and around Johnson Hall, and, observing the look of satisfaction on the sergeant's face, I understood, even before he spoke, that his mission had been, at least in a certain degree, successful.

"It is all right, lads," he said, seating himself by my side. "The general will do what he can; but whether that be much or little depends upon the way in which Thayendanega receives him."

"Are we to march with this command to the village?" Jacob asked.

"Ay, an' remain with it so long as suits our purpose."

It seemed to me we could not in reason ask for anything more; that we were now in the best possible position to learn what Brant's purpose was, and at the same time to aid Peter Sitz, therefore I laid down to rest, contented in mind as I was wearied in body; but poor Jacob, feeling as if he might in some way wrong his father by seeking repose, paced to and fro near the camp-fire until my eyes were closed in slumber.

The soldiers were astir at an early hour next morning; but before the column could be set in motion an Indian strode gravely into the encampment waving a bit of white cloth, and, on being questioned by the sentinels, announced himself as a messenger sent by Thayen-danega with words to General Herkimer.

The fact of his early arrival was sufficient to prove that the wily sachem had known of the movements of the soldiers for a certain length of time, - perhaps several days, - and this might explain why his march from Cherry Valley had been so steady and swift.

It goes without saying that every man in the encampment was eager to know why this painted messenger had come, and I confess to crowding my way among the foremost of the curious in order to hear, if possible, all that was said.

The Indian stood like a statue before the shelter of fir boughs, looking neither to the right nor the left until General Herkimer appeared and said to him, questioningly:

"You have come from Captain Brant?"

It is hardly necessary for me to set it down that, some time before this, Thayendanega had been given a commission in the British service.

The messenger nodded gravely, and, after pausing until one might have counted ten, said:

"Thayendanega asks why so many white soldiers are encamped near his village?"

"I have come to see and talk with my brother, Captain Brant," General Herkimer replied, with the same stiff manner as that assumed by the messenger.

"And do all these men want to talk with the chief, too?"

"They have come to bear me company; they are my followers, as Captain Brant has his."

"And do they also call Thayendanega 'brother'?"

"Ay, and they hope he *is* a brother to them."

The Indian turned slowly in what I thought a most offensive manner, as he looked around at the faces of those who completely encircled him, and then would have moved away, but that General Herkimer asked:

"Is Captain Brant in his village?"

"He will tell his white brother where he may be found, after I can run five miles."

"Meaning that you will go from me to him, and return?" the general asked; but it was as if the Indian did not hear the question, for he said, in a tone which to me was one of menace:

"You will come no nearer Oghkwaga until Thayendanega shall give his permission."

Having said this, he turned slowly about until facing the direction where I knew Brant and his followers encamped the night previous, when he stalked slowly away, giving no more heed to those who pressed closely to him than if he was the only person in that vast wilderness.

To Jacob this enforced halt, at a time when he believed it was vitally necessary he should be making search for his father, was most painful, and despite all Sergeant Corney and I could say or do to relieve his distress of mind, the poor lad paced to and fro, as I was told he had during the long hours of the night, in a nervous condition pitiable to behold.

When half an hour or more had passed, the old soldier said to me, in a more kindly tone than I had ever suspected he could use:

"The lad is eatin' his heart out, an' all to no purpose. Can't you quiet him a bit, Noel?"

"I have said all within my power, an' he turns a deaf ear," I replied, sadly.

"Then I shall try my fist at it," and the old man went up to my comrade, taking him gently by the hand, and leading him into the thicket just beyond view of the encampment.

There the two seemingly conversed for a long time, and I was left comparatively alone, until the soldier who had told us of General Herkimer's doings nearabout Johnson Hall, came up.

Eager to get some idea of what the commander might be able to do with this Joseph Brant, whose name stood in my mind for all that was horrible in the way of cruelty, I asked how it was that General Herkimer could hope to influence one who was such a great enemy to the Whigs of the Mohawk Valley, and, in fact, to all white men save those who wore the uniform of the British king.

He told me that at one time, before Thayendanega had become so powerful a sachem, he and General Herkimer were near neighbors, and quite intimate friends.

It seems, from the story this soldier told me, that Sir William Johnson, Sir John's father, sent the Indian boy to school, and after he had received a good education gave him employment as secretary. During three years this now bloodthirsty savage acted as missionary interpreter, and it was said he did very much for the religious instruction of his tribe. When the colonists revolted against the oppressive rule of the king, Brant took the same side as did his patron, and having received a commission - some have said it was a captaincy, and others that it was a colonelcy - he became one of the most vengeful enemies we, who were devoted to the cause, had.

Now, because of the past, General Herkimer hoped to turn him aside from his chosen path when he was just coming into power, and, boy though I was, it seemed to me a well-nigh hopeless task - one which had better never have been attempted, since in case of failure it would show to Thayendanega that the Whigs of the valley believed him an enemy who should be placated rather than resisted.

However, that was none of my affairs, and I was not so forward as to air my views then when I was only a hanger-on by the sufferance of the commander.

In two hours from the time he left our camp, the Indian messenger returned, still carrying the bit of white cloth, and came among us as if expecting we would bow before him.

He was barely civil when General Herkimer advanced to receive him, and, without greeting the commander, he pointed toward a clearing in the wilderness half a mile or more away, as he said:

"There will Thayendanega meet his brother, the white

chief, and without firearms."

"To-day?" General Herkimer asked.

"When the next sun is three hours old Thayendanega will come with forty of his people, and his white brother will bring no more than that number."

"It is well," General Herkimer replied, and it pleased me that he held himself yet more stiffly than did the messenger. "Say to my brother, Captain Brant, that we also will come without arms, and he and I shall meet as we met years ago, when there was no need to light the pipe of peace, because neither of us had listened to the songs of wicked men."

The Indian stalked away as before, and when he was gone Jacob, who, with Sergeant Corney, had come up to hear what was being said, laid his hand on my shoulder affectionately.

"I am goin' to be more of a man, Noel, havin' come to understand that nothin' can be gained by ill-temper or impatience; but it is hard to remain here idle when perhaps my father may at this moment be suffering torture."

"If it was some one else's father, Jacob, you would say that there was no danger anything of the kind would happen while Brant is makin' ready for the interview with General Herkimer. Until that has come to an end your father is safe, an' perhaps when the powwow is over we shall have him with us."

"So Sergeant Corney has been tryin' to make me believe, an' it must be true."

During the remainder of the day Jacob did not give words to the sorrow which was in his heart, and perhaps it would have been wiser had he not tried to hold his peace, for, strive as he might, again and again I could see how earnestly he was struggling to remain silent.

It is useless for me to attempt to set down all that we did or said while awaiting Thayendanega's pleasure. As a matter of course we indulged in much speculation regarding the outcome of the matter, and discussed at great length the possibility of General Herkimer's being able, even if he failed in other desired directions, to set free the prisoner whom Joseph Brant doubtless intended should suffer death at the stake.

We passed the time as best we might, many of us finding it quite as difficult as did Jacob to restrain our impatience, and not a few openly declaring their belief that Brant was holding us idle simply that he might the better carry out some murderous scheme.

As a matter of fact, it did seem to me no more than prudent General Herkimer should send out scouts to discover what the Indians were doing, and it was whispered about the encampment that one of his officers had suggested that such a precaution be taken; but the commander flatly refused, stating as his reason that it might prove fatal to all his hopes if the sachem should learn he was in any way suspicious because of the delay.

"We must take our chances, remaining here idle and ignorant of what they may be doing, or it were better we faced about on the homeward march at once," the general was reported to have said, and after that he would have been a bold man indeed who suggested any other course.

Well, the day passed, and so did the night, as all days and nights will whether one possesses his soul with patience or frets against that which he cannot remedy, and General Herkimer stood in the opening of his fir camp gazing at the men as if trying to decide whom he should take with him to the powwow, when Jacob stepped out in full view in order to attract the commander's attention.

I knew that he made this move with the hope of being numbered among those who would leave camp to go to the rendezvous; but at the same moment I feared lest the general might be displeased because of his forwardness.

Anything can be forgiven in a lad who burns with the desire to aid his father, however, and General Herkimer beckoned for my comrade to approach.

I could not hear what was said during the brief conversation; but it was easy to guess the purport when Jacob came toward me with sparkling eyes.

"We have the general's permission to go with him to meet Brant," he cried, and I asked with, perhaps, just a tinge of jealousy:

"Meanin' you an' Sergeant Corney, eh?"

"The three of us, so the general said."

"Why did he happen to count me in?"

"He asked how many had come with Sergeant Corney, an' when I told him, he said that all three of us could go with the detachment."

As a matter of course we went, taking our stations at the head of the column just behind the commander, and when the word to march had been given I began to regret having thus been favored, for never one of us carried a weapon of any kind, and if Brant was in the humor he could have us all butchered before those whom we had left behind would get an inkling of what was going on.

When we had come to the edge of the clearing which had been pointed out by the ill-mannered messenger, our further advance was stopped by two Indians who were rigged out in all the bravery of feathers, beads, and robes, - nothing missing in their toilet save the war-paint, - and told to remain at that spot until the sachem and his party arrived.

It was treating General Herkimer rather shabbily, so I thought, to force him to wait like a child until the master was ready to put in an appearance; but there was nothing else to be done, and we squatted on the ferns and rocks a full half-hour before the man who was soon to be the great sachem of the Six Nations was pleased to show himself.

Thayendanega had gotten himself up especially for the occasion, and a more gorgeous redskin I never saw.

He had forty or more savages with him, and strutted on at their head as if he was a king, and we who had been waiting so long no more than the dirt beneath his feet.

Then suddenly, as if until that moment he hadn't the slightest idea General Herkimer was anywhere in the vicinity, he sent one of his company to our commander, he himself continuing to move on until he stood in the very centre of the clearing. His followers ranged themselves behind him in a half-circle, remaining ten or twelve feet in the rear, and when the general went to meet his high mightiness our people took up their stations much as had the savages, thus completely surrounding the two leaders.

Jacob and I stood where we could see all that was taking place, and hear a portion of what was said.

Thayendanega began with compliments, and after General Herkimer had replied in much the same strain, the murdering villain asked bluntly why he had come.

"To meet my old neighbor and friend," General Herkimer replied, whereupon Brant asked:

"And have all those behind you come on a friendly visit, too? Do they also want to see the poor Indian? It is very kind."

The general changed the subject of the conversation by speaking of the past, and wound up by hinting that it might be to Thayendanega's advantage to take sides with the colonists against the king; but he must soon have seen that he was not making much headway, for the sachem began to show signs of anger, and, after quite a long confab, said sharply:

"We are with the king, as were our fathers before us. The king's belts are yet held by us, and we cannot break faith. You are resolute now in your rebellion; but before many days the king's soldiers will humble you to the dust."

When this had been said, Colonel Cox, who was one of the general's party, cried sharply, and heeding not the fact that his voice was raised high:

"We did not come here to listen to threats, and if we are humbled it will not be by such as those who follow Joseph Brant!"

Unfortunately every Indian in the clearing heard the words distinctly, and in a twinkling the savages were running to and fro, giving vent to shrill war-whoops, while they called for those at the main encampment to bring their weapons.

The colonel's incautious words were as a lighted match to gunpowder, and for the instant I firmly believed we would pay for his indiscretion with our lives.

Chapter III.

Disappointment

During this time of confusion, when the life of every white man in the clearing was literally trembling in the balance, General Herkimer passed the word from one to another that we were all to stand firm without show of fear, and at the same time making no move which might be construed as in enmity.

It was no easy matter to remain silent and motionless while the painted villains were running to and fro making a hideous outcry, and, as we knew full well, aching to strike us down.

I know that, as for myself, I trembled like a leaf upon an aspen-tree - so violently that at times I feared the howling wretches would see the quivering of my limbs, and understand that already was I getting a foretaste of the death which they would have dealt out but for the restraining presence of Thayendanega.

It was but natural I should look toward Sergeant Corney, and surely if there was one man in that clearing who obeyed General Herkimer's command, it was he! A graven image could not have been more stolid; one would have said that the uproar everywhere around was as the rippling of waters to him, and the

Indians of less consequence than the dancing shafts of sunlight flickering amid the leaves when they are stirred by the morning breeze.

I question if Jacob realized anything of what was going on around him. All his thoughts were centred upon the one idea of rescuing his father while there was yet time, and the lad waited eagerly for the conference between the leaders regarding the prisoner to be begun, heeding the remainder of the howling gang hardly more than did Sergeant Corney.

Colonel Cox, the cause of all this disturbance, was even more terrified than I, as could be told by the expression on his face, and the finger-nails pressed deeply into the palms of his hands that he might control himself in obedience to orders, while as for the others, I know not how they deported themselves.

At that instant my world was of small dimensions, consisting of only so much carth as that impassive red man and the open-hearted, honest patriot officer stood upon.

Like bees the angry Indians swarmed to and fro between the encampment and our place of meeting, until all were armed with rifles, and it needed but the lightest word to convert that sunlit clearing into a theatre of the bloodiest deed in the history of the tribe whose wildest delight was the shedding of blood.

Not until his followers were in such a frenzied condition that it seemed impossible another's will could restrain them, did Thayendanega speak, and then in a few words of the Indian language, uttered in so low a tone that I could not distinguish a single syllable, he calmed the tempest on the instant, until those who had been howling for our lives became like lambs.

When all was hushed once more, the sachem said to General Herkimer, speaking calmly, almost indifferently:

"The war-path has been opened across the country as far as Esopus, and the Tories of Ulster and Orange will join with the braves of Thayendanega's tribe to quell this revolt against the king, who is their father."

Now it was that General Herkimer spoke earnestly, pleadingly.

"Do not allow so weighty a question to be settled without further consideration, Captain Brant. Why should not you and I discuss it calmly, as we have in the olden days many a matter which was not so grave?"

"You have seen how well inclined my young men are toward anything of that kind," Brant said, with a cruel smile. "Were I to say at this moment that we would consider the matter in council, it might not be possible even for me to restrain them, because their decision has already been made. The hatchet is raised!"

"But surely you and I, Captain Brant, may talk of it among ourselves?"

"Yes, that can be done," Thayendanega replied, indifferently, "and if it gives you pleasure to indulge in what can be of no profit, we will meet here again to-morrow morning; but now it were wiser my young men went back to the encampment."

Then the sachem turned as if to move away, and General Herkimer, remembering what he had promised Sergeant Corney and Jacob, said, in a friendly tone:

"Wait one moment, Captain Brant. I would make inquiries concerning a prisoner from Cherry Valley, whom it is said your people hold at this moment."

"I know of no prisoner in our encampment," Brant replied, stiffly.

"Let us not quibble on words, captain. Whether he be in your camp here, or at Oghkwaga, makes no difference. I ask if you will tell me concerning one Peter Sitz, who, but a few days since, when Lieutenant Wormwood of the American army was killed in ambush, your people made a prisoner?"

"My young men may be able to tell you somewhat concerning him. I will ask them."

"And will you, as a favor to a neighbor and an old friend, do whatsoever you may toward releasing the unfortunate man?" General Herkimer insisted.

"I will ask my young men," was all the reply Brant would make, and then the powwow was brought to a sudden close as the sachem stalked toward the encampment, followed by all his people, and we of General Herkimer's party were left alone in the clearing.

Now the word was given that we rejoin the main body quietly, and in double file, with no man straying from the ranks; but Sergeant Corney and I led Jacob between us, for the lad was well-nigh frantic with grief because no satisfaction concerning his father had been obtained from Thayendanega.

We two said all we could in order to cheer the sorrowing lad, and that all was little. Neither he, nor we, nor General Herkimer himself, could effect anything whatsoever, save through the favor of the Mohawk sachem, and that was withheld for at least four and twenty hours, with the chances that at the expiration of such time we would receive nothing better from the wily savage than a refusal to answer any questions.

I shall not attempt to set down very much concerning this long time of waiting for the second powwow, when it was doubtful if we would be allowed to leave the encampment without a bloody battle.

Even General Herkimer had lost all hope of being able to dissuade Joseph Brant from the course he had already marked out for himself, and shared with his men the suspicion that before the second interview was come to an end we would be the victims of the sachem's treachery. This last we knew from the information which was whispered about the encampment, to the effect that the general had charged one of the soldiers - a man by the name of Wagner - with the duty of selecting two others, that the three might stand directly behind him at the next meeting with the Indians, and at the first show of hostilities shoot down Brant and the two sachems next him in authority.

Wagner selected George and Abraham Herkimer, nephews of the general, and these three were prepared to face the most cruel of deaths, for certain it was that if they were obliged to make an attack upon the

Mohawk chieftain, every Indian under his command would strive most earnestly to take them prisoners in order that they be made to suffer death by torture.

How the day passed I hardly know. The soldiers talked among themselves in whispers, as men do in the presence of death. No one strayed beyond the limits of the encampment; but all waited in painful suspense for that hour to come when it should be known whether Joseph Brant was of the mind that we might return to our homes for the time being, or if he sought immediately to compass our death through treachery.

Sergeant Corney and I spent our time in trying to soothe Jacob, who alternately reproached himself for remaining idle at the moment when he should be straining every nerve to aid his father, and relapsing into moody silence, which to me was far worse than the angry words.

When another day had come we again marched into the clearing, the three who had been selected for the dangerous duty of protecting our leader in case of an outbreak, keeping close by his side.

As I look back now upon what was afterward done throughout the length and breadth of that peaceful valley of ours, I regret most sincerely that those young men did not violate the unwritten laws and usages which the Indians themselves were ever ready to cast aside when it suited their purpose, and kill the blood-thirsty Brant whether his men showed signs of enmity or not.

On this occasion we had not long to wait.

Gathering in a semicircle behind General Herkimer as before, we were hardly in position when Thayendanega, clad in all the bravery of his savage garb, and, what was most ominous, bedecked in war-paint, strode into the enclosure, followed by such members of his party as had accompanied him the day previous.

He did not wait for greetings, but began boastfully, while his painted fiends were yet taking their places, by saying, abruptly:

"I have five hundred warriors with me, armed and ready for battle. You are in my power; but as we have been friends and neighbors, I will not take advantage of you."

Then he made a gesture with his hand, and on the instant there burst from amid the foliage a seemingly endless number of savages, all painted for battle, who, coming down swiftly upon us as if to make an attack, uttered wild war-whoops as they discharged their rifles in the air.

It was as hideous and terrifying a sight as I ever witnessed, and that our little company stood its ground is much to the credit of every man among us.

Thayendanega remained half-turned from General Herkimer, and within two feet of the three men whose duty it was to shoot him with the rifles they had concealed under their blankets in case an absolute attack was made, and there watched the antics of his painted crew until perhaps five minutes had passed, when the savages sank down upon the ground as if exhausted, looking like so many images of demons.

What Thayendanega said when the uproar was thus stilled, I cannot rightly set down, for my brain was in such a whirl, and fear so strong in my heart, as to prevent me from taking due heed of all that was passing - I realized only that death was literally staring us in the face.

As Sergeant Corney afterward told me, Brant advised General Herkimer to go home, thanked him for having come to pay the visit, and said that at some near day he might return the compliment.

"But the prisoner?" General Herkimer cried, when the sachem would have stalked away with a great assumption of dignity.

"My young men will make no reply to my questions," Brant answered, unblushingly, although he must have known beyond a peradventure that we understood full well he was lying.

"Is Peter Sitz yet alive?" General Herkimer asked, sternly.

"There has been no prisoner put to death by my people since they left Cherry Valley," Thayendanega replied, as if irritated by the general's persistence, and, making another gesture with his hand, he sent back into the cover of the forest all his motley crew.

Then he also walked away, as if fearing our commander would detain him with yet further questions, and the powwow, to take part in which three hundred men had marched so many miles, was come to an end without other result than the knowledge that the Mohawk chief would harry us of the valley to the best of his wicked powers.

Thayendanega had hardly gained the shelter of the thicket before black clouds overspread the heavens, and it seemed as if in a twinkling the rain came down in torrents; sharp flashes of lightning zigzagged across the ominous-looking sky, and more than one around me declared it was a portent, a sign, a token of the tempest which was about to break upon our peaceful homes.

When we were in camp once more, and General Herkimer was making his preparations to set off on the return march, Jacob declared that he alone, if we did not accompany him, would go into the Indian village, and there make inquiries for his father.

Sergeant Corney and I spent a long hour persuading the lad of his folly, for after the powwow had come to such an abrupt end there was no question whatsoever but that Thayendanega would kill or make prisoner of every white man who crossed his path.

For a time it was absolutely necessary that we two hold Jacob by force to prevent him from leaving us, and then gradually the boy came to understand that for his father's life he could only hope in the mercy of God, since even had General Herkimer been willing to risk a battle, in which he would have been greatly out-numbered by the savages, there was no hope he might effect the release of Peter Sitz.

Sergeant Corney had an interview with the general after we had succeeded in quieting Jacob to a certain degree, and the commander advised that we return home without delay in order to give information as to what we had seen; but he did us three the honor of requesting, in case our services should not be needed immediately at Cherry Valley, that we would rejoin his force, which was to be stationed at the mouth of Oriskany Creek, without delay.

He promised that we should have every opportunity of serving the patriot cause, and in order that we might be allowed to leave Cherry Valley again, he sent a written message to my uncle, of the purport of which I was then ignorant.

We - meaning Sergeant Corney, Jacob, and myself - set off as soon as the conference with General Herkimer was at an end, on the long journey to our homes, knowing that the advance must be slow and cautious, for we had heard from Thayendanega's own lips that he was fully committed to the work of harrying the patriots.

As I look back upon it now I wonder that we succeeded in traversing the wilderness, when Brant's force was so near at hand, without mishap; but, as it proved, we had more difficulty in persuading Jacob to accompany us than in eluding the foe whom we believed might spring upon us at any moment, and when we arrived home it was to learn that the danger to the inhabitants of the Mohawk Valley was more imminent even than when Thayendanega stalked away from the interview with General Herkimer.

And this was the situation, as I afterward read it in printed letters:

"A few days after this conference with General Herkimer, Brant withdrew his warriors from the

Susquehanna and joined Sir John Johnson and Col. John Butler, who were collecting a large body of Tories and refugees at Oswego, preparatory to a descent upon the Mohawk and Schoharie settlements. There Guy Johnson and other officers of the British Indian Department summoned a grand council of the Six Nations.

"They were invited to assemble to 'eat the flesh and drink the blood of a Bostonian' - in other words, to feast on the occasion of a proposed treaty of alliance against the patriots, whom the savages denominated 'Bostonians' for the reason that Boston was the focus of the rebellion. There was a pretty full attendance at the council; but a large portion of the sachems adhered faithfully to their covenant of neutrality made with General Schuyler, until the appeals of the British commissioners to their avarice overcame their sense of honor.

"The commissioners represented the people of the king to be numerous as the forest leaves and rich in every possession, while those of the colonies were exhibited as few and poor; that the armies of the king would soon subdue the rebels, and make them still weaker and poorer; that the rum of the king was as abundant as the waters of Lake Ontario; and that if the Indians would become his allies during the war, they should never want for goods or money.

"Tawdry articles, such as scarlet cloths, beads, and trinkets, were then displayed and presented to the Indians, which pleased them greatly, and they concluded an alliance by binding themselves to take up the hatchet against the patriots, and to continue their warfare until the latter were subdued. To each Indian were then presented a brass kettle, a suit of clothes, a gun, a tomahawk and scalping-knife, a piece of gold, a quantity of ammunition, and a promise of a bounty upon every scalp he should bring in. Thayendanega was thenceforth the acknowledged grand sachem of the Six Nations, and at once commenced his terrible career in the midst of our border settlements."

I had no more than time to tell my mother what I had seen, when my comrades were ready to set out for Oriskany Creek, counting to make their way over much the same ground we had just traversed.

My uncle, Colonel Campbell, gave his consent to our departure after reading General Herkimer's message, and congratulated me, who deserved no praise, because I had succeeded in so far winning the confidence of a thorough soldier that he should make a personal request for the services of myself and my companions.

It was not in our minds that we would remain very long with our new commander. Sergeant Corney believed General Herkimer had some especial matter in hand in which he thought we three might be of particular service, and when that was done we would be allowed to return home.

Therefore it was that we still counted ourselves Minute Boys of the Mohawk Valley, and left our company in charge of John Sammons, who was to act in my stead until I came back.

It pleased Jacob that we were to return to that portion of the country where we would be near Brant's forces, for he still cherished the hope of being able to aid in the rescuing of his father, if peradventure Peter Sitz yet remained in this world.

Our stay in Cherry Valley was of no more than two hours' duration; but we learned much concerning the war in that time. Our little settlement seemed overrun with people because of the soldiers quartered there, regarding whom I have already written, and the inhabitants from miles around who had come to find a place of refuge.

Already had word been brought in that there were then gathered at Oswego seven hundred Indians and four hundred British soldiers, under command of Sir John Johnson and Colonel Claus, and at Oswegatchie, or, as it is now called, Ogdensburg, were six hundred Tories ready to join Johnson's force.

All that stood between these enemies and the broad bosom of the Mohawk Valley was Fort Dayton, that poor apology for a defence, and Fort Schuyler, not yet completely built and illy manned. That this last named fortification could withstand an assault by such an army as Sir John was evidently making ready to bring against it, few believed, and all with whom I talked during the short time of our stay at home, were looking forward to the future with the gravest fears and keenest anxiety.

When, already weary and footsore, we took up our line of march to traverse the same paths over which we had just come, my company of Minute Boys insisted on accompanying us during the first half-dozen miles of the tedious journey; but it was not in triumph or rejoicing that we, all lads of Cherry Valley, left the little settlement. Our elders were disheartened and afraid, therefore we could well be excused for gloomy

James Otis

looks and timid whisperings, as we spoke of what might take place before I was able to resume command of the company which Sergeant Corney had spent so many hours in drilling.

When the afternoon was well-nigh spent, and we had come to a halt that we might take leave of our escort, Sergeant Corney seemed to think it necessary he should do what he might toward putting courage into the hearts of those who had accompanied us, by saying, as if haranguing a full army:

"You lads are looked upon in the settlement only as boys, and yet already have two of your number shown that they could stand steady, facing the gravest danger without flinching. Now is the time when you may prove yourselves men, as I believe you are in courage and ability. If you are called upon to confront the enemy, remember that there is nothing more glorious than to die in defence of your homes and your country. There is no way by which you can earn more honor than to have it said of you, 'He gave up his life for those he loved.' Better be shot down at the opening of an action, than to live through it in such a manner that your neighbors can point the finger of scorn at you, saying, 'There goes a coward!'"

The old man ceased speaking abruptly, turned about without word or sign, and plunged into the thicket, Jacob and I following close at his heels.

Chapter IV.

On the Oriskany

As we three plodded wearily on day after day, all our senses quickened by knowledge of the many dangers with which we were surrounded, it seemed to me that we had begun our work in behalf of the Cause backward - as if this going to and fro over the same ground was a wilful waste of time when every hour was so precious.

I said to myself again and again, that if General Herkimer really needed such services as we could render, it would have been better had we remained with him, rather than spend so many days and be forced to such severe labor as was required for the march to Cherry Valley and back.

We had accomplished nothing of importance by going home. Colonel Campbell knew even more regarding Brant's movements than we could tell him, and it was by no means necessary he should be informed immediately as to the result of General Herkimer's interview with the Mohawk sachem.

As the days passed, and our every effort was needed to enable us to advance without absolutely running into the arms of the savages, for it seemed as if they were

James Otis

everywhere in the wilderness, Jacob became more resigned, or so it appeared, since he ceased to insist that this or that impracticable move be made. I did not suppose he no longer mourned for his father, but believed and hoped he had come to understand we could not do anything toward effecting a rescue until all the circumstances were favorable.

One day's march was much like another, and many passed before we were with General Herkimer again. We always camped in a thicket, taking good care not to leave a trail leading up to the place, and in this last task we did not consider the time spent as wasted, for on every hand could be seen signs of the enemy, therefore the utmost precaution was needed.

All of us gave ourselves over to slumber as soon as we were stretched out on the ground, for however careful a watch might have been kept, it would not have availed if the enemy was bent on surprising us.

In the early light of the new day either Jacob or I went out in search of small game, for it goes without saying that we could not have brought from home a sufficient amount of food to sustain us during all the time we spent roaming to and fro between Cherry Valley and the Oriskany.

If we were fortunate enough to get so much meat as would serve for one or more meals, we cooked it by digging a hole in the ground, building therein a fire, and screening the smoke as best we might with boughs and ferns. That done, we satisfied our hunger while creeping slowly onward, oftentimes forced to spend an hour or more in making a detour around some particularly dangerous locality.

If, as often happened, we failed of finding game, we buckled our belts the tighter and went on, consoling ourselves with the hope that fortune would favor us before nightfall.

More than once would we have run upon a party of savages - Thayendanega's scouts or hunters - had it not been for the almost excessive precautions Sergeant Corney insisted on taking, and in such case there was no other course than to hide as best we might, and wait until the enemy was pleased to move on.

Fortunately we did not come face to face with the redskins, therefore a detailed story of our march would be dull reading, for it could only be the same thing over and over again until the hour arrived when we entered General Herkimer's camp on the Oriskany, receiving there such a greeting from the commander himself as caused me to believe he really needed us for some important task.

"You have done well to get back alive!" he cried, with a laugh. "It is pleasing to know that lads can do what many of their elders would balk at. So Colonel Campbell was willing to give you up to me?"

"He made no protest, sir," I replied, after waiting an instant for one of my companions to act the part of spokesman. "An hundred and fifty soldiers are quartered at Cherry Valley, and they, with the many who have made of the settlement a place of refuge, are in such numbers that three would neither be needed or missed."

"That would depend on what stuff the three were made, according to my way of thinking. I have some work here which you can do better than any one else of whom I know, and the only question is whether you are willing to lay your shoulders to the wheel when there's a good bit of danger in so doing?"

"We have come, sir, to do whatsoever offered, an' if the task which you have in mind could be performed with safety, then we might as well have stayed at home," I replied, and Sergeant Corney nodded to show that we were of one mind.

"Since I last saw you the enemy has gathered in strong force about Fort Schuyler, and it is necessary we get some word to the commandant, who is, in fact, besieged."

"That shouldn't be sich a terrible hard job, sir," Sergeant Corney said, speaking for the first time since we were received by the general.

"True for you, but the reason why I haven't sent any of my own men before this is, that if the messenger should be discovered while trying to get inside, Joseph Brant would know for a certainty that we on the outside believed the garrison to be hard pressed, which would probably work no end of mischief, for at present the enemy has every reason to suppose Colonel Gansevoort has all the men and stores he can possibly need."

"Why should he think differently if one of us was captured while tryin' to communicate with the besieged, sir?" Sergeant Corney asked, curiously.

"Because you have every reason for going there, even though you had never heard that the fort was invested."

I could not repress a look of surprise, for it was much as if the general was speaking in riddles, and, seeing the question on my face, he continued:

"It is only natural that you from Cherry Valley should be searching for Peter Sitz, and the Indians, in case you were captured, would perforce believe such a story -"

"Is my father in their camp, sir?" Jacob cried, eagerly.

"Ay, lad, so I believe, otherwise I would not think it important you should act as my messengers. One of our scouts brought in word that Brant's immediate followers had a white prisoner with them, and it is reasonable to suppose him to be Peter Sitz, for, since we saw those scoundrels, they have kept out of mischief because of being in camp with the British and Tory soldiers."

There was no need now of urging Jacob to undertake the mission; since he had what seemed like positive information of his father's whereabouts, he would have gone in the direction of the besieged fort whether General Herkimer so desired, or opposed it.

As for my part, having really given up all hope of seeing Peter Sitz again in this world, the probable fact of his being alive quickened the blood in my veins until I forgot that our services were required for anything save the rescue of the prisoner.

Sergeant Corney gave no token either of joy or indifference; he kept in mind only the duties of a soldier, and prepared himself for the dangerous mission by asking:

"Can you tell me, sir, what force the enemy have in front of Fort Schuyler?"

"Near one thousand seven hundred men - regulars, Tories, and Indians. St. Leger is in nominal command; but it is reasonable to believe that Sir John Johnson and Brant have much the same authority as he. Certain it is that they and none other can control their followers. Colonel Gansevoort has nearly a thousand men, with a six weeks' supply of provisions and ammunition for the small arms; but there is in the fort no more than four hundred rounds for the cannon, which is his most important means of defence. The situation is not yet critical, but may become so very soon, and we have more chance now for communicating with the commandant than is likely to be the case a week hence, when the besiegers have settled down to their work."

"When shall we set out, sir?" I asked, as the general ceased speaking.

"As soon as you have recovered from the fatigue of the journey. There is no time to be lost, unless you are eager to encounter more danger than is absolutely necessary."

"There is no reason why we shouldn't set off at once," Jacob said, quickly. "We are not women, to be tired out by a bit of marchin'."

I fancied from the expression on the general's face that it pleased him because my comrade showed himself so eager, and there was a tinge of bitterness in my heart as I understood that, whatever good to the Cause might be the purpose of our task, the commander was, in a certain degree, trading on Jacob's love for his father.

It was not for me, however, to criticize, even in my own mind, anything of a military nature which might be on foot. I had had ample time since the powwow with Thayendanega to decide whether or no I would serve under General Herkimer, and, having come to a decision, it stood me in hand to do whatsoever lay before me without question.

I held much the same opinion as did Jacob, however, although not because of the same reason.

It seemed to me a most dangerous undertaking, this attempt to get a message into a fort which was besieged by so large a body of men; but since it must be done, unless we were willing to show the white feather, then I was eager to be at it, for danger appears greater when one stands idly by looking at it from the distance, than when it is actually encountered.

Sergeant Corney, who had evidently been turning the matter over in his mind, said, after a time, to the commander:

"It strikes me, sir, that we should get all the information we may concernin' the whereabouts of the enemy before settin' out. Not that I am askin' for any long delay," he added, quickly, observing a faint expression of displeasure on the general's face. "I would mingle among the men, to learn what they may know, from now until sunset, when, as it seems to me, our journey had best be begun. By startin' at that time we shall arrive before sunrise, an' thus have all the day in which to lay our plans for approachin' the fort."

Jacob's eyes twinkled with satisfaction when he heard this proposition, and I believed he was thinking that if we lay in hiding a full day in front of the fortification, he might have opportunity to learn something concerning his father.

"I shall leave to you who are most deeply concerned in the matter, the method of doing the work. Pick up all the information you can, and when you are ready to set out come to me for the final instructions."

Then the commander half-turned, as if to show that the interview was at an end, and Sergeant Corney beckoned Jacob and me to follow him, reminding us, when we were comparatively alone, of the promise made at the time we first set out.

"The day we left Cherry Valley on Brant's trail, you lads agreed to follow me without questionin', even when it seemed as if I might be goin' wrong, an' now has come the time for you to keep that well in mind."

"There is no reason why we should not do so," I replied, promptly. "I doubt not but that you, who are versed in military matters, could direct such a task better than any in this encampment."

"I'm not takin' that much praise to myself, lad; but do claim, because of havin' had more experience, to be better fitted for the work, after we are once arrived, than are you. I will go even so far as to say that on the trail or in the thicket you are my superiors, owin' to havin' been brought up to work which, except in this country, would be considered almost unsoldierly. Here is my first order: Mingle with the men of this encampment with the idea of fillin' your stomachs with food, an', that done, lie down to sleep until I shall summon you."

"Sleep!" Jacob exclaimed, angrily. "Think you it would be possible for me to sleep now, when we know that the moment has come in which I may be able to aid my father?"

"Ay, lad, but you must, whether you will or no. You can work for him best by preparin' your body for whatsoever of fatigue we may be called upon to undergo, an' since there is little chance we shall gain any rest durin' four an' twenty hours after leavin' here, it stands us all in hand to be prepared for the exertion."

"Are you countin' on sleepin'?" Jacob asked, fiercely.

"I am more accustomed to keepin' my eyes open durin' a long time than are you; but if it so be I have the chance, you may be certain I shall take advantage of it. Now, remember, eat an' sleep until I seek you out."

Then the old man left us, and, watching for a moment, we saw him enter into conversation with this soldier and that, until it seemed as if he was bent on making the acquaintance of every member of the force.

Jacob and I had little difficulty in finding as much food as we needed, after having explained why we had come into the encampment. The men were more than willing to divide their rations with us, and we might literally have gorged ourselves with the best in the camp had such been our desire.

It was one thing for Sergeant Corney to say that we must sleep, and quite another for us to obey the command.

It seemed to me that my eyes were never open wider than when I threw myself down upon the ground by the side of Jacob, striving my best to cross over into Dreamland. The thought of attempting to force our way through such an army as General St. Leger had under his command; of the possibility that we might, perhaps, come across Peter Sitz; the chances that Colonel Gansevoort would be forced to surrender even before we could arrive with information that reinforcements were near at hand, and, in fact, the numberless happenings which might occur to change the entire situation, served to drive sleep so far from my eyelids that I despaired of being able to summon it until sheer exhaustion should come.

Jacob was lying, with closed eyes, so still that I half-believed he had succeeded in obeying Sergeant Corney's commands, and, bent on moving around among the men in the hope of thereby changing the current of my disagreeable thoughts, I crept softly from his side lest I awaken him.

"Where are you goin'?" he asked, quietly, in a tone which told me he had been no nearer slumber than I.

"I cannot sleep, an' that's a fact. Perhaps after walkin' around a bit I shall feel more like it."

"I'll go with you," Jacob said, rising to his feet. "There is no hope I can sleep, although I am willin', if needs be, to make it appear as if I was unconscious."

Taking heed not to go near Sergeant Corney, whom we could see in the distance, Jacob went from one group of soldiers to the other, and, as may be supposed, the chief topic of conversation everywhere was the possibility that Fort Schuyler could hold out against the large number of men who were besieging it, as well as the chances of General Herkimer's command being able to enter the place.

Thus it was we learned that among Brant's following were savages from all the various tribes of the Six Nations, except the Oneidas, who remained faithful to their agreement to be neutral during the war. It was said that the besiegers were well supplied with everything necessary for the accomplishment of their purpose, including a large amount of ready money, and General St. Leger was willing to pay liberally for the services of those who would join him.

It was also reported - the information having been brought in by scouts - that on the second day of the siege the British commander had sent to the fort a messenger, who, with many high-sounding words, recited the love of the king for those who remained loyal to him, and the punishment which would be inflicted upon those who continued in rebellion. This stream of bombast was concluded by direst threats in case the garrison held out against the demand for surrender, the sum and substance of which was that the savages would be allowed to commit every act of barbarity their ingenuity could devise, if an assault should become necessary.

Nearly all the defenders of the fort laughed these threats and promises to scorn, and it was believed that Gansevoort's men would hold out to the bitter end.

We heard very much in addition, which was really no

more than camp gossip, and it is not necessary I set it down here.

Before the close of the day both Jacob and I really succeeded in going to sleep, and the shadows of night were beginning to lengthen when we were aroused by Sergeant Corney.

"I reckon I've heard all that the men in camp have to tell," he said, when I stood upright in obedience to the pressure of his hand upon my shoulder. "It only remains to get our instructions from General Herkimer before makin' the attempt to have speech with those in the fort."

"Haven't you seen him yet?" I asked, in surprise, for it had been in my mind that the old man would make every preparation before summoning us.

"No, lad. This is a venture in which we share the dangers equally, an' it's no more than right you should hear all which may pass between the general an' me. Therefore let us bring the business to an end as speedily as may be."

Well, we presented ourselves before the commander, announcing that the time had come when we were to leave camp, and, considering all the risks which were to be run, it seemed to me as if the message he would have delivered was exceeding brief and unimportant, as compared with what might result from the attempt at delivery.

"I shall not give you a written message, lest you fall into the hands of the enemy," he said, speaking in a kindly tone, and looking at us, as I fancied, pityingly, much as one would at those who had been selected as sacrifices. "It is in the highest degree necessary you get speech with Colonel Gansevoort, and to such end make disposal of yourselves so that should one, or even two, be taken or killed, the second or third may press on. Having arrived, say to the commandant that I shall leave this camp to-morrow morning, marching slowly toward the fort, and immediately after he has received the information he is to fire three cannon in rapid succession, thus notifying me that he understands the situation. You will not, under the most favorable circumstances, finish the journey in less than four and twenty hours, and by that time I shall be where the reports of the guns can be heard. Once the signal has been given, it is my purpose to attack the enemy, and Colonel Gansevoort is to make a sortie at the same time, when it is to be hoped our forces can be united."

Having said this, the general insisted that each of us repeat the instructions so that he might know we understood them thoroughly, and then, clasping us by hand in turn, he bade us "Godspeed."

I wish I might be able to say that my heart was stout when we left the encampment and were swallowed up by the shadows of the thicket; but such was not the case.

I realized only too well all the dangers which were before us, and the odds against our being able to obey the general's orders. At the same time I knew that in event of failure there would be no possibility of retreat; but we would find ourselves in the hands of an enemy whose greatest delight consists in the most fiendish murder.

As I figured it, out of a hundred chances we had no more than one of getting into the fort, and there remained ninety and nine in favor of our falling victims to Brant's crew.

We had but just set out when I observed that Sergeant Corney had left behind him every superfluous article of clothing, and all accoutrements save the knife in his belt, whereupon I asked the reason for thus laying himself bare to the enemy.

"You lads have each a rifle, which are all the weapons we need, for it can avail us nothing to make a fight. If we win it must be by strategy, not force, and in case of success it will be a small matter to provide ourselves with other arms."

"At the same time it gives me courage to know that I have something with which to defend myself," Jacob said, with a laugh which had in it nothing of mirth.

"Ay, lad, so I counted, otherwise I had advised that you follow my example. It can do no harm to take whatsoever you will, for that which hinders may readily be cast aside. Now let us come to an end of tongue-waggin', for silence is our safest ally."

As the old man had said, either Jacob or I should have known more of woodcraft than did he, but on this night I dare venture to assert that there were not above a dozen in Joseph Brant's following who could have made their way through the thicket with less noise and in a more direct course than did he.

From General Herkimer's encampment in an air-line through the forest to Fort Schuyler was not more than seven or eight miles, and, despite our slow progress, for one cannot travel rapidly when striving to advance without so much as the breaking of a twig, we counted on arriving in front of the enemy's lines by midnight. And this I believe we did.

The first intimation we had that our journey was approaching a close came when we suddenly saw, directly in our line of advance, a faint light amid the thicket in the distance, and Sergeant Corney, who had been leading the way, halted quickly.

"You lads are to remain here while I find out what portion of St. Leger's force is in front of us," he said, in a whisper, and then it was that I ventured to dispute his authority, having, as I believed, good reason for so doing.

"You yourself have admitted that either Jacob or I could beat you out at work of this kind. Let me go, an' do you stay here."

Then it was that Jacob insisted on performing the most dangerous portion of the work, and would have passed by me in the darkness to avoid a controversy, but that I clutched him by the arm, and Sergeant Corney whispered:

"You lads shall lead the way, and I will follow at your heels; but remember what General Herkimer impressed upon us - that one *must* get through, therefore if he who leads is captured, the other two shall leave him to his fate, for the life of a single human being is not to be counted when we are tryin' to save hundreds."

It was not a time nor a place for argument, and in token

of agreement with him I took up the lead.

I did not attempt to go forward rapidly; but, half-lying upon the ground, I crept onward inch by inch, removing carefully with my hands every twig or dry leaf which might be in the path, lest by the lightest rustling of the branches I give warning to the quick-eared enemy of our approach.

In such manner it was not possible to make other than slow progress, and I believe fully half an hour was spent in traversing the distance of a dozen yards, when we were come to where could be had a view of that which had attracted our attention.

Nine Indians were lounging, on the opposite side of a river that we knew to be the Mohawk, around a small fire, over which were being cooked slices of fresh meat. They were talking earnestly among themselves meanwhile, for these red sneaks of the forest do not, when alone, maintain that silent dignity with which so many writers, ignorant of their customs, try to invest them.

They were members of Brant's own tribe, as I knew from the language, with which I was reasonably familiar, and after a few moments it was possible to gather from the conversation that St. Leger had interfered in some way with their plans, or thwarted their desires.

The stream was not so wide at this point but that we could hear fairly well what they said. It seemed necessary I should learn all I might before we crept past the small encampment, and, never dreaming how much of anguish the listening might cause my comrade, I remained silent and motionless, until enough had been said to convince me that their grievance consisted in the fact that they had not been allowed to indulge in the amusement of torturing a prisoner during that same evening.

Then it flashed upon me that it was Peter Sitz of whom they spoke, and involuntarily I moved backward, the one thought in my mind being to prevent Jacob from hearing; but the vigor with which he clutched me by the leg told that it was too late. The lad had heard as much as I, and to his mind the prisoner spoken of could be none other than his father.

For a moment I ceased my efforts at retreat, and then, realizing that if we would take Jacob with us to the completion of General Herkimer's commands, he must not be allowed to hear anything more, I would have backed away rapidly.

To my dismay and sorrow, however, he held me as if in a grip of iron, and, despite all silent efforts on my part, I was forced to remain.

Chapter V.

Divided Duty

I could not find it in my heart to blame Jacob for being eager to learn all he could regarding his father, and it certainly seemed as if we might hear that which would at least tell us who this prisoner was that they were so keen to torture; but surely we were not warranted in lingering for the possible saving of one human life, when by our delay hundreds might be placed in gravest danger.

However, I could not retreat, because Jacob held me firmly in his clutch, from which I would have been unable to release myself save at the cost of betraying our whereabouts.

With the hope that the lad might soon come to realize that we must be attending to General Herkimer's business, I remained silent and motionless, straining my ears to hear what the painted snakes were saying, and at the same time expecting to receive a silent protest from Sergeant Corney because of remaining inactive when the moments were so precious.

In less than a single minute I knew that the savages were speaking of Peter Site, and the tightening of Jacob's grip told that he too was aware of the fact.

Because I can understand only a few words here or there of Brant's native tongue, it would be impossible to set down exactly what the villains said; but I caught enough to understand that the prisoner in whom we were so deeply interested was not far distant, - probably at the main encampment, - and Thayen-danega was protecting him at least from the torture. Why the sachem had taken such an interest in the unfortunate man I could not make out; most likely the savages themselves were ignorant on that point.

It appeared to me, from the conversation, that there was much hard feeling on the part of the Indians because they were not allowed to indulge in an amusement which had been countenanced by more than one officer of the British army, and I fancied that Thayendanega, great sachem though he now was of the Six Nations, would have no little trouble in holding his precious followers in check.

When I had learned as much as has been set down here, I felt a tugging at my shirt, and knew, without seeing him, that Sergeant Corney was not willing to remain at this point any longer.

The savages had begun to speak of St. Leger, and what he might succeed in doing so far as the siege was concerned, therefore it did not seem probable we would hear more regarding Peter Sitz.

This much Jacob must have understood as well as I, for when I forced myself backward, pushing vigorously against him, he gave way, and we thus slowly retreated until having gained such a distance from the feasting murderers that it seemed safe to rise to our feet.

"To what were you listenin'?" Sergeant Corney asked, in a whisper, and with no slight show of anger because I had lingered so long.

In the fewest words possible I told him what we had heard, and when I was come to an end of the brief recital, Jacob asked, as if believing that now all our plans would be changed:

"What are we to do?"

"That for which we came," Sergeant Corney replied, decidedly.

"But we know that my father is near at hand, and, if Thayendanega grows careless or indifferent, will be tortured to death."

"Ay, lad, an' I could be no more sorry if Peter Sitz was my brother; but we cannot now do anything to aid him, even though the way lay clear before us," and the old man laid his hand on Jacob's shoulder as if to give emphasis to the words. "We are to push on toward the fort, an' must not heed any other duty."

"But we stand as much chance of rescuing my father as we do of gettin' speech with Colonel Gansevoort, an' surely you will not leave a friend to be tortured to death?" Jacob said, pleadingly, and speaking incautiously loud.

"Lad, we have no choice in the matter. If General Herkimer was in your father's place I would turn my back on him until after our work had been done. Can't you see that by loiterin' now we may be sacrificing all those brave fellows who are making ready to march from the Oriskany in the hope of aiding in holdin' the fort?"

"That is your final word?" Jacob asked, sharply, and Sergeant Corney replied, feelingly:

"It cannot be otherwise. We are bound first to obey orders, even though a dozen of our best friends were bein' led to the stake, an' -"

"Then you will obey them without me," Jacob said, in a tone which I knew full well betokened a purpose from which he would not be turned by words. "Two will stand a better chance of gainin' the fort than three, an' *my* duty calls me to Thayendanega's camp."

"But surely you will not attempt to go there alone!" I cried, in horror. "Even though you should come face to face with your father, you could not hope to set him free!"

"I would rather die by his side than have him believe I remained idle while he was in such terrible danger."

"If you cannot be persuaded, we must leave you, an' that without delay," the old man said, sadly. "God knows I would do all a man might to aid Peter Sitz; but if he was here at this minute, knowin' that the stake was bein' made ready for him, he would say that we were bound to keep on toward the fort regardless of his fate."

"I shall go to him," Jacob replied, quietly, and Sergeant Corney turned aside with a sigh.

But that I knew beyond a peradventure it was useless, I

would have said all in my power to keep him with us; but his mind was fixed, and, to tell the truth, I could not well blame him for doing as I would have done, regardless of any duty I might owe to General Herkimer.

"We can say nothing more, lad?" Sergeant Corney said to me, inquiringly, and I shook my head, for so great was the grief in my heart that just then I could make no reply.

I believe Jacob understood how keen was my sorrow at thus parting, when the chances were that we would never meet again in this world, for, as if to put an end to the agony, he turned abruptly, not even stopping to press my hand, and in an instant was lost to view amid the gloom of the forest.

Already had our venture, so it appeared to me, cost the life of one of our small party, and mentally I reproached myself bitterly for having left Cherry Valley to take service with this General Herkimer, who could as well have sent some other in our place, for surely all in his command were not known to Thayendanega's following. I, as captain of the Minute Boys stationed at Cherry Valley, could not have been accused of refusing to aid the Cause had I failed to serve under the general, so far from my post of duty.

As it was, however, we had come a long distance from our friends, and already sacrificed a life uselessly, so it seemed to me then in my bitterness of spirit.

"Come, lad," Sergeant Corney whispered, shaking me roughly by the shoulder as if he would drive from my mind the painful thoughts. "We cannot do as Jacob would have us, and there is an end of that matter. Get to work, and it may be that 'twixt now an' morning but one of us will remain to carry the message."

I had never before heard the old man speak in so despondent a tone, and it seemed an evil omen, coming as the words did when we were ready to plunge into the most dangerous portion of the work.

In silence I led the way once more, making such a detour as I thought would carry us safely past that party of savages from which we had gained such painful information, and perhaps half an hour was spent in advancing at a snail's pace; but in the direction where we supposed the fort stood.

Now it was I realized that some one well acquainted with the locality should have been sent with us, for we were obliged to go on blindly, as it were, trusting that chance, and what we might see of the disposition of the enemy's forces, would bring us to the point we desired to gain, for neither of us had ever visited Fort Schuyler.

At the end of half an hour I came to a sudden standstill, for we were within a few paces of half a dozen white men, as could be told even in the darkness by the outlines of their clothing.

These last appeared to be stationed at that point, for none of them made any attempt to go away during the two or three minutes I remained motionless, although why so many should have been placed there as sentinels, when one would have served the purpose, I failed to understand, and it perplexed me not a little, for it was necessary that we should know whether we were inside the lines, or simply confronting their outlying pickets.

There was nothing for it, however, but to crawl backward half a dozen yards, and then make another detour, and while this was being done Sergeant Corney had only a single question to ask, which was as to whether I had seen white men or Indians.

"White men," I replied, "and no less than half a dozen standing in a group, as if stationed there."

The old man paused an instant, as if quite as much perplexed as I, and then whispered:

"Go on. We are like to run across more than one such snag, an', what is worse, don't have a clear idea of whether we shall come plump on to the fort, or go a considerable distance to one side of it."

Again I advanced, making an even wider detour than before, and in ten minutes, perhaps, we were come upon a single sentinel, - a soldier, - who stood leaning against a tree as if half-asleep, and I was less careful in passing him because he did not appear to be particularly on the alert.

Again and again we nearly stumbled upon a squad of men, small parties of Indians, or a single sentinel, until it seemed to me as if all St. Leger's force must be distributed throughout the thicket, and I began to despair of ever making our way through.

Now we were where it seemed as dangerous to retreat as to advance, and I strove manfully to keep from my mind all thoughts of the perils that surrounded us, lest I grow faint-hearted at the very time when all my courage was needed if we would save our lives.

To do this it was only necessary I think of Jacob and his hazardous venture, which could serve no good purpose even though he succeeded in avoiding the enemy, therefore my mind dwelt on the perils which confronted him, causing me in a measure to forget where I myself stood.

To go on in such a manner was most wearisome, and I was well-nigh at the end of my strength when a faint lightness in the eastern sky gave warning that the day was near at hand.

At the same moment I observed this fact, the sergeant gripped me by the arm, and, understanding he would have speech with me, I halted.

"It is time we went into hidin', lad, although I did count we would come within sight of the fort before bein' obliged to call a halt."

"Where can we hide here?" I asked, bitterly, and, strange as it may seem, I began to realize, for the first time since the general had explained what he would have us do, that we must remain concealed from view during all the hours of daylight, and that while we were literally surrounded by the enemy.

"We must take our chances in the first dense thicket, wherein may be found a stout tree, that we come across," he replied, "an' now instead of tryin' to get a sight of the fortification, turn all your efforts toward findin' a hidin'-place."

This promised to be as difficult a task as I had ever undertaken, for how would it be possible in the darkness to say whether one thicket was denser than another, and, without spending precious time in the examination, to learn if there was a stout tree within any certain clump of bushes?

Because the sergeant had said we were to halt where was a tree, I believed he proposed spending the day amid the branches, and any one who has ever been in a forest can readily understand how few there are of such hiding-places.

However, we were there, and within another hour must be screened from view after some fashion, therefore it was useless to grumble, or say this or that movement was impossible; but rather I should do the best I might, and trust to the chapter of accidents that I did not lead my companion into what would prove to be a trap.

All the thicket looked dense in the night, but when I was finally come to a clump of bushes through which it was difficult to force my way, I stopped and whispered to Sergeant Corney.

"This seems to be such a place as you would have; but who can say whether it will answer our purpose?"

"So much the worse for us if it does not," the old man replied, grimly. "Make your way in, an' if there be no tree to give us a roostin'-place, we must take our chances on the ground, for the day is comin' on apace."

And indeed he said no more than the truth; already was it possible for me to see surrounding objects, dimly, to be sure, but more clearly than when we first began searching for a place of refuge.

Unless we were concealed from view within half an hour, we might as well march straight to the nearest sentinel and give ourselves up as prisoners.

There was much to be desired in this thicket which we had chosen by chance, as was learned when we were well within it. Several large trees grew amid the clump of bushes, to be sure; but the foliage was not so dense that one who passed near at hand with reasonable alertness would have failed to discover us lurking there.

"It is better than the open country," Sergeant Corney said, when I would have found fault with our blind choice. "We will burrow amid these small bushes until daylight, an' then, if necessary, go to roost."

I had in my pocket a small piece of corn bread, and, when I would have divided it with the old man, he showed me about the same quantity, which he had saved in event of just such an emergency, and we munched the dry food with no very keen appetites, but eating at this the first opportunity, in order to keep up our strength for the struggle which must ensue before we gained speech with those in the fort.

My sorrow because Jacob had left us on a venture from which I did not believe he could ever return, was so great that I felt no desire for food, but ate it from a sense of duty, even as I had turned my back on my comrade when he needed aid.

One does not make haste with such a meal, and when I had swallowed the last dry crumbs, which were like to have choked me, the day had fully come.

It can readily be imagined that we crept even nearer the edge of the thicket than was really safe in order to get some idea of our position, and to my great surprise and delight I found that we had come in as direct a course as if we had followed a blazed trail.

There before us, and less than three hundred yards distant, was the fortification over which was floating the flag made from Capt. Abraham Swartwout's cloak, and because we were on high ground it was possible to see the Americans moving about within, bent on this task or that duty.

After one hasty glance we crept back into the middle of the thicket, and there, surrounded by hundreds of enemies, we two held a whispered conversation regarding the situation.

It was only natural we should first congratulate each other on our good fortune in having come unwittingly to the very spot we most desired to gain, and then I said, simply giving words to the thoughts which had entered my mind as I gazed upon the fortification:

"He who crosses the clearing between here and the fort, even though it be in the night, needs to wriggle along like a snake, else will one of Thayendanega's painted beauties lift his scalp."

"It is a bit open jest in front of here; but I took note that further to the westward was a little more of green," Sergeant Corney said, half to himself, and I knew he was picturing in his mind the two of us making the attempt where was not a blade of grass to give shelter, for the "green" of which he spoke was nothing more than the fragment of a bush near the stockade.

"How are we to attract their attention, providin' we succeed in creepin' up under the wall?" I asked, after a long pause, and he replied, grimly:

"I'll answer that question after you've told me how we're goin' to stop 'em shootin' at us while we're tryin' to get across."

Then it was I understood that even though the enemy did not see us while we were making our way over the plain, the sentinels in the fort were doubtless on the alert against just such an attempt on the part of the Indians, and there was little question but that they would fire at any moving thing which came within their line of vision.

"It seems to me that we'll be between two fires," I said, with a feeble attempt to speak in a jovial tone, and Sergeant Corney's reply was much like a bucket of cold water full in my face.

"That's exactly the case, lad, an' I'm countin' that betwixt 'em we'll be peppered in fine shape, else there are some mighty poor marksmen hereabouts."

"Why didn't you tell the general that we couldn't carry his message? Didn't you think of all this at the time?"

"Ay, lad, it was pictured in my mind much as we see it now; but he said we were to do the job, an' it wasn't for me to point out the danger."

"Why not, if you felt certain we would be shot?" I cried, angrily.

"Because a soldier has good reason when he enlists to

expect he'll stop a bullet, else what would be the need of powder an' ball?"

Having said this, the old man relapsed into silence, as if he was trying to figure out how the work might be done with less of danger, and I sat staring at him in a rage, for to my mind he had much the same as compassed his own death and mine by not speaking of all the perils in our path.

Now it was that I almost envied Jacob his position. It is true the odds were strongly against his being able to make his way through the camp without being captured, yet it was possible for him at any time to give over the attempt and retrace his steps, whereas we were absolutely penned up in the thicket, where retreat was even more perilous than advance.

Fume and fret as I might, it was not possible to mend matters, and I stretched myself out at full length under the bushes, with the idea in mind that it would be better if we were captured at once, for then we would be spared just so much suspense, yet when Sergeant Corney suggested that we were not as well hidden from view as we should be, I was alarmed on the instant.

How that day was passed by us I can hardly say even now, when I look back calmly upon all the incidents which were then so terrifying.

We had eaten the last crumb of our corn bread in the morning, without appeasing the hunger which assailed us, and now could only chew the twigs of the bushes, striving to make ourselves believe we extracted nourishment therefrom.

More than once straggling soldiers or Indians passed near where we were hidden; but no one thought of searching the thicket for those who were friendly to the garrison, because none save idiots like ourselves would thus have ventured into the lion's mouth.

Screened as we were from the lightest breath of wind, it was cruelly hot in that hiding-place. Tiny streams of perspiration ran down my face, wetting the leaves beneath my head, and I chewed them in the vain hope that the suspicion of moisture might serve to quench my thirst.

I rejoiced when the sun began to sink in the west, even though it was, as I believed, bringing the hour of my death so much the nearer; but I soon came to understand that Sergeant Corney was not disposed to make the perilous venture without first having taken all possible precautions for our safety.

When the day was within an hour of its close, I suddenly became aware that the old soldier was stripping the fringe from his shirt, and immediately I sat bolt upright, fancying for the moment that he had lost his reason.

"What are you doin'?" I asked, sharply, and he replied, with a faint smile:

"If the sentinel who stands on the wall of the fort facin' us is 'tendin' to his business as a soldier should, then there's a chance I can let him know these 'ere bushes shelter decent people."

While speaking he had been cutting cautiously with his knife one of the longer branches which helped to screen us from view, and when it had been severed he trimmed it with infinite care, as if our welfare depended upon its being smooth and clean.

When this had been done to his satisfaction, and it seemed to give him greatest pleasure to keep me in suspense as to his purpose, he tied to the smaller end of the stick the fringe from his shirt.

"You're goin' to creep out an' wave that!" I cried, in the tone of one who has made a great discovery.

"You can set it down as a fact that I won't creep very far out," the old man replied, with a smile. "It's only the ghost of a chance that anybody will take heed of it, an' yet there's no harm in the tryin'."

When finally he crept cautiously out toward the edge of the thicket, I watched him as eagerly as if all our troubles would be over in case we succeeded in attracting the attention of those in the fort, whereas, no matter how many of our friends might see the waving fringe, we would still be in the same danger of getting a bullet from the besiegers.

"It ain't any ways certain that some of these sneakin' Injuns don't see my signal before one of the garrison does, in which case we won't have to puzzle our heads about gettin' into the fort; but if they should jump on me, you'd best take to your heels. There's a bare chance you might give 'em the slip in the squabble, for I shouldn't knock under while there was any fight left in me."

Then, peering through the branches, I could see the sentinel on the wall near the sally-port, and it goes without saying that I watched with my heart in my mouth for some gesture which might tell that he understood what was of so much importance to us.

It was fortunate that we had blindly stumbled upon a hiding-place a few yards in advance of the enemy's line of watchers, otherwise the scheme could never have been successful. Even as it was, I expected each instant that some painted snake would take it into his wicked head to wander around in front of the thicket, when the game would come to a speedy end.

Sergeant Corney waved the bit of fringe slowly to and fro in such a manner that the dull color of the deerskin might offer a contrast against the green of the foliage, and when five minutes or more had passed without any movement on the part of the sentinel, I said to myself that there was no possibility we could catch the man's eye.

The old soldier was not one easily discouraged. During ten minutes more he continued his efforts, now moving the stick to and fro, and again giving to it an up-and-down motion, and then, at the very moment when all hope had fled from my heart, I saw the man straighten himself suddenly, as he shaded his eyes with his hand.

Then there could be no doubt but that Sergeant Corney had succeeded in his purpose, for the soldier waved his hand twice, and bent over as if speaking to some one on the inside.

Now it was that I expected the old man would return to my side and chuckle over our good fortune; but he remained at the edge of the thicket while I might have counted twenty, and then a second member of the garrison had clambered up beside the first.

Another hand was waved in reply, and then, having finished his task in good shape, Sergeant Corney crept back to me as he whispered, gleefully:

"I reckon we needn't fear that any of the garrison will shoot at us this night, an', what's more to our advantage, we won't be called on to lay behind the walls very long tryin' to attract attention."

"It was a great plan!" I replied, as if all our troubles were at an end, and then again came the thought that it would be necessary for us to creep out from the thicket under the very noses of those who were on guard, and straightway all my fears returned.

It no longer seemed to me as if we had gained any great advantage from the old man's efforts.

Chapter VI.

Between the Lines

As the sun slowly sank behind the hills in the west, I forgot the thirst and the hunger which had assailed me. So great was the fear in my mind because of what we were about to attempt, that bodily discomforts seemed as nothing.

It was a most daring venture we were to make, and one wherein the chances were no less than ninety and nine out of an hundred that we would be killed or captured before having well started on the enterprise, and yet the attempt must be made, however faint-hearted we might be, for, as I have already said, there was as much danger in retreating as advancing.

The only thing in our favor was that the night promised to be dark. Already were clouds hiding the setting sun, the wind was growing stronger, and it was reasonable to believe that within an hour the heavens would be covered as with a black veil.

After having succeeded in attracting the attention of the sentinels, Sergeant Corney crept back to my side, lying there at full length and in silence. I believed his anxiety as to the outcome of this mad venture was so great that he did not dare indulge in conversation, and because of such idea was I even more cast down in spirit.

I tried to count the seconds in order to have some knowledge of the passage of time; but could not fix my mind upon such a simple act.

When it seemed to me as if the night was considerably more than half-spent, I whispered tremblingly to my companion:

"Have you given over tryin' to gain the fort?"

"Why should you think so, lad?" he asked, as if in surprise. "We had best make the venture after midnight, rather than now while the enemy is astir."

So great was my fear as to what the future might have in store for us that I had failed to hear the hum of voices, until my attention was thus attracted, and then I realized that it was yet quite early in the evening, instead of well toward morning, as I had supposed.

Because he did not speak again I understood that Sergeant Corney was not inclined for conversation, and I lay there motionless and silent until it was as if twice four and twenty hours had passed, when the old man, rising to a sitting posture, whispered, cautiously:

"I reckon, lad, that the time has come for us to make a try at deliverin' the general's message. As I figger it, we had best bear off to the westward, strikin' the fort on that side nearabout where the fragment of a bush stands, than to push on for the main gate. It seems reasonable the enemy will watch that part of the works closer than any other, in order to guard against a sortie, an' if Colonel Gansevoort has been told of our signals, every sentinel will be on the alert for us."

"Well?" I asked, as he ceased speaking for an instant.

"We'll do the trick after this fashion: You shall go ahead, an' I'll keep two or three paces in the rear."

"Why do you propose such a plan as that?" I asked, suspiciously, and the old man replied, hesitatingly, as if averse to having his reasons known:

"In case they see us before we are well on our way, he who is in advance stands the best show of escapin'."

"But why should my chances be made any better than yours?" I asked, angrily, for even though I was afraid of the venture, it was not in my mind to be treated like a child, as seemed to be the case when the old man was considering my safety rather than his own.

"Well, lad, there are two reasons, 'cordin' to my way of figgerin', but the last is the strongest. First off, I have a much shorter time to live in this world than you, therefore, if one life is taken, it had best be mine, so far as the patriot cause is concerned. Then agin, an' this has weight to it, in case we are chased you should be able to run faster than me, an' we must bear in mind the fact that to deliver the message is the one important thing - our lives amount to very little compared with that."

I could not well make protest after this explanation, and, in fact, it seemed to me that there was little choice of position. If the enemy discovered us at any time while we were between the lines, our fate was well-nigh certain, and he who was three paces in advance would have no more show of escaping the bullets than the one who remained in the rear.

"Are we to go now?" I asked, striving earnestly to prevent my voice from trembling.

"Ay, lad, I reckon it's time," and the old man tightened his belt as he spoke. "Throw away your rifle, or strap it on your back where there's no chance it will hinder the progress, an', once havin' started, keep your mind well on the fact that we must get there, heedin' not what lies behind."

Then he gently forced me to the edge of the thicket, where we halted an instant to make certain there was no one in the immediate vicinity, after which was begun such an advance as I hope never to be forced into again, for of a verity it was nerve-shattering.

Strive as I might it was impossible, during the first two or three minutes of the painful journey, to prevent myself from fancying that half a dozen of Thayendanega's painted wolves were creeping up close behind me, enjoying the mental torture caused by my suspense, and then suddenly my mind was cleared of fears, even as the heavens are of clouds after a storm, as I ceased to think of what lay behind, remembering that my efforts *must* be successful else patriot blood might flow in streams.

We were lying flat upon the ground, pulling ourselves painfully along by our hands, and pushing with our toes whenever it was possible to get a leverage on the hard earth, moving perhaps no more than twelve inches each moment.

Had St. Leger's sentinels kept the strict watch which the siege demanded of them, we would not have gone a dozen paces before being discovered.

But that we did move out from the thicket without causing an alarm was, as I believe, due to the fact that the enemy contented themselves with watching the main gate of the fort, fancying that only from such quarter could any danger menace them. They had so many scouts out between the fort and Oriskany that it probably seemed to be an absolute impossibility any of the patriots could come through their lines undetected.

However it may be, we did succeed in crossing that open space without being seen by those who would have delighted in torturing us to death; but it was as if I lived a full lifetime before coming within the deep shadows cast by the walls on the west side, at the point decided upon by Sergeant Corney.

Some moments before we arrived I understood, and my heart literally bounded with joy, that those on the inside were already aware of our approach, and waiting to receive us, for we heard subdued voices from the sentinels on the walls, as if they were giving information to those below of our progress.

"It's a big thing we have done, lad," Sergeant Corney said, as he drew himself up by my side while both of us hugged the earthworks as limpets do a rock. "It stands to reason we'll be in danger many a time before we go out from this world, unless it so chances that we come to grief here; but I dare venture to say we'll never be nearer death than we have been since leaving the thicket."

James Otis

The relief of mind was so great, and the knowledge that we had come thus far undetected under the very eyes of a watchful enemy was so overpowering, that I could not for a moment make reply, and by the time I had gathered my scattered senses - scattered through very joy - we heard voices from the inside which told that the men were seeking to learn exactly where we were.

"Keep right on till you come to the horn-works," I heard a voice whisper, and the words had little or no meaning to me, for I was not familiar with the names of different portions of a regular fort; but the sergeant seemed to understand the command, for he began to creep in a southerly direction, still keeping within the shadow of the wall, until we arrived where was a stockade.

This, as I afterward came to know, was the "horn-works," which as yet was in an unfinished condition, and protected by a stockade of logs, between each of which last were spaces, in some cases two or three inches wide.

By lying with our faces against these narrow openings, it was possible to hold converse with those on the inside almost as well as if we were within the walls.

"Who are you, and where did you come from?" a voice asked, and Sergeant Corney took it upon himself, much to my relief, to act as spokesman.

"Messengers sent by General Herkimer, who have come from Oriskany."

"When did you leave there?"

"Yesterday."

"We thought the woods were overrun with Indians and Tories."

"So they are; but by some lucky chance we have come through thus far in safety, and would have speech with the commandant."

"I am Colonel Gansevoort. My people saw your signal this afternoon, and I myself have been watching for your arrival, but supposed you to be fugitives, for I never dared hope there was a possibility of reinforcements so near at hand. Will you make an attempt to get in by the sally-port?"

"Is there any other entrance, sir?"

"Yes; but the enemy have been keeping sharp watch there since noon, as if thinking something of this same kind might be attempted."

"We will deliver our message, sir, and then decide what to do," the old man said, grimly. "The words had best be repeated now, for we may be unable to utter them half an hour later."

Then Sergeant Corney delivered the message with which we were charged, and during a full minute after he ceased speaking the commandant remained silent.

When he spoke again, it was to say:

"It would be folly to give him now the signal of your arrival, since to discharge one of the cannon when there is no direct target in sight would be to apprise St.

James Otis

Leger of all the facts. If it were possible for you to return, I would say that we will signal the moment my men are ready for the sortie."

"I am of the mind that there will be no more danger in going back than in trying to enter the fort," Sergeant Corney said, half to himself. "Doubtless the enemy are watchin' the sally-port so closely that we would be seen tryin' to gain it, for on that side the shadow is less than here, and if there be large numbers posted to prevent an entrance, then must we come to grief."

"Meaning what?" Colonel Gansevoort asked, with no slight tinge of impatience in his tone, as if he did not care to hear the old soldier summing up all the situation.

"Meanin' that we are runnin' no greater risks in goin' back to General Herkimer, or at least not many more, than by tryin' to gain admission to the fort."

"It will simplify matters if you choose to return; but I would not ask any man to do so, in view of all the danger."

"What do you say, lad?" Sergeant Corney asked, laying his hand on my shoulder, and, although I would have given anything I possessed to have been at that moment behind the walls, I was not minded to show that my courage was less than his, therefore I replied:

"It is for you to say, accordin' to the agreement we made."

"But I would not set off against your wishes, because of the danger in the road, although I claim it would be quite as great if we attempted to enter the fort at once."

"Then it is decided you will return to General Herkimer," Colonel Gansevoort said, quickly, as if fearing lest we might repent of our decision. "Tell him that within five minutes after giving the signal we will make a sortie from the main gate in the direction of Oriskany."

"An' if it should be that we didn't get through alive?" Sergeant Corney said as if to himself, and the commandant replied, quickly:

"In such case, without means of knowing what has happened to you, we shall make the sortie and shed much blood uselessly. Is there anything I can do for you before you start?"

The old soldier hesitated, as if unable to think of anything we needed, and I, remembering the hunger which had assailed us while we lay hidden in the thicket, replied:

"If it so be you could spare us a bit of corn bread, we would be the better able to make a hurried journey."

"That you shall have, and in plenty," the commandant said, as if relieved at knowing our wants could be gratified with so little trouble, and Sergeant Corney added:

"Only so much as we can put in our pockets, for this is not the time to encumber ourselves even with provisions."

Some of the soldiers who had been standing near by

hurried away, returning a few moments later with as much bread as would have served to satisfy our hunger for a week at least.

When such a quantity as we needed for one meal had been pushed out between the logs of the stockade, my companion whispered to the commandant:

"We shall strike into the thicket to the westward, making a circle to the south around the fort, until coming to the road leading to Oriskany, crossing the river just below here, and now, sir, if you have no further demands, we will go."

"May God have you in His keeping," the colonel said, fervently, and without waiting to hear more the old soldier set off, this time leaving it for me to bring up the rear.

Now it was I came to understand that the rain was beginning to fall; the wind came in spiteful gusts, betokening a storm, and I could have hugged myself with glee at the thought that the elements were favoring us in the attempt which, at the outset, had seemed doomed to failure.

Before we had traversed half the distance from the fort to the thicket on the westerly side, the rain was falling heavily, and the wind whistling at such a rate as to have drowned any ordinary noise we might make in forcing our way through the foliage.

Never had a storm, which promised much bodily discomfort, been so warmly welcomed by me; never had one been more sadly needed by those who fought against the king and his savage followers for the cause of American liberty.

It is well known that Indians, like cats, are averse to exposing their bodies to rain, and when we set out on the return I had but little fear, believing that every one of Thayendanega's followers would be hugging his lodge closely, while the Tories would find it difficult to discern us from any great distance as we lay prone upon the ground.

Lest I spend too many words in the telling of it, let me say, in short, that we gained the thicket without causing an alarm, and, what was really strange, made our way through it in a westerly direction for fully a mile without meeting any living being.

Then it was that Sergeant Corney came to a halt, and, taking the corn bread from his pocket, began to munch it greedily as he said to me, speaking indistinctly because of the fulness of his mouth:

"I reckon, lad, we've passed the Britishers' lines, an' can begin to circle southward from this point."

While we were creeping away from the fort, beginning the second journey before having had time to rest from the first, I had said to myself again and again that it was the act of madmen for us to make any attempt at gaining General Herkimer's forces. In the first place there was no real necessity for such dangerous labor, because the signal could have been given by Colonel Gansevoort at a reasonably early hour next morning, and thus our commander would have known that the message was delivered. We were risking our lives foolishly, and when the old soldier spoke of making a circle from that point, in a tone which told that he was very well contented with himself and what he had done, I lost my temper, and replied, sharply:

"Ay, we have got through the lines safely because of the storm, which was a lucky chance in our favor, and one we could not have foreseen when you were so foolish as to propose that we go back to-night."

"It would have pleased you better had we made the attempt to get into the fort?"

"Ay, ten times over, for then instead of roaming these woods, taking a fool's chances of bein' shot down, we might be comfortable and in safety."

"An' remained there so long as pleased Colonel Gansevoort, for once inside that fort we placed ourselves under his command."

"Well, and why not?" I asked, in surprise.

"Because it does not please me to linger when there is other work to be done."

"But there was no real need of undertakin' this task," I said, with irritation.

"Yet it gave us an excuse to which he would listen for leavin', when, had we told the truth, I question if he had not tried to stop us."

"Well, what is the truth?" I cried, sharply.

"Is there nothin' in your mind that we are bound to do, now the message has been delivered?"

"Do you mean to aid Jacob?" I asked, as a sudden light began to dawn on me.

"Ay, lad, all of that. Neither you nor I would have let him gone alone in the hopeless task of rescuin' his father, had it not been that duty demanded of us to keep our faces turned toward yonder fort. Now we have done that which General Herkimer required, we can set out to fulfil our duty toward the lad, an' this goin' back on the road to Oriskany is but little more than we would be forced to do in order to gain the spot where we parted with him, for I'm countin' that he was then near by the place where his father is held prisoner."

I could have hugged the old man, but that he might have fancied I had lost my senses.

When we parted with Jacob there was no thought in my mind that Sergeant Corney had the slightest idea of joining in what was a most desperate venture, and I even fancied he felt a certain sense of relief in having such a good excuse for not sticking his nose into the Indian encampment. But now I understood that all the while he held firm to the determination to do whatsoever he might toward aiding Peter Sitz, and I began to feel real affection for the noble old man.

Whether we might be able to find Jacob or not, and the chances were that he had already been made prisoner, we could say to ourselves that the poor lad was not deserted by us in his hour of need, and, if the worst happened, it would be no slight satisfaction to us in after years.

The storm increased each moment, and we were soon

wetted to the skin, but hardly conscious of the discomfort because of the safety which this downpour brought to us.

I had never given Sergeant Corney credit for any great knowledge of woodcraft, because he came to us from over the seas where his life had been spent fighting battles in the open, and could not be expected to cope with the savage foe, as did our people who had always been accustomed to the skulking methods of warfare practised by the redskins.

Now, however, I was forced to give him credit for being wiser than I in the forest, since in the darkness and amid the tumult caused by the wind and rain he made the detour as if a broad trail stretched out before him under the sunlight, and we half-circled around the fortification, at the distance of a mile or more, without varying, so far as could be told, a single hair from the true course.

Not until we were come to the trail which led to Oriskany did the old man halt, and then it was to say to me:

"From this on I'm allowin' we had better be cautious how we move."

"But surely there is no danger of meetin' any of the savages now," I said, like a simple, and he replied, with a laugh:

"True for you, lad; but General Herkimer was to begin an advance on the mornin' after we left camp, and he should be nearabout. To run upon his sentinels in the darkness might not be agreeable."

From that on, until half an hour had passed, we pressed forward cautiously, and well it was that we did so, for suddenly I came upon a levelled musket, which would have been discharged but for my crying out quickly, as I swerved to one side:

"We are messengers for the general! We are friends!"

"You come from an odd direction if that be true," was the reply, and at the same instant a vigorous hand seized me by the shirt-collar.

Then it was that Sergeant Corney stepped forward, as he asked:

"Are you of General Herkimer's force?"

"How much will it benefit you to get such information?"

"Nay, nay, friend; there is no need of bein' over-cautious with us. We are two of the three messengers who left camp at Oriskany to go to Fort Schuyler, and are now returnin'."

"Returnin'?" the soldier said, for it was indeed one of General Herkimer's sentinels whom we had come upon. "It must please you to skulk around among the Tories and savages, if, after having once gained the fort, you come back."

"That is exactly what we have done, my friend," Sergeant Corney replied, gravely, "and for the good reason that Colonel Gansevoort had a message for us to deliver to the general. You are right in questioning us, for under such situations a soldier had best be overcautious than too credulous. But now we ask to be sent to the commander."

"Have you seen any of the enemy near at hand?" the man asked.

"I can swear there are none within half a mile."

"Then come with me," and the sentinel deserted his post to lead us into camp, a proceeding which called forth harsh criticisms from Sergeant Corney, despite the fact that he was being benefited thereby.

Chapter VII.

Insubordination

It was near to daybreak when we followed the soldier to where General Herkimer lay under a shelter of pine boughs; but owing to the storm the gloom was quite as profound as at any time during the night.

To my surprise, the general came out from his poor apology for a tent on hearing our voices, although we spoke cautiously low, and even then I could but ask myself why it was that an experienced soldier such as he was not giving more heed to his bodily welfare, for men on the eve of encountering a strong enemy surely need all the repose which can be had.

I was soon to understand why the commander slept so lightly, and to learn for the first time that even patriots may be insubordinate.

General Herkimer did not at first recognize us in the gloom; but when Sergeant Corney made himself known, the leader said, in a tone of bitter disappointment:

"Then you did not succeed in getting there?"

"Ay, that we did, sir," the old soldier replied,

emphatically; "but Colonel Gansevoort had the desire to send a message to you, and we have brought it, hopin' to be excused from further duty for a short time."

"What had Gansevoort to say?" General Herkimer asked, impatiently, and Sergeant Corney repeated the message twice over, in order that there should be no misunderstanding as to its meaning.

"Very well. We will be on the alert if these hotheads can be restrained," the general replied, and his words were a riddle to me until half an hour later.

Then he asked what the old soldier meant by wishing to be excused from duty, and the sergeant, in the fewest words possible, gave him an account of our proceedings since leaving the camp at Oriskany, concluding by saying:

"There is no question but that Jacob Sitz will make his way through the Indian encampment, if it can be done by any person. Yet the lad is blinded by love for his father, an' will take altogether too desperate chances, unless there be some one at hand who can restrain him."

"Is it in your mind that the prisoner may be taken out of Thayendanega's camp?" General Herkimer exclaimed.

"We do not count on any such good fortune; but follow the lad simply that he may know he has not been forgotten. If it so be you need us, sir, we will wait until you have gained the fort before making any effort to join him."

"No, no, it was not from such motives that I spoke," the general interrupted, hastily. "With a force as large as this two men would not make much of a count either way. Go where you please, Sergeant Braun, and when you are once more at liberty report to me."

"We reckon on resting our legs a bit, sir, before settin' out. You will not advance for some time to come, sir?"

"How far do you count we are from the enemy's pickets?"

"Not above two miles, sir."

"Then we shall remain here, unless matters get beyond my control, until having heard the signal."

Having made this, to me, odd remark, the commander disappeared from view inside the shelter of boughs, and Sergeant Corney led me a dozen yards or more from what might by courtesy have been called "headquarters," when he halted to say, gravely:

"It appears that things are not just as they should be in this camp, lad."

"How do you mean?" I asked, in surprise.

"You heard what the general said?"

"Ay."

"Well, who of his men are making the trouble?"

Before I could so much as make a guess at the proper answer, I must needs be told that there was trouble, for, through having failed to understand exactly what the commander meant, I had not suspected that there was anything serious brewing. But Sergeant Corney, experienced as he was in such matters, seemed to know as if he had been informed in so many words that insubordination was rife in the camp, and at a time when it was in the highest degree necessary the men should move in harmony.

Since I could not even so much as hazard a guess, the old man, forgetting his weariness and the need of gaining repose, led me out to where he had been halted by the sentinel, and, finding him at his post, began his investigations by saying:

"We two have just come from Fort Schuyler, an' knowin' full well how strong a force is in front of the place, have a better idea of the kind of work in hand than you who haven't seen the enemy."

"Did the general send you over here to tell me that?" the man asked, in a certain tone of irritation, and Sergeant Corney replied, soothingly:

"Not a bit of it, my friend; but while we were having an interview with the commander it struck me that matters here were not just as pleasant as they should be, an' instead of awakenin' some one who might need more slumber, we thought to come to you for an explanation."

"Of what?"

"That we cannot say; but there is a question I would ask you, as between man and man, for mayhap the lives of us all depend upon the general sense of good fellowship. Tell me plainly, is there insubordination in the camp?"

"I know not if you may call it by that name," the sentinel said, somewhat moodily; "but certain it is we would have relieved the fort four and twenty hours ago had General Herkimer not held us back. With such a force as we have here, it cannot be a hard matter to do about as we please. Look you," the man continued, growing more confidential, "the general has no less than eight hundred men under his command, and what may not a company of that number do?"

"Very much, my friend; but your eight hundred would be weak indeed unless the advance was made at the proper time and in a soldierly fashion. So your people have been complaining because the commander holds them back?"

"Ay, and with good cause. When Colonels Cox and Paris say openly that it is cowardly for us to loiter here, surely there must be some reason in their words. A full third of this force believe we should have come in front of Fort Schuyler yesterday mornin', an' think you all those can be mistaken, an' only General Herkimer stand in the right?"

"Then it *is* insubordination!" Sergeant Corney said, sadly, and the sentinel replied, angrily:

"It is only common sense and a desire to aid the Cause. If we are eager to begin a battle which will drive the Tories and their painted allies from the valley, surely that man is a criminal who would hold us back."

"If you had been where this lad and I have just come

from, able to see what was seen by us, you would talk in a different strain," the old soldier said, hotly. "Why, man, Colonel Gansevoort himself sent us back to request that you remain here until he signals, so that everything may be prepared for your comin', and we, knowin' how important it was you delay until the proper moment, risked our lives twenty times over in the effort to bring the word."

"Then Colonel Gansevoort is as great a coward as General Herkimer, for we are of sufficient strength to march whithersoever we will."

Sergeant Corney turned as if to go, and then suddenly wheeling upon the sentinel, said:

"I do not read my Bible, as a man should; but yet I remember that in it can be found these words: 'Fools die for want of wisdom,' an' I'm allowin', my friend, if you have any desire to linger in this 'ere world, that you take the statement home mighty strong."

With this cutting remark, which for a moment I feared would provoke a downright quarrel, Sergeant Corney strode off into the darkness, I following meekly at his heels.

"Surely there can be nothing which would work harm in this desire of the men to go forward," I said, when the sergeant had come to a halt, throwing himself down under a tree as if to rest. "It should be a good sign when soldiers are eager to go into battle."

"Insubordination, wherever you find it, is the most dangerous condition of affairs that can be figgered out. When a man puts himself under a leader, whether to fight or to till the land, an' then sets up his opinions against those of the one who is supposed to know best, else he wouldn't be in command, matters have come to a mighty dangerous pass. Instead of helpin' the men inside the fort, this regiment is likely to bring them to grief, unless things are changed, an' that right soon. Now get what sleep you can, lad, before the encampment is astir," the old man added, changing his tone very suddenly, and before I could obey he drew out his rifle from the hiding-place where he had left it when we set off for the fort.

I laid myself down by his side; but it was not to sleep, for I realized that the old soldier would not have spoken in such a tone unless matters, according to his belief, had been in a most serious condition.

I was still speculating upon the situation, sorrowing because the men would, at such a time, while the lives of so many depended upon concerted action, set up their individual opinions against those who had been put in authority over them, when a bustle on every side told that the soldiers were awakening to a day of noble struggle for their country, or worse than criminal bickerings.

If Sergeant Corney had really closed his eyes in slumber, which I doubted, he was now awakened by the many noises, and a plan of action must have been presented to him in his dreams, for he spoke like one who is determined upon some decided course, as he said to me:

"Now, lad, we'll fill ourselves up with one good hearty meal, if it so be this mutinously inclined army has a proper store of provisions, and then it is for us to decide whether we stay among those who are like to come to grief if they have their own way, or push out for ourselves."

I did not understand fully what he meant; but it was sufficient for me that he was no longer in doubt as to what was best, and right willingly did I obey his orders, for my stomach was uncomfortably empty.

There was no lack of food in this command which seemed to be divided against itself, and the breakfast would have been to me most enjoyable but for the sauce with which it was served.

Every man's tongue was loosened as if its owner was the only man amid all the company who knew exactly which was the wisest course to pursue, and I dare venture to say never a commander had under him at a critical moment, such as this certainly was, so many pig-headed recruits.

Only once during the brief meal was Sergeant Corney asked for information, although the word had passed around the encampment that he and I were but just come from Fort Schuyler, and then it was that the old soldier gave those insubordinate men such a tongue-lashing as they deserved and I dare say had never before received; but, storm as he might, it seemed as if all the arguments he brought up in favor of General Herkimer's carrying out the plans suggested by Colonel Gansevoort, only served to make those imitation soldiers more fixed in their opinions.

And for all this unseemly wrangling, when it was almost a crime to raise one's voice against an order of the commander, I lay the blame upon the two colonels,

Cox and Paris, who, instead of holding their men firmly in check, as was their duty, openly declared that General Herkimer was in the wrong; thus fomenting what promised to be a most serious disturbance, and what was finally paid for over and over again in blood.

It was perhaps half an hour after daybreak when Colonel Cox, the same officer who by injudicious use of his tongue had well-nigh compassed the death of us all during the powwow with Thayendanega, approached General Herkimer while the latter was walking slowly around the encampment as if on a tour of inspection, and said, in a tone so loud that all in the vicinity might hear it:

"Are we to go forward, sir, as men should who set out to relieve a besieged fort, or must we loiter here until the enemy has worked his will?"

For an instant the general made no reply, and Sergeant Corney whispered to me, angrily:

"That man deserves to be shot, an' all the more so because he is high in command. I've seen troops in many a tight place durin' my life, but never before heard any thin' that quite come up to that."

When, after a pause of fully a moment, General Herkimer spoke, it was to ask:

"Do you know that messengers have come from Gansevoort, asking that we hold our hands until he shall give the signal?"

"I have heard that it is pretended such a message has come," Colonel Cox replied, in a most offensive tone, and I could see Sergeant Corney clenching his fists tightly, as if thereby the better to hold himself in check, for surely were we two entitled to make reply to such an implied accusation.

"The garrison will make a sortie immediately after giving the signal, and we can thus go into action with some hope of success," General Herkimer said, mildly and firmly. "To advance before Gansevoort is ready would be to imperil the lives of all this command."

"Speaking more particularly for yourself, sir, I suppose," Colonel Paris said, with a sneer, and it would have given me the greatest pleasure to have struck him down for that insult.

Then the three officers, still disputing, or, I should have said, the two colonels still insulting their commander, who continued to bear with them beyond that point where forbearance ceases to be a virtue, passed out of earshot for the time being, and the men in the immediate vicinity took up the subject, until, to my surprise, I found that nearly all of them sided with the insubordinate colonels.

Five minutes later the three officers had approached so near where Sergeant Corney and I were sitting that we could hear their words once more, and then, to my indignation and the old soldier's anger, Colonel Cox cried, in a fury, as he planted himself directly in front of the commander:

"You are not only a coward, sir, but a Tory!"

I shall always hold that General Herkimer was a brave man, because, after a severe effort which was evident to us all, he so far mastered his righteous anger as to say, quietly:

"I am placed over you as a father and guardian, and shall not lead you into difficulties from which I may not be able to extricate you."

Unless the soldiers of the command had been literally beside themselves, such words would have brought them to a proper frame of mind; but as it was, the temperate reply seemed to inflame their anger, and on the moment there was a very babel of outcries, amid which it was only possible to distinguish the demand that the force be led toward Fort Schuyler without delay, regardless of any message which the sergeant and I might have brought.

I could see, rather than hear, for the tumult was exceeding great, that the two colonels continued to demand that the commander follow their plans rather than adhere to his own, and it was a veritable fishwoman's squabble during twenty minutes or more, when General Herkimer apparently lost his temper for the first time, and cried, in a tone so loud that the words could be distinctly heard all over the encampment:

"I will give the command to march forward, and you shall soon see that those who have been boasting loudest of their courage will be the first to run on meeting the enemy."

"I was afraid it would come to that," Sergeant Corney whispered to me, with a sigh. "It don't stand to reason that any man could hold his temper a great while under such a tongue-lashin' as those curs gave the commander, an' I'm predictin' that every mother's son of 'em will rue this mornin's work."

Immediately the unwilling permission for them to do as they pleased had been given, the men set about making ready for the advance as if each moment was of the greatest value, and in an incredibly short time after General Herkimer had been bullied into agreeing to that which his better judgment told him to be wrong, the company was ready for the march.

"Are we to go with them?" I asked of the sergeant, believing for the moment that it would be wiser for us to form an independent command of two.

"Ay, lad, I'm thinkin' that we had best stand by the general, for he may be needin' us before this mornin's work is done, an' we sha'n't be takin' a great deal of time from Jacob, because, in case of arrivin' before Colonel Gansevoort is ready for us, the scrimmage will soon be over."

The two colonels, who were responsible for this unsoldierly method of conducting a campaign, busied themselves with getting the men into lines, and all the while telling what it was possible for them to do to St. Leger and his force, as if anything of value could be done when the idiots did not have sufficient sense to make inquiries of those who could give them full information regarding the strength of the enemy whom they were so soon to meet.

Even had Sergeant Corney not decided to follow the commander before the line of march had been arranged, he would have done so later, because General Herkimer beckoned us to approach when he took his place at the head of the column.

"Are you counting on coming with me, despite the unnecessary danger which we know will be encountered?" he asked, and Sergeant Corney replied, promptly:

"Ay, sir, that we are, and had already settled it in our own minds."

"Which portion of the besieging troops are we likely to meet first, if we follow the trail?" the general asked.

"Thayendanega's camp lies southeasterly from the fort; but how far it may be from the trail, I cannot say."

At this moment the report of a rifle from the direction of where the outermost sentinels were stationed startled every one, including those bloodthirsty colonels, and for a moment all stood silent and motionless, waiting to learn the cause of the alarm.

Then it was that the sentinel with whom the sergeant and I had already spoken, came running into camp, for it seemed a favorite trick of his to desert a post of duty whenever inclination prompted.

It was Colonel Cox who asked, advancing:

"Did you fire that gun?"

"Ay, sir; I saw two Indians in the thicket, coming as if from the direction of this camp."

"Did you kill either of them?"

"I do not think I even scratched 'em. The wood is too dense for much good shooting."

Colonel Cox wheeled around as if the information was of no especial importance, when even a boy like me understood somewhat of its import, and, carelessly saluting the commander, reported that the troops were ready for the word to march.

The general, who was mounted, spurred his horse on to the head of the column, Sergeant Corney and I following as best we might, and once in the lead he gave the command.

"Is nothing to be done toward finding out whether the Indians whom the sentinel saw, succeeded in getting back to their own camp?" I asked of my companion, and he replied, grimly, with what was very like a smile of satisfaction on his wrinkled face:

"These officers who have so much wind to spare in camp cannot afford the time to consider such trifles as a few scouts skulkin' around to make certain of what we are doin'."

"An' we are like to find ourselves ambushed!" I cried, in dismay.

"Ay, that's what we are, lad, an' I'm thinkin' there will be no way out of the difficulty until some of these insubordinates are killed off, which will be greatly to the advantage of the command, accordin' to my way of thinkin'."

I will set down here that which I read in a book several years after the day Sergeant Corney and I followed

General Herkimer on what we believed to be a most ill-advised and hazardous march, in view of Colonel Gansevoort's request, and from the words it will be seen that I am not the only person who lays blame of all that happened upon those loud-mouthed, imitation soldiers who were so soon to show themselves cowards.

"The morning was dark, sultry, and lowering. General Herkimer's troops, composed chiefly of the militia regiments of Colonels Cox, Paris, Visscher, and Klock, were quite undisciplined, and their order of march was irregular and without precaution. The contentions of the morning had delayed their advance until about nine o'clock, and the hard feelings which existed between the commander and some of his officers caused a degree of insubordination which proved fatal in its consequences.... A deep ravine crossed the path of Herkimer in a north and south direction, extending from the high grounds on the south to the river, and curving toward the east in semicircular form. The bottom of this ravine was marshy, and the road crossed it by means of a causeway of earth and logs. On each side of the ravine the ground was nearly level, and heavily timbered. A thick growth of underwood, particularly along the margin of the ravine, favored the concealment of the enemy."

All the colonels of this small army were on horseback, a fact which caused me no little astonishment, for I had heard my uncle say again and again, and there can be no question but that he was a brave and skilful soldier, that the man who went in the saddle to meet savages was courting his own death.

So great was my indignation against these men who

had badgered the commander that I mentally hugged myself with delight because of their folly, not only in thus riding, but in moving the column without scouts ahead to learn the whereabouts of the enemy, or to ascertain what might be in front of, or on either side of them.

It is true that Colonel Visscher's regiment was detailed as a rear-guard, and I question if even such a precaution would have been taken but for the fact that the provision and ammunition wagons, which were not able to move at as rapid a pace as the men, needed something in the way of protection.

It was not until we had advanced half a mile or more that I bethought myself of the position in the column which Sergeant Corney and I occupied because of attempting to follow General Herkimer closely.

In event of an ambush being prepared for our reception, and I confidently expected that such would be the case after the sentinel had seen Indians lurking nearabout the camp, we two would be in a most dangerous position, and I made mention of that which was in my mind to the sergeant.

"Ay, lad, you may be right, an' yet I am questionin' whether we shall be any worse off here than further in the rear, for if it so be Thayendanega's sneaks count on ambushin' us, I can tell you to a dot just where it'll be done. They will let this gang of men - you can't call 'em soldiers after what we have seen - get well into the ravine before makin' any attack. Consequently it will be about the centre of the line that suffers most."

"You mean that if trouble comes it will be at the ravine

over which is the causeway?"

"Ay, lad, an' there's no question about our gettin' it hot there!"

Chapter VIII.

The Ambush

I am willing to confess that I grew more and more frightened as we neared the ravine, and but for the disgraceful scenes of insubordination which occurred earlier in the morning, I would have cried out against the folly of thus going blindly into such trap as Thayendanega's murderers had probably prepared for us.

As it was, however, I would not let these mutinous men who called themselves soldiers see that we from Cherry Valley would question a commander's orders, whatever might be the situation, and I held my peace, but with much effort and inward fear.

There was little attempt made by these representatives of the Tryon County militia to hold in military formation during the march, each man trying to outstrip his neighbor, as if this advance upon a foe of superior strength could have no more serious consequences than that some might be left behind, and when one of the company came up to my side with words of complaint because the general would not move faster than a walk, I said, angrily:

"It can make but little difference if you are not killed at

the first volley, for the savages will have ample time to finish us all off after we have walked into their trap."

"So you are one of the weak-kneed, eh?" the man cried, with a sneer, and my anger was too great to permit of my making reply; but Sergeant Corney, who had heard the insulting words, said, sharply:

"You may talk to that lad about bein' weak-kneed after you have shown the courage he has within the past four an' twenty hours. You an' your mutinous comrades prate loudly of bravery when there is no enemy in sight; but I'll lay odds that not one out of an hundred like you would dare go alone from here to the fort!"

"Oh, you are the messengers who claim that Colonel Gansevoort asked us to remain idle until he should give the signal, eh?" the fellow said, in an offensive tone, and Sergeant Corney raised his rifle clubwise, as if to strike him down, but held his hand as he said, slowly, and in a tone which was full of menace:

"But that you are already so near your death at the hands of the enemy, I would make certain you never again questioned my word! We did go to the fort, while you were engaged in the manly sport of badgerin' your commander, an old soldier who knows his business, an' had you been with us it is certain you'd never made the attempt to get back. Go on to your death, you fool, an' I'll hope it don't come so soon but that you'll have time to realize you did all in your power to bring it about the more speedily."

By this time we were well within the ravine which has already been described, and the old soldier had hardly ceased speaking when from amid the foliage ahead and on every side came a circle of fire like unto the lightning's flash, followed by the crackling of firearms, which served to drown the death-cries from every portion of our lines.

We had marched like children into the ambush, and on the instant a blind rage took possession of me because I had followed the mutineers when I knew full well to what they were hastening.

Even as the flashes of light sprang out from among the leaves, I saw Colonel Cox, he who was responsible for all that flood of death, leap high in the air, only to fall back dead, and at the same moment General Herkimer's horse reared and screamed in a death-agony.

It was as if every second man of the command fell before that withering fire, and in the midst of the tumult of groans, screams, and savage war-whoops could be heard shouts behind us, telling that the rear-guard, who a few moments previous were prating of their bravery, had turned and fled like cowards that they were.

More than the rear-guard would have beat a retreat at that moment, but for the fact that the baggage-wagons hemmed us in so that flight was well-nigh impossible.

It seemed as if I lived a full hour during the terrible ten seconds that elapsed after the first volley was fired by the hidden foe, and then I heard Sergeant Corney crying in my ear, his voice sounding as if afar off:

"It is for you an' I, lad, to look after the general! He

is wounded!"

Then it was that I realized the commander was pinned to the earth by his dead horse, and, without being really conscious of my movements, I ran to his side.

The old soldier and I had no more than bent over General Herkimer to learn how we could best release him from his dangerous position, when a second volley came from amid the foliage, and those alleged soldiers of the command who were yet alive ran wildly to and fro like frightened chickens, seeking some way of escape, rather than standing up like men to battle for their own lives.

Without really seeing it, I was conscious that all this was taking place around us, and then I heard Sergeant Corney say to the general, in a matter-of-fact tone:

"That's a bad wound in your knee, sir."

"Ay, but there's no time to think of ourselves just now. The cowards must be brought to their senses, or every one of them will be shot down," was the reply of the man whom his own soldiers had taunted with cowardice not an hour previous.

Acting under Sergeant Corney's commands, for the old man was as cool as if he had been born amid just such scenes of carnage, I helped raise the body of the horse until it was possible for General Herkimer to roll himself out from beneath the dead animal, and, while we worked to aid him, the commander was crying to his men to stand firm if they would save their own lives.

"Rally, there!" he shouted, yet lying, unable to move, upon the ground. "Stand firm, and we yet have a good chance of holding our own!"

All the while Sergeant Corney and I worked over him he continued to cheer the frightened men, until, by the time we had dragged him to where he could sit upright with his back against a huge tree, placing his saddle beneath him to serve as a prop, the men were beginning to understand that the only chance for life was to fight desperately.

The wagons in the rear, and the horde of savages which had closed in upon us, prevented any save those who had first fled, from retreating, and by the time a full third of the command had been killed or disabled, the remainder understood that it would be well to turn to the man they had so lately reviled, for possible safety.

Sergeant Corney and I gave no heed to what was going on around us until we had bound up the general's knee in such a manner that there was no longer danger he would bleed to death, and when this had been done I noted that our people had taken shelter behind the trees, where they could strike a blow in their own defence.

The Indians, understanding that the first daze of terror had passed away, leaving their intended victims in condition to do considerable execution, fell back a short distance to where they could find shelter, and thus, thanks to General Herkimer, it was no longer a massacre, but a battle.

When Sergeant Corney and I had done all we could to

render the commander more comfortable, we took our share in the fight, remaining close beside General Herkimer meanwhile, lest the Indians make an attempt to take him prisoner.

Within half an hour from the time the first volley had been fired, our people were doing good execution, and yet the enemy's line was closing in upon us slowly but surely.

"Tire 'em out, lads!" the general shouted, encouragingly. "You never yet saw a painted snake who could take much punishment, an' it's only a question of holding your own awhile longer. Make every bullet count, for, although we have ammunition in plenty, there is no good reason why we should waste any."

Then the commander, most likely in order to set his men an example of coolness, rather than because he needed the fumes of tobacco, quietly lighted his pipe, and, seeing this, our people cheered at the same time they shot down every feather-bedecked form that was exposed to view.

A few moments later General Herkimer gave the word that our force form a circle, in order to meet the foe at every point, and after this had been done the enemy were the better held in check.

Even at the moment I was surprised when I found myself thinking of the danger to which Jacob must be exposed, rather than of my own desperate plight. While on the alert for a living target, I speculated whether he was yet free, and if he had discovered the whereabouts of his father.

I had no idea as to the flight of time, and could not have told whether we had spent ten minutes or sixty in that struggle for life, when, without warning, the floodgates of heaven were opened. The rain came down literally in torrents; it seemed as if the water descended in solid sheets rather than drops, and, no matter how bloodthirsty a man might have been, he could no more have continued the battle than if he had been neck-deep in the river.

Savages as well as white men were forced to cease their efforts to kill, and for a time we crouched beneath such poor shelter as the trees afforded, but drenched to the skin in a twinkling.

General Herkimer was in no better plight than those who were the most exposed. The fire in his pipe was drowned out; but he continued to hold it between his teeth as he said, in a low tone, to Sergeant Corney:

"Pass the word quietly for our people to close in where it will be possible to hear what I say. Thus far I've noted that the savages have watched until a rifle has been discharged, when they rush up and use their hatchets. We can put an end to that kind of butchery."

The old soldier did as he had been bidden, moving to and fro without fear of exposing himself, for the downpour was so great that no man could have loaded a musket with dry powder, and even while the storm continued the circle was contracted until the commander was enclosed by a living hedge.

Then it was that orders were given for the men to take their stations in couples, and, when one had discharged his rifle, the other was to wait until the Indians came up to kill the supposedly defenceless soldier, when a second bullet would be ready for them.

Much to my surprise, I heard General Herkimer say that a full hour had elapsed from the time the first volley had been fired, and it stiffened the courage of all to learn that we had been able to hold the foe in check so long.

Immediately the summer storm had so far sub-sided that the weapons could be loaded, the battle was continued, raging with even more fury than before, as the enemy tried to overwhelm us by a sudden rush, and in a very few seconds the painted fiends came to understand that it was no longer an easy matter to tomahawk a man immediately after he had fired a shot.

When the savages found that their tactics were guarded against, it seemed as if they lost courage, and gradually fell back a little, having had quite as much of Whig marksmanship as was pleasing.

Because we could no longer see as many targets before us, the fire was slackened considerably, and then some one on the outer lines of our defensive circle shouted:

"They are bringin' up the Tories! Here come the Johnson Greens!"

Although I was standing well in the centre of our force, it was possible to see the uniforms of that band of renegades which Sir John had armed and equipped that they might kill their neighbors, as the men came up to take the place of the retreating redskins, and, if anything had been needed to stiffen the backs of our people, surely they got it when seeing those whom they had once called friends, moving into line to compass their death.

I had thought that the men under General Herkimer's command fought bravely after the cowards were weeded out, and those who were left understood that, but for the mutiny in camp, the ambush would not have been successful; but now they seemed like veritable tigers as the Tories came into the battle.

There was no longer any thought of fighting from behind trees, but each man pushed forward intent only on vanquishing the renegades, until none save Sergeant Corney and I were left to guard our wounded commander.

I will set down here that account of the battle from this point, which I found some time since in a book containing the story of the fight in the ravine, sometimes called the Battle of Oriskany:

"Major Watts came up with a detachment of Johnson's Greens to support them (the savages), but the presence of these men, mostly refugees from the Mohawk, made the patriots more furious, and mutual resentments, as the parties faced and recognized each other, seemed to give new strength to their arms. They leaped upon each other with the fierceness of tigers, and fought hand to hand and foot to foot with bayonets and knives."

While this portion of the battle was at its height, we suddenly heard the reports of firearms from the direction of the fort, and my heart leaped into my throat, for I understood that Colonel Gansevoort was making the sortie for which we should have waited.

Nor was I the only one who thus realized that the Britishers and their painted allies were at the end of their rope, so far as this fight in the ravine was concerned, for our people pressed the foe yet more hotly, and in a short time the savages raised the cry of "Oonah! Oonah!" which told that they had had enough of the battle.

So far as my experience goes, and I have had considerable from first to last, Indians are only brave when they have the advantage; but, let the tide turn against them, and they are veriest cowards.

Hemmed in as we were, our ranks thinned by death and the desertion of the rear-guard, it should have been possible for the enemy to cut us down to a man, and yet the retreating cry of the savages sufficed to send all that force back to the encampment, leaving us in possession of the field, even though we might not rightly be called victors.

Some of our people, upon whom the fever of battle had fastened more firmly, would have pursued the cowards, even though it might have been to come directly upon the main army, who were then, doubtless, engaged in checking the sortie from the fort; but General Herkimer sent a squad of the cooler soldiers after them, with the result that the valiant Johnson Greens were allowed to continue their retreat unmolested.

And it was high time we had a breathing-spell. More than two hundred of General Herkimer's force lay dead among the trees, while even a larger number were so seriously wounded as to be unable to defend them-selves, therefore it was impossible for us to act in concert with those who were making the sortie, and the commander issued orders to fall back.

The contents of the baggage-wagons were thrown out to make room for our wounded, and, while the uproar of the battle near the fort rang in our ears, we retreated from that valley of death.

Now those who had raised their voices against the general, accusing him of cowardice, did all within their power to make atonement by their care of him, and willing hands bore him on a litter that he might be spared the pain of transportation in the lumbering wagons.

It was a sorry train that left the ravine, not stopping to bury the dead because of the certainty that St. Leger's army would come to finish the bloody work as soon as the force from the fort had been driven back, and when it was in motion Sergeant Corney gripped me by the arm, as he said:

"Our road is not in that direction, lad. Yonder men may take the repose which they do not deserve after havin' brought about all this disaster; but we must face danger once more, an' perhaps for the last time."

"Meanin' that we're to go back in search of Jacob?" I asked, feeling for the moment as if it would be impossible for me to voluntarily turn my face in the direction of the enemy, now that I was no longer animated by the fever of battle.

"Ay, lad, our duty is now toward him, havin' done all we may under General Herkimer's command. As I figger it, we're free to do as we choose, for we can no longer aid those who are goin' back when, but for rankest mutiny, they might have entered the fort amid the cheers of victory. If Colonel Gansevoort is forced to surrender, it can all be set down to the credit of those who howled so loudly this mornin' that they could march straight through the enemy's lines."

"There is little hope we can find Jacob after so long a time has passed," I said, thinking of the perils that must necessarily await us while we tried to make our way through Thayendanega's camp.

"I grant you that, lad, an' yet we are bound to make the venture, or let it be said that we deserted a comrade when he needed us."

"We did that same when we pressed on toward the fort," I suggested, feebly.

"Ay, an' because we were in duty bound to carry the general's message. Now that work has been done, we are free."

I could not well say anything more against his plan without laying myself open to a charge of cowardice, - and at that moment I really was a coward, - therefore I stood ready to follow him.

There were provisions in plenty strewn on the ground, having been thrown out of the wagons to make room for the wounded, and from such store Sergeant Corney gathered up as much as would serve us during four and twenty hours.

This we stuffed into the pockets of our shirts; filled our powder-horns and bullet-pouches from the ammunition on the dead bodies, and then we were ready to leave that valley of death.

All this while it was possible to hear the din of that battle which was being fought near the fort; but as we advanced it became evident that the conflict was subsiding.

It would have been folly for the besieged to do other than beat a retreat, when it could be seen that General Herkimer's men were not in a position to take advantage of the sortie, and as soon as might be the brave fellows sought the shelter of the fort once more, leaving twenty of their comrades between the lines as victims of the mutiny among the Tryon County militiamen.

Much to my surprise, Sergeant Corney appeared sadly disappointed when the tumult of battle died away, and I asked if he believed that the people from the fort should have made an attempt to inflict more punishment upon the enemy.

"Not a bit of it, lad," the old soldier replied, promptly. "They have already done more than could have been expected; but yet I had a hope that the scrimmage would have lasted a bit longer."

"Why?" I asked, in surprise.

"Because we stand a better chance of circlin' around to where we left Jacob, while the villains have somethin' to keep 'em busy. Now there's no longer any need to fight, they'll likely keep sharper watch. Yet I count that Peter Sitz, if they haven't killed him already, has a bigger show of livin' a spell longer than he had last night."

"Why?"

"Because it stands to reason that Thayendanega's beauties have taken more than one prisoner, an' will have a better supply of livin' material for the stake than before. Peter may be lucky enough to keep his hair a spell longer; but there'll be many a poor wretch who'll taste of torture this night."

"An' perhaps Jacob may be one of them!" I cried, in an agony of apprehension, and from that moment it was not necessary the old soldier urge me forward, for I burned with the desire to do all I might to find our comrade before it should be too late.

When we left the ravine in search of the lad, it was necessary we advance over much the same course as when we carried General Herkimer's message, and it was slightly in our favor that we knew fairly well at how great a distance from the general encampment of the enemy we must keep in order to avoid running into the Indians.

Then, again, it seemed probable we had a better chance of making our way around this circle than when we first traversed it, because just at this time Thayen-danega's villains had received such a drubbing at the hands of the patriots as would most likely prevent them from having any keen desire to come upon more white men.

It was also probable, as Sergeant Corney had suggested, that they had taken a number of prisoners during the fight with the garrison of the fort, as well as at the ravine, and the murderous scoundrels would be so occupied with making preparations for torturing such poor unfortunates as to neglect their duties as St. Leger's allies.

When I had thus viewed the situation, it did not appear such a difficult matter for us to gain a station to the southward of Thayendanega's encampment; but coming across Jacob was quite a different proposition. Finding a needle in a hay-stack seemed much more simple than running upon a lad who was doing his best to remain hidden from view, unless, perchance, he had already been captured.

"It ain't any easy job, figger as you will," Sergeant Corney said, when I had put the situation before him from my point of view. "But I'm reckonin' that we're goin' to come somewhere near succeedin'. We can count on doin' pretty much as we please from now till to-morrow mornin', providin' we don't stick our noses into the camps of the Britishers or Tories, for you can set it down as a fact that every red-faced wretch will have considerable on hand this night. The only trouble will be that we may have to keep within cover while they're torturin' some poor fellow under our very shadows. You'll have to keep in mind that Peter an' Jacob Sitz are the only white men we're after, an' shut both eyes an' ears to every one else."

"Suppose Jacob has been made prisoner? Would you risk your life to save him?"

The old man made no reply until I had repeated the question, and then he said, slowly:

"If there was any show of bein' able to work the trick,

you could count on me to the end; but if he *has* fallen into their clutches, unless some wonderfully big turn of affairs comes in our path, we would be only throwin' away the lives of both without chance of helpin' him. I've heard long-tongued boasters tellin' how they'd rescued a prisoner from an Indian camp, but I never believed anything of the kind, for it ain't to be done more'n one time in a thousand, an' then you'd have to find a lot of red-skinned idjuts to work on."

Sergeant Corney had used a good many words in replying to my short question, and I believed he had done so to the end that I might not fully understand what he meant.

As I made it out, however, he would turn his back on poor Jacob in case the savages had him in their power, and I asked myself again and again what course I should pursue in such a situation.

We made a long detour around the battle-field in order to avoid as much as possible the danger of stumbling upon the enemy's scouts, and, when the afternoon was half-spent, had come, as nearly as we could guess, to a point due south from Thayendanega's camp.

"How far do you reckon we are from St. Leger's force?" I asked, when Sergeant Corney threw himself on the ground within shelter of a clump of bushes, as if for a long halt.

"Three miles or more from their lines of sentinels, if they've got any out, an' we're none too far away, 'cordin' to my figgerin'. After sunset we'll work in toward 'em; but there needn't be any hurry, for I'm reckonin' that we don't want to do much work till after midnight. If Jacob is still free to do as he pleases, there's little danger he'll come to grief 'twixt now an' mornin'."

"Unless he should see them torturin' his father, an' then it's certain he'd make a fight, no matter how great the odds against him," I suggested, thinking of what I would be tempted to do under similar circumstances.

"In that case we're better off where we are. I don't allow that a lad has any right to deliberately throw away his own life, an' that's what Jacob would be doin' if he showed himself when the villains had his father at the stake."

"He couldn't stand still an' see it done."

"True for you; but, no matter how he might feel, it's his duty to think of his mother, an' surely she would say that it was better one came home, than for both to be killed."

"It's a mighty hard outlook," I said, with a sigh.

"You're right, an' at the same time you ain't makin' matters any better by chewin' it over. A man don't fit himself for a fight by figgerin' out all the possible horrors."

"An' you think we'll have a fight before this venture is ended?"

"I'll leave it to you if somethin' of the kind don't seem reasonable," the old man replied, grimly, and then he set about making a dinner from the supply of provisions we had found in the ravine.

After that I made no more effort to keep up a conversation, and tried very hard to force from my mind any speculations regarding Jacob and his father, but with poor success. It seemed as if every subject had some bearing upon the matter, and so disagreeable was the constant harking back to what was beyond my control, that I really felt glad when the shadows of night began to lengthen, for almost any kind of action was better than remaining there in hiding, eating one's heart out.

Sergeant Corney gave no sign that he realized night had come, until I called his attention to the fact, and then he said:

"Ay, lad, the time is drawin' nigh; but I reckon that we'll be wise to hold on as we are a spell longer."

Then he lay back as if bent on going to sleep, and I held my peace, determined to say no more even though he remained there until sunrise.

It must have been ten o'clock before he showed signs of life, and then he rose to his feet as he said:

"I allow that we'd better be movin', though there ain't any great need of hurryin'. We'll be able to cover three miles in an hour, an' even then be a bit early for good work."

"How will you set about findin' Jacob?" I asked, giving words to the question which had been in my mind ever since we came to a halt.

"Our only chance is to keep movin' nearabout Thayendanega's camp, an' trustin' to accident for comin' across him."

Sergeant Corney strapped his rifle on his back, as if believing he would have no use for it; but he made certain his knife was loose in its sheath, and I understood that if we had trouble it would be at close quarters.

At last we were ready, and this time the sergeant did not propose that I lead the way.

He strode off in advance, with never a glance backward to see if I was following, and in silence we went on toward the danger-point at a swift pace, until the old man halted to say, in a whisper:

"There should be sentinels nearabout, unless Thayendanega believes he has killed all the decent men in the Mohawk Valley; so have your wits about you, lad, for a mistake now will cost us dearly."

Chapter IX.

The Indian Camp

I claim that it is nothing to my discredit when I say that there was a great fear in my heart while we advanced at a snail's pace, after having come to that point where we might reasonably expect the Indian sentinels would be posted.

In the darkness, moving amidst the dense foliage, where it required the utmost care to avoid betraying one's whereabouts, advancing blindly into you knew not what peril, was well calculated to make even the most courageous feel a bit timid.

At any moment we might literally stumble over a party of warriors in such numbers that there could be no possibility of making our escape, and in case we should come face to face with no more than four or five of the enemy, it would be well-nigh useless to show fight, because of the hundreds everywhere around who could be summoned to the assistance of their comrades.

Before we had advanced an hundred paces, I became convinced that it was impossible we should be able to reconnoitre the camp and return to the point from where we had set out without being killed, or, what was worse, taken prisoner, and yet, had I known for a certainty that such fate awaited us, I would not have let Sergeant Corney know of my unwillingness to follow him.

Sorely did I blame Jacob for having forced us into such a position of danger, when there was little hope any good could be effected by our coming, and more than once I promised myself that, if by any fortunate chance I succeeded in arriving at Cherry Valley again, no one could tempt me to leave it.

It was useless, however, to mourn over what could not be cured. We had come there voluntarily, and, unless both of us were willing to write ourselves down as cowards, must perform the task.

It was well-nigh midnight before we heard anything of the enemy, and then a faint hum of voices in the distance told that Sergeant Corney had led the way truly and wonderfully well. Never again would I say that he was not thoroughly versed in woodcraft.

The old soldier gripped my arm to make certain I understood that we had come near to the enemy, and then inch by inch we moved forward, halting a few moments every time we incautiously caused a rustling among the foliage.

How long that slow progress continued I cannot rightly say; but it seemed to me as if the morning was near at hand when we were arrived, having miraculously passed such stragglers, scouts, or sentinels as might have been in the vicinity, at a point where we could have a view of this particular portion of the encampment.

Three or four hundred Indians were dancing wildly around a huge fire, while half as many more were feasting, preparing their own food by cutting it from the carcasses of two oxen which lay near at hand, and broiling it on the live coals.

I knew sufficient of savage customs to understand that, if there had been any torturing of prisoners during the evening, such fiendish work was at an end, and that which we were witnessing was but the ending of the barbarous sport.

Now it was that I mentally thanked Sergeant Corney for having delayed so long before starting, for it would have been agony indeed had we been forced to witness the horrible spectacle of a white man suffering under the knives and by the fire of these wolves in human form.

We remained there stretched out at full length on the ground, with no possibility of gaining information which might be of service to us in the future, ten minutes or more, and then, suddenly, I was forced to exert all my will-power to prevent a scream of fear from escaping my lips, for what was unmistakably a human foot had been planted directly upon my leg.

Like a flash, after I succeeded in restraining myself from giving an alarm, came the knowledge, I know not how, that he who had stumbled upon me was no less frightened than I, and, clutching Sergeant Corney's leg nervously to attract his attention, I sprang upon the newcomer, believing him to be some Indian straggler whom it was absolutely necessary we should silence in order to save our own lives.

James Otis

So quick had been my motions that the fellow had no opportunity to get away, save at the cost of betraying himself to us, and by what seemed to be the most fortunate chance, I succeeded, when leaping blindly forward, in gripping him by the throat.

We went down together, I on top striving most earnestly to strangle him to death, and he fighting quite as strenuously to throw off my hold.

Before one could have counted ten I began to realize that this stranger who was at my mercy appeared quite as much afraid of making a noise as did I, and involuntarily my grasp was loosened ever so slightly, for I understood that had it been an Indian he would have done his best to attract the attention of those near the camp-fire.

With this thought came the knowledge that I had beneath me one clad much like myself, and not the half-naked body of such villains as marched in Thayendanega's train.

Then it was, and just as Sergeant Corney came up to us, that I loosened my grasp entirely in order to pass my hands over the stranger's face and head.

There were no feathers, no daubs of paint, which should have been apparent to the touch, and I whispered, with my mouth close to the fellow's ear, while yet pinioning his arms in such a fashion that he could not well move:

"Who are you?"

"A white man," came the reply, the words sounding

thick and muffled because of the squeezing which the speaker's throat had received.

Then like a flash came to me that which I should have suspected before!

It was my comrade for whom we had been searching that I was grappling with, and, just as the old soldier knelt by my side knife in hand to put an end to the struggle, I whispered, for the darkness was so intense that I could not even see the face which was but a few inches from my own:

"Are you Jacob Sitz?"

"Ay; an' you?"

"It is the sergeant an' Noel, lad, an' right glad am I that we came to know each other just as we did, else would your blood have been on our hands."

Jacob apparently gave no heed to the close shave which had been his, so great was the delight at knowing we were with him once more, and we three sat with our heads close together in order that we might question and be questioned without fear of betraying our whereabouts.

"Where have you been all this time?" I asked, and Jacob replied, softly:

"Hangin' around this camp. Twice have I come near bein' discovered, an' of a verity I believed, when you clutched my throat, that this was the last - the endin' of it all."

"Have you seen your father?" Sergeant Corney asked, and the lad replied, triumphantly:

"Ay, an' had speech with him."

"Where is he?"

"In a lodge near Thayendanega's, an' until to-night there has been no great danger he would be tortured, as I believe because of the sachem's promise that he shall not be killed."

"How did you get to speak with him?" I asked, in surprise.

"Within three hours after leavin' you I was hereabout, an' saw him. That night I crept through the village undiscovered, for even the dogs failed to bark at me, I know not why, an' there talked with my father as I now talk with you."

"If you got away, why could not he have done the same?" I asked, surprised that Jacob should have succeeded in making his way among the lodges.

"I urged him to make the attempt, but he claimed that there was no hope we two could leave the village undiscovered. First he was bound hand an' foot, an', although I might have cut my way through the lodge to release him from the fetters, he forbade it because of the risk, sayin' I must not endanger my life on account of mother, an' insistin' that at some future time escape would be more easy than then. He ordered me to go home at once, providin' I could not find you, an' I would have done so this night but for the battle of the mornin'."

"Why did that stop you?" I asked. "Surely you had no part in it?"

"No; but the savages were so infuriated that I feared even Thayendanega himself would be unable to prevent the wretches from leadin' my father to the stake, therefore I remained on watch. Three prisoners have been murdered in a most barbarous manner, but yet he was left unmolested in the lodge. Have you somethin' to eat?"

I took from my pocket all the food remaining, and the lad devoured it like one famished, whereupon Sergeant Corney asked:

"Have you had nothin' to eat since we left you?"

"I gathered some roots an' berries, but not enough to satisfy my hunger."

"An' yet you would have stayed here longer in danger of starvation?"

"Ay, until havin' satisfied myself that father was as safe as one can be who remains in the power of such as are encamped here. Did you come for no other purpose than to find me?"

"Nothin' more," I said, not minded to let him know that if he could show any reasonable chance of rescuing Peter Sitz it was our purpose to give him aid.

"Where have you been all this while?"

"That is too long a story to tell now," Sergeant Corney interrupted. "If the savages are not likely to do more than dance from now till mornin', we may as well find a shelter in which to spend the morrow, an' then I'm of the opinion that the three of us had best make tracks for Cherry Valley, as Jacob's father advised."

As he ceased speaking, Sergeant Corney would have led us out of the thicket; but Jacob whispered, softly:

"Not half a mile away is a small cave - no more than a hole in the hillside, an' there we may remain hidden durin' the hours of daylight."

"Lead the way, an' we will follow," the old man said, in a tone of command, and straightway Jacob did as he was thus ordered.

Knowing, as the lad did, very nearly where the Indians might be found, we advanced with reasonable rapidity, until having come to the place of which he had spoken.

It was indeed no more than a hole in the ground, and so small that when we three were lying at full length inside with our heads toward the opening, it would have been a very small cat who could have found a chance to lie down comfortably with us.

Some bushes and a tangle of creeping vines hid the entrance most admirably; but, after we were once inside, I questioned to myself whether we had not been reckless in coming directly to this place without taking precautions to cover our footprints, for, should a keen-eyed savage chance to see our trail, there was good reason for believing he would follow it up.

However, we were there, and the mischief might not be undone readily, therefore I held my peace, saying mentally that if Sergeant Corney and Jacob were satisfied with having taken no especial precautions, then of a verity ought I, the least experienced in woodcraft of the three, be content.

When Jacob had eaten all the small store of provisions which I gave him without having apparently satisfied his hunger, he insisted on our telling him what we had done since he left us, and I related the story much as it is set down here, spending a full hour in the recital.

When I had finally come to an end, the old soldier proposed that as soon as another day had passed we should turn our faces toward Cherry Valley, for, after receiving the commands of his father, Jacob could do no less than go home.

I understood full well that the lad would have encountered any danger or suffered every privation rather than leave this place where his father was held prisoner, even though there was little or no hope he could aid him; but yet he did not argue against the plan, and thus was it settled that when night came again we would start on our journey.

"Save for the fact that father himself insisted I should go, no one could force me to leave here," Jacob said, after a long pause, and Sergeant Corney added, soothingly, saying that which I question if he himself really believed:

"You can do no better, lad. If Thayendanega has given his word to save your father's life, so will it be, despite all the howlin' wolves in his followin'. But if you should stay here and be discovered tryin' to rescue him, there is little doubt that it would result in the death of both."

With that we fell silent once more, and I was right glad of an opportunity to sleep.

Jacob insisted that the old soldier and I give ourselves up to slumber while he kept guard, for he did not need the rest as much as we.

Therefore it was that I slept soundly and sweetly until a full hour past noon, and when I awakened the sergeant was peering out through the leafy curtain in front of the cave, while Jacob was enjoying his turn at sleep.

"Can you see the camp?" I asked, wriggling forward until my head was close beside his, and then it was not necessary he should make reply, for we had from this place of vantage a fairly good view of the red-skinned portion of St. Leger's army.

It is true that the trees and bushes screened certain portions of the encampment, but the greater number of the lodges were in a clearing, and Sergeant Corney pointed out to me that shelter which Jacob had told him was the one where his father was confined.

The Indians were lounging about lazily, some stretched at full length sleeping, others gathered in little companies, squatting on the ground as they smoked and talked, and not a few moving slowly to and fro; but never one who appeared to have any business on hand.

There were both women and children in the camp, which struck me as being odd, for when savages set off on the war-path it is not customary for them to take their families; but I explained this peculiar state of affairs to myself by the supposition that the women had been brought that they might do the work, which is deemed unfitting a warrior.

"Jacob counts on payin' one more visit to his father before we start," Sergeant Corney said to me, when, having wearied with gazing at the scene, I turned away.

"To what end?" I asked, with somewhat of irritation, for it did not seem to me wise the lad should run the chances of capture when nothing was to be effected by taking such risks.

"Only that he may speak with him."

"But it is folly!" I said, sharply. "It has been possible for him to go into the village twice; but of a certainty it cannot be done many times in safety."

"You are right, lad, an' yet how can we refuse him? Fancy if your father was in the same tight place, an' ask yourself if, when about to turn your back on him, perhaps forever, the desire to hold converse with him once more would not be stronger than the fear of disaster?"

To this I could make no reply, as a matter of course; yet I was still firmly convinced that it was a foolhardy venture. If there had been a possibility of his doing the prisoner any good, then would I have said that we would stay on until further efforts were of no avail. As it was, however, Peter Sitz himself had said it was wiser for Jacob to go, and surely he, the most interested and the most experienced in such matters, should be the judge.

I held my tongue, even though rebelling against the scheme, because of knowing that the lad was prompted only by love, and yet my heart grew heavy within me, until I had become convinced that something of evil would follow.

So disturbed was I in mind that it was impossible to close my eyes in slumber again, even though knowing that my best preparation for the journey would consist in getting all the rest I could.

Sergeant Corney had fallen into what seemed to me a moody silence; I looked out now and then at the painted forms of those human wolves, who would lay waste our happy valley, and wished most fervently that I had the power to destroy them all with one blow.

When one has seen, as have I, women and children butchered in the most fiendish manner which a wicked man can devise, he cannot consider bloodthirsty the person who would, if he could, wipe out the entire race. It would only be an act of mercy to the colonists, who lived in momentary fear, not so much of sudden death as of barbarous torture.

Jacob slept until nightfall, and when he awakened the first thought in his mind was to set off on his dangerous and useless venture; but Sergeant Corney advised that he wait until the night was well advanced, and to this I agreed, although chafing against the expenditure of time, because he would but have ensured his own capture had he ventured among the wretches while the entire encampment was astir.

We did not have supper for the very good reason that we had no provisions, but buckled our belts a bit tighter, because already was hunger beginning to assail us.

As we waited for the lengthening of the night, Jacob went over in detail his experiences while Sergeant Corney and I were with General Herkimer, and this served to make the time seemingly pass more swiftly.

The savages evidently had no fiendish sport on their programme for this evening, most likely because of having exhausted themselves the night previous, and at a reasonably early hour this portion of St. Leger's army was in a comparative state of quietude.

"Now, if ever, is the time when you can go, lad; but remember that I advise against it, as would your father," Sergeant Corney said, gravely. "I am not minded to argue you out of what your heart is set upon, but ask that you give the matter due weight before goin' so far that retreat will be impossible."

"I must speak with my father once more," Jacob said, in a tone so piteous that I did not have the heart to make any protest.

"Then God go with you," the old soldier said, solemnly, and in a twinkling my comrade had slipped out of the cave, being lost to our view almost immediately amid the foliage near at hand.

When we were thus left alone a silence fell upon us. Because of the forebodings in my heart I was not inclined for conversation, and I dare venture to say the sergeant held his peace for much the same reason.

During half an hour, perhaps, we listened intently, fearing each instant lest we hear those sounds which would betoken the capture of Jacob, and then did it seem probable he had succeeded in the venture, at least so far as gaining the village was concerned.

Regarding him I had no further anxiety, and, without being aware that slumber was weighing heavily upon my eyelids, I fell asleep.

I could not have been unconscious many moments, for it seemed as if my eyes had but just closed, when I was aroused by the pressure of Sergeant Corney's hand upon my arm, and as I would have sprung up he forced me down, whispering:

"The savages are comin' this way, an' it looks to me mightily as if they counted on stoppin' hereabouts."

Involuntarily I parted the vines at the mouth of the cave, for I had been lying with my head close upon them, and gazed down the side of the small hill, where it was possible to see, even despite the gloom of the night, no less than ten forms coming up the incline as if following a trail.

"They have taken Jacob, an' he has told them where we are," I said on the impulse of the moment, not meaning to cast reproach upon the lad, but knowing what fiendish means those wretches employed in order to extort information.

"We would have heard the noise of a squabble if he had been captured, an' I have stood watch ever since he left," Sergeant Corney said, decidedly.

"Can they be followin' our trail in the darkness?" I cried, and my companion replied, grimly, drawing his rifle nearer to him:

"It makes no difference to us, lad, why or how they are comin'. The question is whether, in case they find this place, we shall fight to the death or submit without resistance."

It was a question I could not answer. I knew full well that we could not hope to hold the cave any considerable length of time, and that if, during the fight, we killed any of the villains, our end at the stake would come before morning, even though Thayen-danega himself should do all he might to prevent it.

I remained silent, the Indians approaching nearer and nearer each instant, and, when they were half-way up the hill, within perhaps thirty yards of the mouth of the cave, the sergeant said, as if speaking to himself:

"All we can hope for, if we should put up a fight, is to die with weapons in our hands, for death in some form would come to us within a few hours. While there's life there's a chance."

"Meanin' that we had best give ourselves up?" I asked, in alarm.

"Ay, lad, that is my idee, unless you can show me something better."

There was little time for reflection. Already were the Indians so near that I fancied I could hear them breathing. I knew that the cave had no other outlet than this one at which we crouched, but also that two determined men might hold half an hundred in check as long as their ammunition lasted - but then?

The foremost of the red-skinned snakes were within a dozen feet of us when I whispered, with tremulous voice:

"It shall be as you say, sergeant!"

Chapter X.

Prisoners

I believe if at that critical moment I had decided it was best we hold the cave against the foe, regardless of the ultimate consequence, Sergeant Corney would have done my bidding. But immediately I declared myself willing to act as he thought best, the old man threw down his rifle, and, with upraised hands, stepped out from amid the screen of foliage into the very arms of those who were coming up the slope.

Just for one instant there was in my mind the thought that I might slink back into the further end of the cave, and possibly escape detection, unless it so chanced that the savages knew exactly how many were hidden there. But, fortunately, before there was time to do anything so cowardly, a realization of what it meant to thus hang back when I had spoken the words which sent my comrade forward came upon me with full force, and I followed him so closely that he could not have had any suspicion of that which, for the merest fraction of time, found lodgment in my heart.

It was too dark for me to see the look of triumph on the faces of our captors; but I knew they wore such expressions, because of the cries of satisfaction and shouts of delight which burst from them when we, unarmed, stood in their midst.

I was satisfied in my own mind that they had seen the trail, even in the darkness, which had been made when we three entered the cave, or by Jacob as he went out, and had followed it rather from curiosity than the belief that white men were in the vicinity.

This idea of mine, although there was in it nothing favoring to us, gave me no little relief of mind, for it led to the conclusion that Jacob was yet free.

After the first outburst of rejoicing at having taken two captives at a time and in a place where they least expected to find them, the Indians set about securing us in the most businesslike manner.

Some one of the party brought strips of rawhide, by which our hands and arms were bound tightly to our sides, and with so large a surrounding that it would have been impossible to escape even had we been unfettered, they led us down to the village, where we were greeted by the squaws and the children with fiendish cries of delight.

I knew enough of savage customs to understand that we would be forced to submit to a certain amount of ill-treatment from the female portion of the band before the warriors decided upon our fate, and nerved myself to bear it as best I might, realizing that any show of weakness at such a time would work to our disadvantage later.

We were tied to a tree, Sergeant Corney on one side and I on the other, within twenty paces of Thayen-danega's lodge, where the light of the camp-fire shone full upon us.

The braves of the tribe seated themselves in a circle, as if holding a council to determine our fate, while the squaws and the young boys amused themselves by holding stout sticks in the fire until one end was a living coal, and then placing these against our hands, until the pain was so great that only by summoning all my strength of will could I prevent myself from screaming.

Even at such a time, when our lives were literally hanging in the balance, I found somewhat of comfort in the thought that Sergeant Corney was with me, and not very far away Peter Sitz could probably see us.

It may be difficult to understand why knowledge of that kind should serve to cheer one at such a horrible moment, and I myself cannot explain it. It simply remains a fact that I seemed in less danger of being murdered than if I had been the only prisoner in the encampment.

"It's plain that Jacob was not captured, else we would see him near by," Sergeant Corney said to me, and I tried my best to enter into conversation with him, to the end that I might in some slight degree take my mind from the torture which, perhaps, was but a foretaste of what I would be forced to suffer.

"He will be overcome with grief on knowin' that by lingerin' to speak once more with his father we were captured, an' I fear the lad may be led to some foolishly reckless move," I said, at the same moment trying to stifle a groan.

"If he will but stop a moment to rigger the matter out, he'll understand that only by keepin' clear of this camp can he hope to help us," the old man replied, and I asked, sharply:

"Do you really believe, sergeant, that any one can aid us now?"

"Tut, tut, lad; do not give yourself up for dead yet awhile. So long as there's life there's a chance. Peter Sitz has been in the clutches of these villains many a day, an' yet, 'cordin' to Jacob's story, he's as sound an' hearty as when he left Cherry Valley."

"Ay; but his life has been saved because Joseph Brant knew him before the dream of bein' made great sachem of the Six Nations turned that redskin into the most bloodthirsty of savages."

"Yet had you been in Peter Sitz's place when he was first taken prisoner, your despair would likely have been as great as it seems to be now."

I knew that Sergeant Corney would say many things which he himself did not believe, if he thought thereby he might strengthen my courage for the terrible ordeal which was probably before us; therefore his words of cheer had less weight than might otherwise have been the case.

Not until it seemed to me every square inch of my hands had been burned to a blister, and there was a livid, red mark across my forehead, where an old hag had scorched me with a burning brand, did the squaws tire of their cruel sport, and then we were left comparatively alone, with sufficient of pain to keep us so keenly alive to the situation that weariness of body did not make itself apparent.

"We came to aid Jacob, and now ourselves are standing in need of assistance," I said, bitterly, for this seemed like the irony of fate.

"True for you, lad, an' yet we won't look at it in that light. But for marvellous good luck we would have been made prisoners before this, therefore let us reckon it simply as the fortune of war, and not count Jacob the cause of our trouble."

I would have replied yet more bitterly than before, but for the fact that at the moment it so chanced my eyes were fixed upon the lodge wherein our comrade had said his father was held prisoner, and I saw the flap pulled cautiously aside.

Then the face of a man could be seen close to the ground, and I said, eagerly, to my companion, who, perforce, had his head turned in the opposite direction:

"Peter Sitz is lookin' at us."

"I would he had remained ignorant of our where-abouts," Sergeant Corney muttered, and I asked, in surprise:

"Why?"

"Because, in addition to his own sufferin', he must believe that we've been brought to this plight through tryin' to aid him, an' it only serves to make his troubles greater, without lessenin' ours."

Sergeant Corney was rapidly becoming a hero in my eyes, for surely it is a brave man who, when he stands in most imminent danger, can think rather of others than himself.

We spoke but little from this time on, the sergeant and I. The rawhides, which were tied so tightly as to nearly stop the circulation of blood, were eating their way into our flesh, and the pain thus caused became greater than the smarting of the blisters raised by the burning brands.

We knew that those who formed that circle of painted forms but a short distance away were deciding whether we be put to torture immediately, or reserved for some especial time of rejoicing, and there grew upon me such a fascination as is sometimes brought about by keenest peril, until I almost forgot the desperate situation as I watched those who held our fate in their hands, trying to discover from the expression on their hideous faces what might be the result of the conference.

As the moments passed I sank into a sort of apathy, until it was as if some other lad's fate trembled in the balance, and I myself was looking down upon the encampment from a secure place of refuge.

The fires burned dim. One by one Thayendanega's heathens stalked away to his lodge, until the council was finally brought to a close; a deep silence came over the encampment, as if all, save that white face which I could see just beneath the flap of the lodge in front of me, and we two who were bound to the tree, were wrapped in slumber.

"We can count on remainin' alive at least until to-morrow night," Sergeant Corney said, as if imparting some cheering information, "for these wretches do not torture a prisoner in the daytime."

"Unless some change is made speedily I will not be in their power, for of a verity I am dyin', Sergeant Corney," I said, and he, thinking, of course, to cheer me, laughed almost merrily as he replied:

"Nonsense, lad, you are a long ways from bein' dead. I allow your body is numbed, but that's all. If these strips of rawhide were slackened a bit, you'd soon find yourself feelin' as well as ever, save, perchance, for the blisters upon your hands."

"If we *could* stretch them a bit," I cried, trying vainly to change the position of my arms.

"Ay, but you can't, lad, an' by makin' the effort you'll only cause them to bind the tighter."

How that long night passed I cannot well say. The agony of mind, together with the bodily pain, benumbed all my senses until I was like one in a trance, hearing nothing, seeing nothing, save the gleam of that white face beneath the flap of the lodge where Peter Sitz kept mournful watch upon us.

The morning came, and like one under the influence of some hideous nightmare I became aware that the savages were loosening the rawhide thongs. Faintly, with but little curiosity regarding the matter, I wondered if we were to be killed at once, regardless of the usual customs of such wretches.

When the bonds had been removed the sergeant and I sank down upon the ground helpless, unable to move hand or foot, and in that condition we were dragged into the lodge where was Jacob's father.

There we were bound quite as securely and cruelly as before, the thongs cutting fresh welts into our wrists and ankles; but the relief caused by the change of position was so great that it seemed as if I had every reason for thankfulness.

Here, when our captors had made certain we could not by any possibility escape, we were left alone with Peter Sitz, and his first question was as to why we had ventured within reach of the enemy.

Sergeant Corney, minded to save our neighbor from the self-reproach which might be his if he knew we were in such plight through desire to aid his son or himself, replied that we had been sent into the vicinity by General Herkimer, and then explained how we came across Jacob, as well was the manner in which we had been taken prisoners.

"Will they torture us to death?" I asked, giving words to that question which had been uppermost in my mind from the moment we saw the painted sneaks approaching the cave, and Master Sitz replied, with a painful effort at cheerfulness:

"It's for you to believe that they won't, lad. Remember how long I've been in their power, an' yet have come to no real harm, so far as life is concerned, although this bein' trussed up like a chicken ready for the roastin' is by no means pleasant or comfortable."

Then it was that Sergeant Corney, minded as I now believe only to change the subject of conversation, asked Master Sitz why it was we had failed to see him during the march from Cherry Valley to the Indian village.

The explanation was simple, and at the same time served to show, to my mind at least, that Jacob's father would not be led to the stake.

It seems that when he was first captured, at the time Lieutenant Wormwood was killed, he came face to face with Thayendanega, and that savage recognized him at once, speaking in such a friendly tone that Master Sitz immediately appealed for mercy.

The sachem declared that if he remained with the war party it might be impossible to save him, and even went so far in his friendliness as to explain that it were better he be sent ahead to the Indian village, for, having once arrived at that place, there was little fear of the warriors demanding his death until on some especial occasion.

Therefore, within half an hour after having been made prisoner, Master Sitz was being hurried forward to Oghkwaga, under charge of two savages, and was well on his journey before we started.

When, immediately after the interview with General Herkimer, Thayendanega hurried his tribe on to join St. Leger's forces, he so far submitted to the demands of his followers as to allow them to take Peter Sitz on the war-path with them.

"More than once have the red devils insisted on

torturin' me; but each time Joseph Brant has prevented them, although I question if he could have done so but for the unfortunate men who were captured in the battle with General Herkimer's troops."

Peter Sitz ceased speaking very suddenly, and I had not the courage to ask him how those prisoners suffered; I could imagine that they came to a most horrible end, and knew that my worst picturing of it would fall far short of the reality.

Then Jacob's father spoke of the possibility that we might escape with our lives; but it was evident he did so with an effort, and I had it in mind that he only tried to cheer me, while he was convinced that his end, as well as ours, would come at the stake before the siege was finished.

And now I do not propose to make any effort at giving in detail all that occurred while we lay cruelly bound, during a greater portion of the time, in this lodge, situate almost in the centre of the Indian camp.

For eight days we were kept thus close prisoners, without a ray of hope, and then came the unexpected.

At least once in every twenty-four hours, and some-times twice, the bonds were taken from our arms that we might feed ourselves on such food as savages cast to their dogs. Perhaps thrice in that long term of captivity were we permitted to walk around the lodge, and, save for that short respite from our suffering, I believe of a verity we would have lost the use of our limbs.

Half-starved, suffering oftentimes the keenest pangs of

thirst, and believing that all this torture was the preface to something yet worse, it can well be imagined that we were indeed a sorry party. Even Sergeant Corney ceased trying to animate us, for despair had seized upon him.

When we did hold converse among ourselves, it was usually regarding Jacob. We had neither seen nor heard anything of the lad since the hour he left us in the cave to get speech with his father, and it was to me wondrous strange that he who had been so eager when there was but one prisoner, had apparently lost all desire to render aid after two more had been captured.

During the first two or three days we believed he was skulking around somewhere near at hand, with the vain hope that he might be able to effect our escape; but as the time passed on it became certain that such could not be the case, otherwise he would have succeeded in making his way to the lodge, as he had done when his father was the only occupant of it.

So far as I could make out, there was no more vigilant guard kept after we were taken than before, and the lad must have succeeded in getting speech with us had he made the effort during those times when the savages gave themselves up to dancing or feasting, as occurred at least once in every eight and forty hours.

Then we decided he had gone in search of General Herkimer's men, thinking to enlist a sufficient number of them in our behalf; but if such had been the case we should have heard something from him, at least when eight days were passed, and after that time we made no mention of the lad, believing he had been discovered near the encampment and killed outright.

And now it must be understood that during all this time St. Leger's army was laying close siege to Fort Schuyler, and, strange as it may seem, we, closely confined in that lodge of skins, had a fairly good idea of what was happening.

More than one of the Indians spoke English, and, not unfrequently, the Tories or British officers came to visit Thayendanega in his own lodge, when we could overhear a goodly portion of the conversation.

Thus it was we knew that Colonel Billinger and Major Frey, officers from General Herkimer's force, who had been taken prisoners by some of the British during the battle of Oriskany, had been compelled, under threats of torture, to write a letter to Colonel Gansevoort, misrepresenting St. Leger's strength, and advising him to surrender.

We also knew that this letter, written under pressure, was delivered by Colonel Butler, who went to the fort with a flag of truce, and, when the commandant flatly refused to surrender, the Tory officer threatened that, in case it became necessary to take the fortification by force, the women and children inside would be delivered over to the mercies of the Indians.

Fortunately Colonel Gansevoort was too brave a man to be frightened by such threats, and when Colonel Butler told him that Burgoyne had already taken possession of Albany, he became thoroughly well convinced that the officer was deliberately lying to him.

At all events, he refused to surrender, and two days later General St. Leger sent a written demand, the reply to which contained the emphatic statement that it was Colonel Gansevoort's determined resolution with the force under his command, to defend the fort to the last extremity.

We learned also, through different friendly visits which were paid to Joseph Brant by the officers, that General St. Leger was continuing the siege in true military fashion, advancing by parallels slowly but surely, and it was the belief of all our enemies that they must of a necessity soon succeed in their purpose.

The information which we thus obtained did not tend to make us feel any more comfortable in mind. In case the fort was taken, the utmost we could hope for would be to escape death, but at the cost of remaining, no one knows how long, as slaves to the savages.

If, however, the garrison made such a resistance as we believed they would, and then were finally overcome, the Indians being allowed to wreak vengeance until their thirst for blood was satisfied, then was it probable we would go to the stake with a goodly company and little chance of escape.

However, I am not minded to set down here all our fears. One can readily understand how many and great they were, and how we twisted and turned each additional bit of information which we gathered by eavesdropping, until it seemed as if matters which had no bearing whatsoever on our condition were a direct and deadly menace.

I have said that we were eight days closely confined in this one lodge, and then came the night when we were lifted from out the mire of despair into which we had fallen, so suddenly as to make us literally dizzy with hope.

During the afternoon of this day Thayendanega's warriors had spent their time laying on an unusual quantity of paint, and arraying themselves to the last feather of their finery, therefore we knew that something of considerable importance was on foot. When they marched out of the encampment, the medicine-men leading the way, with the beating of drums and blowing of horns, we believed a council of war was to be held, in which these wretches, most likely to tickle their vanity, had been invited to take part.

When, just as they were setting out, the rain began to fall heavily and the wind to blow in a manner which betokened a summer storm, I found the wildest delight in picturing to myself the discomforts which would be theirs unless St. Leger had tents sufficient to provide them all with shelter.

At another time I would have given little heed to such a trifling matter, but now it seemed of so much importance that I spoke to my companions in misery regarding it, picturing the bedraggled condition of the fine feathers after they had become thoroughly saturated, and was talking with more of animation than at any time since having been made prisoner, when suddenly a sound, as of some one scratching on the skin of the lodge, caused my heart to bound until it seemed positive its furious beatings could be heard a long distance off.

"It is Jacob!" I cried, speaking incautiously loud.

A warning hiss from Peter Sitz brought me to my senses, and in a fever of suspense I listened for the sound which had first attracted my attention, to be repeated.

The silence remained unbroken, save for the lightest rustling of the skins, until, in the dim light to which my eyes had been so long accustomed, I saw Jacob's head and shoulders inside the lodge.

It was only with difficulty I restrained myself from crying aloud with joy, for now it seemed, even surrounded by enemies though we were, that because my comrade had come were we rescued.

James Otis

Chapter XI.

The Escape

So great was my delight at seeing Jacob slowly working his way into the lodge, that there was no room in my heart for surprise. I entirely forgot to be astonished because after so long a time he had returned, or to question why it was he dared venture within the encampment.

Only the fact that he was there presented itself to my mind, and I gave no heed to anything else.

I struggled violently to reach the dear lad, intent on throwing my arms around him in order to show how deeply I felt this devotion of his which had brought him back, perhaps, to a terrible death; but Master Sitz and Sergeant Corney remained silent and motionless until Jacob was well within the lodge. Then his father said, conveying reproach even in the whisper:

"Why have you come here after once having gotten well away from the place? You can do us no good, an' only hope to add to the savages' list of victims."

"They have not got me yet," Jacob replied, cheerily, and I understood that his courage had been greatly stiffened since the night he crept out from the cave.

"There's a big powwow goin' on over at St. Leger's camp, an' no one is on guard hereabouts. This is the time when, if ever, you can escape."

It seemed to me as if the lad talked the veriest nonsense in speaking of our escape by simply crawling away from the lodge, situate as it was in the very midst of the encampment; but Jacob had the whole plan in his mind, and was not to be disheartened, however much cold water we might throw upon it.

It may seem strange, but such is the fact, that even when thus surrounded by danger my curiosity was so great that I asked him, even before he had time to explain how he hoped to effect our rescue, where he had been so long.

"At Cherry Valley," he replied, as if a journey there and back was the most simple thing imaginable.

"Meanin' that you have been home since the night you left the cave?" I repeated, in astonishment.

"Ay, no less than that."

"But why did you do it?" I cried, speaking so loudly as to call forth a warning groan from Sergeant Corney.

"Because I believed it might be possible for you to escape, providin' we had help enough near at hand," he replied, and I said, even more mystified than before:

"Surely you could not expect to get help for us from Cherry Valley?"

"Ay; and that is just what I did."

"Is my uncle here?"

"No, indeed; he believed my scheme to be so wild that he would hardly listen to me, and said you three had the same as come to your death already, therefore it was useless to raise a finger in your behalf while there were so many hundred people near at hand needin' assistance."

"Who then did you expect would come to our aid?" I asked, and Jacob replied, with what sounded very like a chuckle of satisfaction:

"Who else, save the Minute Boys of the Mohawk Valley?"

But for the rawhide ropes which held me so cruelly immovable, I would have leaped to my feet in astonishment; as it was, I involuntarily gave so violent a start as to cause myself considerable pain, and then asked, in great heat:

"Why do you play upon our hopes, so lately raised, by declaring that the company of lads is here?"

"Not a bit of play about it, Noel," Jacob replied, in so cheery a tone that my heart became wondrously light. "Four an' twenty of our company, with John Sammons still acting as captain, are within an hundred yards of this lodge, an', what is more, we count on takin' you away with us before another day shall dawn."

Then it was as if Jacob believed he had satisfied our curiosity so much as was necessary at such a time, for without delay he moved from one to the other, deftly cutting the rawhide which held us motionless, and three minutes had not elapsed from the time he first showed himself inside the lodge until our limbs were freed.

We were no longer bound, but yet remained helpless. I could move neither hand nor foot, struggle as I might. It was as if my limbs were dead while my body yet remained alive; but Jacob, who had in his wild plan considered just such a probability, set about chafing my arms and legs until the feeling began to return.

He performed the same office for Sergeant Corney, I aiding in the task before it was finished; but a good ten minutes elapsed before we had command of our limbs, and then it was that even Master Sitz began to believe it might be possible for us to escape from the encampment.

While he worked over us, Jacob, understanding that we were being literally overwhelmed with curiosity regarding his movements during the long absence, explained that he was but a short distance from the cave when we were made prisoners, and at first almost gave way to despair because of what seemed to him the hardest stroke which an ill fortune could deliver.

During that night he kept us in view, until learning that we would not be put to death immediately, and then the lad searched in his mind for some plan which might give promise, however slight, of success.

He could not hope that those in the fort, closely besieged as they were, would be willing to make a desperate venture in order to aid three men, when so many hundred were in peril, and, even though the chances might be in favor of Colonel Gansevoort's being ready to make a sortie in our behalf, they were decidedly against Jacob's being able to communicate with the garrison.

Then it was he bethought himself of the Minute Boys, who were not absolutely needed in Cherry Valley after the hundred and fifty soldiers were quartered there, and, without knowing how they might be able to aid him in the almost hopeless task, he set off at full speed for our home, travelling by night as by day, with no more halts than were absolutely necessary in order to recruit his strength.

Colonel Campbell, my uncle, was much averse to Jacob's wild plans. He believed that, because of the danger which threatened all the inhabitants of the Mohawk Valley, it was in the highest degree foolhardy to make any such effort toward saving the lives of three people as might jeopardize an hundred times that number. However, while saying flatly it was a boy's scheme, and not worthy the attention of men, he stated that he would not put any obstruction in the way of those who chose to make the hazard, save to state openly that whosoever left on such a mission was but hastening his own death.

It quickened the sluggish blood in my veins when Jacob said that, after he had summoned the Minute Boys and explained to them in what peril we three were, never one showed the slightest disinclination to do as he proposed.

John Sammons, the lad who was acting as captain in my absence, insisted that it was plainly the duty of every member of the company to do whatsoever he might in our behalf, and the result was that the lad had been in Cherry Valley no more than half an hour before every member of the company was armed and outfitted for the perilous venture.

At the very last moment, however, eight or ten of the number were dissuaded by their parents; but the remainder started hotfoot for Fort Schuyler, arriving an hour before this last day had dawned.

The only plan which Jacob had formed in his mind was to get speech with us as speedily as possible after arriving. Then, if needs be, he would make a dash upon the encampment, and trust to the Minute Boys fighting their way out with us in their midst.

Fortunately, however, he saw very speedily after daybreak that something of import was taking place, and wisely waited until it could be seen that every warrior was making ready for a grand powwow.

Now, so he told us, the Minute Boys were waiting hardly more than an hundred yards distant, and, if it should be possible for us to make our way through the encampment to that point, it was the determination of every lad to fight to the best of his ability, with the hope of being able to retreat meanwhile in case the Indians were aroused.

He who would not have done his best at escaping after all Jacob's work, and in face of the pluck shown by our comrades, deserved of a verity to remain prisoner even until he was led to the stake; but, as can well be imagined, neither of us three hung back from the hazard, for surely it was better to die fighting than be tortured as Thayendanega's wolves could torture a human being.

Master Sitz made one stipulation, however, which was that Jacob should lead the way as we crept out from the lodge, and, in event of our attempt at escape being discovered while we were yet within the encampment, the lad was to save himself without giving heed to us.

"There shall not be another victim added to our number," Jacob's father said, in a tone of determination. "Strike out for your comrades, in case the alarm is given, my boy, and if we are taken again leave us to our fate."

Jacob made no reply to this; but I believed that if the need arose he would disobey his father's command without compunction.

There was no time to linger. At any moment the powwow might be brought to an end, or some warrior return to the encampment, therefore it stood us in hand to move quickly, and so we did.

Not until Jacob was well outside the lodge did either of us three make any move to follow him, and then Sergeant Corney would have pushed me under the skins, which he raised slightly, but that I hung back, declaring it was Master Sitz's place to go first; but the old man forced me forward.

How my heart beat when for the first time in eight days I had full command of my limbs, and wriggled myself out into the clear air! It seemed as if every movement of my arms or legs caused so much noise that the few who remained in the lodges must be alarmed, and that I moved at even less than a snail's pace, when every muscle was being strained in the effort to advance rapidly.

The perspiration came out upon my forehead in great drops, caused, not by the heat, but by the mental anguish, and again and again I said to myself that Jacob had labored for naught, since it would be impossible I could crawl undetected even over the short distance.

And when, in my excited frame of mind, it seemed as if the escape was but just begun, I found myself in the thicket amid those lads who had been my playmates since I could remember, while each strove to show in silence how delighted he was that I had come safely.

Then ensued another time of keenest suspense, when we strained our ears to hear the lightest sound which should betoken that the squaws of the encampment had been alarmed, and once more our hearts leaped up in joy as Master Sitz came behind the screen of bushes.

Now we had only to wait for Sergeant Corney, and, having seen what he could do in the wilderness, I had no doubt but that he would succeed in his purpose, which he soon did.

Perhaps no more than half an hour had passed from the time we first saw Jacob until we three, so lately prisoners, were surrounded by that brave band of lads who, by calling themselves "Minute Boys," had excited the mirth of the elders of Cherry Valley, and yet never one who was not prepared to sacrifice his own life for the welfare of the others.

"What are we to do?" Sergeant Corney said, turning to me, as if I should resume command of this company of mine, and I replied, promptly, with never a thought of claiming my rights as captain:

"It is for you to lead, sergeant, an' we will obey. There's not one in this company so well fitted as you to take us out from amid the dangers which surround us."

"Yet my idea of what is safest may seem to the rest of you like veriest folly," he replied, as if he would shirk the responsibility, and Master Sitz said, eagerly:

"It all seems to me like a piece of folly, Sergeant Corney, even though because of it are we brought out from the power of our enemies. You can do no more hairbrained things than has already been done by my son."

"Then, if the command be left to me, we shall make our way into Fort Schuyler, provided that be possible."

"Fort Schuyler!" I cried, in dismay.

"Ay, lad, an' we shall be there before another day dawns if we live, provided we make the start."

"But why not put as many miles between us and this place as is possible?" I cried, with no slight show of irritation, for the imminence of the danger set every nerve tingling until I could think of nothing save the most hurried flight.

"It stands us in hand to go there, first, because they are in need of our help, and, secondly, because we shall stand a better show of finally escaping from the savages."

"How do you make that out?" John Sammons asked, and I understood from his tone that he was not inclined for the hazard.

"Think you Thayendanega's wolves will lose the prisoners whom they counted on seeing at the stake, without some effort to retake them?" the old man asked, sharply, and John Sammons replied:

"All that we understand; but reckon on puttin' a goodly distance between us an' yonder encampment before to-morrow mornin'. Unless there is an accident the escape will not be known for many hours, and then should we have so much the lead that we could count with some degree of assurance upon gaining Cherry Valley."

"In that I do not agree, lad, an' for many reasons. We cannot advance at full speed, because it will be necessary to spend some time in learnin' whether there be an enemy in the road; but the savages followin' the trail may come as fast as their legs can bring them, therefore will they travel three miles to our two."

"Ay; but we should be able to hold in good play as many as may overtake us."

"That must be accordin' to the fortunes of war. It is hardly to be reckoned that we could fight a pitched battle without losin' some portion of our company, and I would have this brave rescue of yours accomplished with as little cost as may be. Therefore have I in mind to enter Fort Schuyler."

I cannot truly say that Sergeant Corney convinced us his plan was the best; but certain it is we were silenced, as was no more than proper, since it stood to reason he knew best about such affairs.

After this, having made up our minds that we must attempt the perilous task, came the question of how it should be done, and on this point the old soldier gave us very little opportunity for discussion.

"It is my plan that we circle around the encampment, even beyond St. Leger's quarters, in order to get a general idea of what may be goin' on, an', havin' arrived at the road westward of the fortification, you lads shall get in hidin' while I try once more to open communication with the garrison."

"Why should you go alone?" I asked. "We might remain in a body, and thus save just so much time. If one can do the trick, then may it be possible for two, or a dozen."

"Yes, to make one's way across the open country, I grant you; but remember, lad, how long it would have taken to gain admission when we were there before had the garrison not been warned that we were in the vicinity. This time they will look upon us as enemies until we are near enough to make ourselves known, and such a force as is here would appear to them like an attackin' party."

The sergeant was right, as I now understood full well, and, although I craved not the dangerous work, because my comrades were near at hand I desired they should see that I shirked not peril.

However, all seemed to understand that, if the sergeant's plan was to be carried out, he should arrange the details, and therefore I held my peace.

In order to gain the westerly side of the fort from the Indian encampment, in the vicinity of which we then were, and learn what might be going on at St. Leger's headquarters, it would be necessary to cross the river and traverse at least two-thirds of a complete circle around the fortification.

Much time might have been saved had we crossed the Mohawk to the southward, without venturing near the camps of the British.

Sergeant Corney seemed to consider that it was more important to get a general idea of the disposition of St. Leger's forces before entering the fort, than to save ourselves so much labor, therefore he led the way eastwardly half a mile or more, until we were come to the narrowest part of the river, when we swam over, afterward heading directly for the main encampment of the besiegers.

Still acting under Sergeant Corney's directions, the greater part of the company kept at a respectful distance when we were come within the vicinity of St. Leger's headquarters, while he, Jacob, and I crept forward to reconnoitre.

Because of the many fires and the apparent confidence of the enemy that no attempt would be made to surprise them, we had ample opportunity to see all that was required.

The biggest kind of a feast, or powwow, or council, or whatever it might have been called, was in progress, and so deeply interested were the Britishers, Tories, and Indians alike that I believe of a verity we could have approached within fifty feet and not been discovered save by purest accident.

"Whatever they've got on hand seems to be somethin'

that'll last well through the night," Sergeant Corney said, as he lay amid the bushes watching the various groups of men, both white and red. "If Colonel Gansevoort could only know what's goin' on at this minute, I allow he'd make such a sortie as would raise this siege in quick order. We couldn't have a better night for enterin' the fort, an', if we don't succeed, it'll be our fault, or through the blundering of some fool sentinel."

To one who had not been in this vicinity, as had I, the old soldier's words might have induced the belief that we were really not exposed to danger in making the proposed venture; but I knew full well he believed, as did I, that, however many might be feasting and dancing in the encampment, there were a certain number watching the fort, and if one of them should catch a glimpse of us the business would be at an end right speedily.

When Sergeant Corney had satisfied himself with a scrutiny of the camp, he led the way to the northward, where the Minute Boys were in hiding, and, arriving there, explained in few words the situation, to the end that they might be encouraged for that which was to come.

I question if, after showing the bravery they already had, the lads needed any words to stiffen their backs; but it pleased the old soldier to make it appear as if we had clear sailing before us, and did no real harm.

Then we started on the march, which would be long because it was necessary, after passing the encampment, to make considerable of a detour in order to avoid, first, a battery of three guns, then one of four mortars, and, lastly, a battery of three more guns, all of which extended northwesterly from St. Leger's headquarters.

After this distance had been traversed, we passed within less than two hundred feet of the line of trenches which had been begun as an approach to the fort, and then bore to the southward again, crossing the Albany road.

Finally, at perhaps two o'clock in the morning, we arrived at a broad elevation, the easternmost slope of which came very near to the outer walls of the fort.

Here it would be necessary to advance without cover for perhaps an hundred yards, and it was this last and most dangerous work that Sergeant Corney insisted on doing himself.

My company found fairly good hiding-places in the thicket near at hand, Jacob and I creeping out to the edge of the foliage in order to keep watch upon the old soldier as he made his way like a snake over the plain, which was almost entirely destitute of vegetation.

He set off without delay, for, owing to the lateness of the hour, there was no time to be wasted, and our hearts were literally in our mouths as we watched him make his way slowly along, at imminent danger each second of being fired upon by the sentinels inside the fort.

Chapter XII.

In the Fort

Everything was in our favor on this night, otherwise Sergeant Corney's attempt would not have been the simple matter which it appears as set down by me.

True it is we had previously visited the fort, and that while many of the enemy's sentinels were on the alert; but because a task has once been done is no proof that it may be accomplished a second time. In fact, it is by trying a hazardous venture again and again that it becomes yet more dangerous, or, in other words, "The pitcher that goes often to the well will one day return broken."

I question if there could have been found in the entire Mohawk Valley a man who would have performed the task better than did Sergeant Corney. The night was not particularly dark, and we who were watching from the undergrowth knew exactly where to look for him, but yet there were many times when I failed utterly to distinguish his form, although, as I have already said, there was nothing in the way of vegetation to screen his movements.

Only when he half-raised himself to make certain he was advancing in a direct course could we see him, and when, after perhaps twenty minutes of such stealthy approach, the deeper shadow cast by the fortification itself had been gained, he was entirely lost to our view.

Then was come the time when I feared most for his safety, although, if the sentinel had failed to see him making his way across the open space, we might have reasonable hope that the remainder of his scheme, less dangerous, could be worked without mishap.

It seemed to me as if an hour elapsed from the time he disappeared before we saw any sign of him again. The minutes passed laggingly, although while there was no outcry we knew full well he had come to no harm; but yet I trembled with anxiety until we finally saw a figure upon the wall waving its arms, and I said to Jacob:

"That is the signal for us to advance."

"Advance where?" he asked, in perplexity. "Surely it is not possible for us to get in at any point."

"We can at least hold communication with those inside if we creep to the new portion of the fort, which as yet is only a stockade - the same place where the sergeant and I had converse with Colonel Gansevoort."

It appears, as I finally learned, that the sergeant believed I would have sufficient sense to understand it was at this place we must effect an entrance, if anywhere, and I ought to have known at the time, for, after waving his arms to attract attention, he walked along the wall, disappearing near what was known as the "horn-works," which as yet were enclosed only by a stockade of logs.

To summon the Minute Boys and bring them to the edge of the clearing was but the work of a few moments, and then was done that which I venture to say has seldom been accomplished during such a siege as was then in progress.

For an armed party of nearly thirty to cross an open plain, supposedly under the very eyes of the enemy's sentinels, without being discovered, is something of which to boast, yet we Minute Boys of the Mohawk Valley did it without raising an alarm.

When the foremost of us, among whom I was, gained that portion of the fortification of which I have already spoken, the sergeant was lowering a long ladder over the stockade, and up this we clambered without delay, the entire party getting inside the fort within two minutes after the ascent was begun.

What a time of congratulation that was! The garrison pressed around to praise us and pat themselves on the head, because we had come at what was, for them, an opportune time. Not only was the fort reinforced by no inconsiderable number, but we brought with us fairly good information as to the condition of affairs in the enemy's camp.

The men were yet praising and thanking us for having come at such a time, when an officer approached with the word that Colonel Gansevoort wished to speak with the leaders of the party.

"That means you, Noel," the sergeant said, patting me on the shoulder. "The colonel quite rightly believes that we can give him valuable information, an' is eager to have it."

"But I am not the leader of the party," I said, finding time to be a bit bashful, now that the imminent danger was passed.

"Who is, if not the captain of the company?" the old man asked, with a smile.

"You, an' you always were when we were at home, Sergeant Corney, therefore are you doubly the leader now, after having brought us safely in from the encampment."

The old soldier flatly refused to present himself as being in command of the Minute Boys, and there is no saying how long we might have wrangled among ourselves had not Colonel Willett, impatient to see us, come up just at that moment.

After asking a few questions, he settled the matter by saying:

"If you lads who have accomplished so much which men might well have feared to attempt, are not willing that one should have more praise than another, let all those who have been in command at different times present themselves to Colonel Gansevoort, and then, mayhap, we shall hear that for which we are so eager."

I am free to admit that it was childish in any of us to hang back at such a moment, but, thanks to Colonel Willett, the matter was arranged as he suggested, Sergeant Corney, John Sammons, Jacob, and I going to the commandant's quarters, escorted by the colonel and the messenger who had been sent for us.

There was no real occasion for us to have been timid

James Otis

regarding the interview with the commandant of Fort Schuyler, for a more pleasantly spoken, neighborly-like man it was never my good fortune to come in contact with.

One would have said that he was interested personally in each and every one of us, from the questions he asked concerning our having organized a company of Minute Boys, how we had been drilled, and such like homely matters.

Then, having shown himself to be a friend, as it were, he began getting that information which was necessary for the safety of the garrison. First he was eager to learn regarding the battle of Oriskany, for those inside the fort knew nothing whatsoever of that disastrous ambush, save such as could be guessed by the reports of the firearms and the bearing of the Indians after they beat a retreat.

Sergeant Corney flatly refused to tell the story, insisting that I was the better able to do so, and, in the presence of Colonel Gansevoort and all his principal officers, I related the events of that day when an able soldier and a brave man was forced by the prating of cowards to lead his soldiers where he knew, almost beyond a peradventure, he had no hope of winning a victory.

Then Jacob and I in turn gave an account of what had been done, bringing our story up to the time when Sergeant Corney took the lead in the attempt to gain the fort, and the old man could not well refuse to describe what he had seen that night regarding the disposition of the enemy's forces.

That Colonel Gansevoort and his officers were deeply interested in our recital may be understood by the fact that day had fully come before we were at an end of our stories, and yet never one of them had shown the slightest impatience or a desire to cut us short.

"I know of no greater favor which could have been done the garrison, save that of bringing in additional stores and larger reinforcements, than what has come to us through you," Colonel Gansevoort said, when we had imparted all our information. "I hope you will not regret having made this effort to aid us, and, if it so be an opportunity ever offers, I will see to it that, so far as is within my power, the Minute Boys of the Mohawk Valley shall receive substantial credit from their country-men because of services rendered. We will give you as good quarters as we have; but if the rations seem scanty now and then, you must remember that we are not in position to get all we may require in the way of eatables."

"Will you answer me one question, sir, an' not deem it impertinent?" Sergeant Corney asked, with a degree of humility such as I had never before seen him exhibit.

"An hundred if you please. We can hardly refuse anything to those who have given us so much encouragement this night as have you and your comrades."

"I would like to know, sir, simply from curiosity, an' not because it would make any difference with my desire to go or stay, if you have a good show of holdin' the fort against so strong a force as is under St. Leger's command?"

"I believe we have," the colonel replied, thoughtfully.

"At all events, I promise you that we will not surrender; but, if the worst comes to the worst, I shall sally out at night with the idea of cutting my way through the enemy's lines. Our provisions are running low; the enemy has advanced by parallels within an hundred and fifty yards, and the store of ammunition is by no means as great as we could wish. Our only hope is that General Schuyler may be able to succor us."

"If a company of thirty boys can move through Thayendanega's camp, spy upon the British, and force their way into this fort unharmed, then of a surety can I do half as much," Colonel Willett said, vehemently. "I will undertake to make my way to General Schuyler, setting out when another night shall have come."

"And I will go with you!" an officer, whom I afterward came to know was Lieutenant Stockwell cried heartily, whereupon the sergeant, puffed up because of what we had already done, declared that Jacob, he, and I would act as messengers.

"It is enough for you to have shown us that the task can be accomplished," Colonel Willett said with a smile. "I have been the first to volunteer for such service, and claim the right to go."

At this point the commandant suggested in the most friendly manner that perhaps we who had lately arrived might be in need of food, and I fancied he made this suggestion in order to be rid of us while he and his officers discussed the proposition.

At all events, we left headquarters and were conducted by Lieutenant Stockwell to a portion of the barracks which was set aside especially for the Minute Boys, to the end that we might all be together.

"Rations shall be served you at once," the lieutenant said, as he turned to leave us, and, although he kept his word, it was past noon before we had an opportunity to break our fast, because it seemed as if nearly every man in the garrison was eager to hold personal converse with us in order to learn what he might concerning the besieging army.

No matter however much we as a company might succeed in doing in the future, certain it is we could not be petted or praised more than we were during that first day in the fort.

We had not accomplished anything remarkable, so far as I could see; aided by all the circumstances, and particularly by the fact that St. Leger's force had concluded to hold a powwow with the Indians on that certain night, we had come across the plain when, at another time and under other conditions, we might have made an hundred attempts without succeeding.

It was, as Sergeant Corney would put it, the fortune of war, or the accident of war, which enabled us to do as we had done, and only the old soldier himself could take personal credit for our being there.

If the garrison was on short allowance, we never would have suspected it during the first four and twenty hours of our stay, for every man inside the walls who had anything in the way of food which he thought might tempt our appetites, offered it to us, and the wonder of it all is that we were not so puffed up with pride as to behave very foolishly.

Late in the afternoon, on the day after we arrived, Colonel Willett came to our quarters, and, sitting down among us regardless of his rank and high attainments as a military officer, talked in the most neighborly fashion with us concerning the surrounding country, the different routes we had pursued when coming to or going from the fort, and, particularly, concerning what we might have heard regarding the movements of the enemy between Fort Schuyler and Oswego.

Of course to this last question we could give no satisfactory reply; but certain it is that he gained very much of useful information which would serve him in his attempt to reach General Schuyler. Having come to an end of his inquiries, he told us that it had been determined between himself and the commandant that on the next stormy night he and Lieutenant Stockwell would make an effort to leave the fort on their way to Stillwater, where it seems he believed the general would be found.

Sergeant Corney begged hard to be allowed to accompany the two officers, but the colonel said, laughingly:

"You will remain where you are, sir, unless it is in your mind to leave here because of the danger which threatens. Already have you done enough in the way of scouting."

"I hope you do not think, sir, that I would run away because of anythin' like that?"

"No, my man, I am quite certain you never would; but you are not to gain all the credit in this siege, for I count on taking some of it myself, unless, peradventure, the enemy treat me worse than they did you."

Then the colonel left us, and right glad was I that he had not accepted the sergeant's offer, for I might in some way have been dragged into the venture, and of a verity I had had enough in that line of work to last me so long as I might live. It is all very well when a fellow is beyond reach of danger to speculate upon what might be done to gain a name for himself; but quite another matter to take his life in his hand any oftener than may be absolutely necessary.

On the following morning I presented myself to the commandant with a complaint, having been prompted thereto by Sergeant Corney. We had not yet been assigned to any duty, and each member of the garrison seemed particularly averse to allowing us to even help ourselves.

There was not a member of our company who wished to remain there idle, and I visited headquarters to ask that we might be called upon for the regular garrison work, the same as if we were enlisted men.

Colonel Gansevoort very kindly assured me that there was no real reason why we should do duty while the force was so large; but promised, if we insisted upon it, to consider us when making a detail, exactly as he would any of the others.

Colonel Willett had not long to wait before beginning his perilous journey. By noon of the second day after our arrival the wind veered around into the south, bringing heavy clouds across the sky, and even the poorest weather prophets among us knew that a

James Otis

summer storm was close at hand.

Once during the afternoon the colonel passed near where I was furbishing up my rifle, and halted to say:

"The lieutenant and I count on leaving the fort shortly before midnight. If you and your friends have any desire to see us set out, go down to the new works at about that time."

By the "new works" he meant the stockade over which we had come, and I hastened to impart the information to Sergeant Corney and Jacob, knowing full well that they would be as interested in the venture as was I.

The volunteer messengers could not have asked for a better night. When the day had come to an end the storm burst with no inconsiderable fury, and it was safe to predict that it would not clear away before sunrise.

Had I been going on the venture I would have set out much before the appointed time, because while the rain came down so furiously there was little chance the enemy's sentinels could see what might be going on at the southerly end of the fortification, and it seemed as if my opinion was shared by Colonel Willett, for he and the lieutenant were ready to leave at about ten o'clock.

I considered it very friendly in him to send us word as to his change of plans, that we might not miss seeing them set forth, and thus it was we beheld the two brave men as they imperilled their lives voluntarily and solely in the hope of aiding their comrades.

They carried no weapons save spears, wore no clothing except what was absolutely necessary for comfort, and, stripped to the lightest possible marching trim, they went out into the blackness of the night like true heroes, with a smile and a jest upon their lips.

There were not above twenty of us who witnessed the departure, but it is safe to say that no more fervent prayers for their safety could have been offered up if the whole garrison had bent the knee.

The darkness of night had literally swallowed them up, and the downpour of rain drowned every noise that might have been made by their advance. It was a brave venture, more particularly because, without chance of being accused in the slightest degree of cowardice, they might have yielded their places to others.

During half an hour or more we remained exposed to the storm, as we listened with painful intentness for some sound which should tell us that they had been discovered, and when at the end of that time we had heard nothing, it was believed they were on their way in safety.

Later in the day we learned that it was Colonel Willett's intention to push on to German Flats, and there, procuring horses, ride at full speed down the valley to General Schuyler's headquarters.

Having once got clear of the fort and its vicinity, as we believed to be the fact, the only thing which might prove the undoing of the venture was that the general had gone to some other section of the country, and they would not succeed in finding him until St. Leger had accomplished his purpose.

Well, we settled down to garrison duty, taking our turn with the squads of from fifty to an hundred men who remained constantly on the alert to shoot such of the enemy as might be sufficiently obliging as to show themselves, and ready to give warning of any signs of an attack.

This last was not believed probable. The officers of the garrison argued that neither the Indians nor the Tories could be depended upon to make a direct assault on such a fortification as Fort Schuyler, and that all St. Leger's efforts would be directed toward advancing his parallels until he was sufficiently near to mine.

And yet how true is the old maxim that "it is always the unexpected which happens!"

On the third morning after we had entered the fort Sergeant Corney and I were on duty as sharpshooters, and, before we had been upon the walls many moments, I called his attention to what seemed like an unusual hurrying to and fro on the part of the enemy. It was as if they were making ready for some important movement, and, according to my way of thinking, that could only mean an assault, improbable as our officers believed it to be.

As a matter of course, we gave immediate information to the officer of the day of what we fancied had been discovered, and within half an hour more there could no longer be any doubt but that St. Leger had made up his mind to see what might be accomplished by a direct attack.

I was disposed to make light of the matter, not believing it possible the enemy could effect anything of importance, but lost somewhat of my confidence on observing the grave expression on the faces of the officers.

"What is it?" I asked of Sergeant Corney. "Do they fancy for a moment that, even though the Indians should be willing to take part in the assault, the fort could be carried?"

"No, lad, I reckon they're not sich fools as that; but it has come to my ears that ammunition for the cannon is runnin' mighty low, an' to repel an attack, even though there be no danger come from it, will be a serious matter."

Even then I failed to understand what the old soldier meant, and asked him to explain more fully, which he did.

Then I came to realize that to expend our ammunition for the big guns at that time might result disastrously for us later, when, the parallels having been brought nearer, an assault would be vastly more menacing.

However, St. Leger had the right to do whatsoever he might, and he could not have chosen a wiser course had he known exactly the amount of powder in our magazine.

The gunners were sent to their stations, the remainder of the force disposed here or there as they might be the most useful, we Minute Boys being stationed near the sally-port, which, as Sergeant Corney said, was a great compliment, because at about that place might the hottest work be expected.

It was not pleasant, this making ready for a battle. When we went into action with General Herkimer it was done quickly; we suspected something of the kind might happen, but were not certain of it. Now there could be no question but that, in a short time at the most, we would be striving to kill human beings, and unable, except at the cost of being branded as cowards, to do anything toward saving our own lives.

Chapter XIII.

The Assault

If I have not spoken of Peter Sitz since he was rescued by the Minute Boys, it is because he did not remain in the barracks with us from Cherry Valley, but messed with some of his acquaintances from German Flats, therefore we saw very little of him until the garrison was mustered to repel the threatened attack.

Then I noted that Colonel Gansevoort had entrusted to him the charge of a certain portion of the wall nearly opposite where the Minute Boys were stationed, and because he had been placed in command, even though it was of course only temporary, I judged, and truly, that Jacob's father was accounted an able assistant in such work as we most likely had before us.

Sergeant Corney remained with the Minute Boys, as was his duty. I believe of a verity my company would have grumbled almost as loudly as had General Herkimer's men on the morning before the fight at Oriskany, had the old soldier taken station elsewhere, and yet it would have been but natural for him to go into the fight side by side with those of the garrison who were most experienced in warfare.

As I have said, we were given a post which had in it no

206   James Otis

inconsiderable honor, since it was at that point where the most fighting might be expected, and from where we stood it was possible to have a fairly good view of the plain immediately surrounding the fort.

Within twenty minutes after the alarm was first given, we could see the British and Tory soldiers forming in line, while to the southward, below the bend in the river, the Indians were crossing hurriedly, which last fact caused me to say to the sergeant:

"I am of the mind that the savages count on attacking the stockaded portion of the fortification," and the old man replied:

"Ay, lad, an' one might have guessed that without stopping to see from which direction they were comin'. Thayendanega may prate as much as he pleases about the bravery of his warriors, but he cannot find a corporal's guard among the whole crowd that would dare march up to a direct assault upon earthworks."

"What portion of the force is on duty in the stockade?" Jacob asked, but none of our company could answer him. It was reasonable to suppose Colonel Gansevoort had stationed there those of his men who were most experienced in savage warfare, and we whose duty it was to hold the walls in the vicinity of the sally-port had no need to trouble our heads concerning them.

The one thing which puzzled me was as to why St. Leger was making this attack, since he had begun to approach the fort by parallels. I was eager to have some expert opinion as to whether the British were apparently abandoning the slow method of reducing the fortification, or if, having learned perchance that we were running short of ammunition for the big guns, they were making an attack in order to provoke us to waste powder which would be more sadly needed at some later day. Therefore it was that I asked Sergeant Corney what his belief was regarding the matter.

"It looks to me much as if Colonel Willett an' Lieutenant Stockwell had been captured."

"How do you figure that out?"

"Because an assault is evidently about to be made. If they are not prisoners, the enemy has learned that they left the fort."

I was still in darkness as to why he arrived at such conclusion, but found the reason exceedingly plain when he said:

"If St. Leger knows that a man of Colonel Willett's rank was eager to take the chances of leaving the forti-fication to summon assistance, he must believe the garrison is in sore straits, an' therefore it is that I believe the mistake was made in allowin' him to go out when there were plenty of others here willin' to take the chances."

It grieved me sorely to think that the brave officer might be at that moment in the hands of the savages, or, what amounted to much the same thing, in the custody of the Britishers, for it was charged openly that, in order to keep the Indian allies in good temper, prisoners taken by his Majesty's troops were often delivered over to the red-skinned wolves for torture.

However, there was but little time left me in which to

speculate upon this painful matter, for even as Sergeant Corney and I spoke together the British troops, supported by the Johnson Greens, came out into view from amid the encampment, marching directly toward the fort.

"There is more in this than an ordinary assault," I heard the sergeant mutter, as he looked to the priming of his musket. "St. Leger would not expose his men to the slaughter which must follow without good and sufficient cause. I'm not overly given to praising the Britishers; but we must admit that he who's in command here is a thoroughly good soldier."

Under ordinary circumstances I would have been conscious of a certain chill along my spine, and felt my knees trembling beneath me at the certainty of soon being engaged in a life or death struggle; but after my experience as a prisoner there was but one thought in my heart, and that of repaying the enemy for some of the sufferings I had undergone.

The desire for revenge was greater than the fear of death.

Before many moments passed Sergeant Corney hit upon what I firmly believed was the true answer to my question of why an assault was to be made at this time.

The Britishers and Tories advanced in good order until facing the northerly and westerly sides of the fort, within musket-shot range, and from that distance poured their bullets into us without doing much execution; but calling for strict attention on our part lest a charge be made, for the ditch was not so wide or deep but that a body of trained soldiers could have overcome the obstacle.

Only twice were the guns, which could be trained in that direction, discharged, and then we inflicted no slight injury upon the foe; but Colonel Gansevoort soon showed that he was far too prudent a commander to shoot away all his powder at one time, even though it was possible to punish the enemy severely.

It looked much as if the king's forces were bent on continuing the battle with small arms at short range, for they discharged their pieces as rapidly as it was possible to reload them, making a great din even though the execution was slight.

Then it was that Sergeant Corney hit upon the meaning of this odd move. Without a word he leaped down from the wall where he had been stationed, running swiftly toward the unfinished portion of the fortification, and was gone no more than three or four minutes when he returned with more show of excitement than I had ever known him to exhibit.

"Yonder Britishers and renegades are but holding our attention in order to give Thayendanega's wolves a chance to scale the stockade," he said, hurriedly. "The force there is all too small. I will take half of the company, at risk of disobeying orders, to that point, while you go with all speed and tell the commandant what I have learned."

I understood the situation without further explanation, and, realizing the necessity for haste, went as rapidly as my legs would carry me to the northeast bastion, where I had last seen Colonel Gansevoort.

Fortunately for my purpose he was still there, giving directions as to the firing of the guns, and in a twinkling I had acquainted him with the situation as described by Sergeant Corney, at the same time explaining that half the Minute Boys had been withdrawn from near the sally-port.

"The sergeant has done well," the commandant replied. "Ten of your number should be more than sufficient there, if matters are as they seem. Tell Sergeant Braun I will join him as soon as possible."

Then I ran with all speed to my company, and, explaining to John Sammons my purpose, took with me half the number remaining under his command. With this small force I set off at full speed, and we arrived none too soon at the place where the most desperate fighting was going on.

At the beginning of the action no more than forty men had been stationed in the "horn-works," and it seemed to me as if the entire stockaded portion was surrounded by a dancing horde of howling, maddened Indians, who, bringing with them tree-trunks or stout branches, were throwing up such a heap of odds and ends as admitted of their gaining the top of the logs despite the fire which our people were pouring upon them.

It must be set down here that there were no cannon in this unfinished portion of the fortification. The so-called rebellion against the king had broken out before this very necessary adjunct to the strength of the fort could be completed, and, consequently, it was the weakest portion of our defence.

When I arrived with my comrades at this point, our

people were engaged in a hand-to-hand struggle with the savages, three score or more having succeeded in effecting an entrance, and it needed no experienced eye to say that unless the onrush could be speedily checked, the capture of the fort might be effected at a time when we had believed St. Leger was simply making a feint.

Exactly what happened during the next half-hour I am unable to state of my own knowledge, for I had no sooner entered the horn-works than it became necessary to put forth every effort in the saving of my own life.

A gigantic savage discharged his musket with seemingly true aim directly at my head; but, strangely enough, missed the target, and then he came at me, hatchet in hand, with such fury that for an instant it seemed as if I was at his mercy.

So excited was I that my bullet, which should have found lodgment in his heart, went as wild as had his, and then was I forced to use a clubbed musket for defence.

Had any one asked me on that morning if I believed it possible to withstand the attack of an Indian, the two of us using the weapons I have just described, my answer would have been a decided "no," and yet now I held him in good play, although realizing that each moment I was growing weaker and he gaining the advantage.

Already were my eyes becoming suffused with blood; my brain was in a whirl, as I leaped here or there, parrying with the butt of the musket the blows of his hatchet, and all the time he continued to press me nearer and nearer toward the wall, where my resistance would have been overcome within a very short time.

I wondered why it was that Colonel Gansevoort delayed in the coming, and could see, without looking in any direction save at my foe, that the number of savages inside the stockade was increasing each moment.

Only a brief delay now on the part of the commandant, and they would gain so great an advantage that such portion of the garrison as could be withdrawn from the walls where the Britishers were making the pretended attack, would not be able to dislodge them.

Then suddenly, at the very moment when it seemed impossible I could struggle any longer, the painted villain sank down upon the ground as if having received his death-blow, and I dimly heard Sergeant Corney cry, cheerily:

"That was a narrow squeak, lad, an' we'll hope there'll be many more of 'em before the last one comes! Keep yourself well in hand, for of a verity our work is cut out for us here!"

Now it was I knew that a shot from the old soldier's musket had put an end to the combat in which I was most deeply interested, and I strained every nerve to gather myself together as he had commanded.

By this time I dare venture to say no less than two hundred of the howling demons had scaled the stockade, and we who were defending this weakest portion of the fortification were pressed back and back until we stood massed against that opening which gave entrance to the main fortification.

We were in good position for the enemy to mow us down with bullets, and in such close formation that only those in the outermost ranks could use their weapons to advantage.

"It is all over," I said to myself, realizing that within a very few moments we must be killed or disabled under such a fire as Thayendanega's scoundrels were pouring upon us. Then from our rear I heard ringing cheers, the trampling of many feet, and realized that assistance had come at the most critical moment.

Sixty seconds later we had all been slain like sheep in the shambles!

"Give way, give way, lads in front!" I heard Colonel Gansevoort shout, and, hardly understanding the words, instinctively we surged either side of the passage, having hardly done so before a shower of grape-shot came hurtling between our ranks, dealing death to scores of the feather-bedecked wretches.

"Stand to your muskets, you Minute Boys!" Sergeant Corney shouted, and the sound of his voice stiffened my courage wonderfully. "Now is the time to pay back some of our old scores, and every bullet should cut short a life from among those who would harry us of the valley."

He had hardly more than ceased speaking when a great uproar could be heard from the distance, and, without turning my head, I understood that the British regulars and the Johnson Greens were pressing the attack on the west and the front, in order to hold our men at the walls that we might not be able to regain possession of the stockade.

Now the fight was on in good earnest, and a bloodier one or a more desperate struggle I hope never to see again.

After the single cannon which Colonel Gansevoort had caused to be brought in was discharged, the reinforcements betook themselves to their muskets, for our frontiersmen were more accustomed to the use of small arms than big guns, and the tide surged this way and that, with the fate of the fort trembling more than once in the balance, until I had before my eyes only great billows of feathered forms, which rose and fell, advanced and were forced back, until I was well-nigh bewildered.

Before this portion of the fighting had come to an end, fully half the garrison was engaged in repelling the attack of Thayendanega's forces, and during such time the white portion of the enemy's army might have made a successful assault upon the walls, I verily believe, but for the cowardice displayed by the Tories.

How long we struggled there hand to hand, stumbling now over the lifeless forms of our comrades, and again finding our way checked by the dead bodies of the savages, I cannot say; but certain it is that we finally drove the last of the hated foe over the stockade, and gave Thayendanega's boasting braves such a lesson as they would not need to have repeated for many days.

I was not less wearied with the carnage than those around me. Even Sergeant Corney, to whom such scenes were not strange, leaned against a portion of the earthworks as if for support while he dashed the perspiration from his eyes, and then we knew by the sounds that the battle was being waged severely over against the sally-port.

Then it was I called for the Minute Boys to follow me, as I ran at the best pace possible in that direction, for there was our post of duty.

Now Colonel Gansevoort no longer husbanded his store of ammunition intended for the cannon, and every piece in the northern and eastern bastions was being worked with the utmost rapidity, sending among the Tories such a shower of iron as their cowardly hearts could not hold out against, and, when they turned with cries of fear to flee, the British regulars, understanding that they were too few in number to effect anything against us, joined in the retreat.

The assault had come to an end, and we of the garrison were triumphant, but at such an expense of life that we could not well afford many more such victories.

During that night we buried our dead, - four and twenty men, - committing them to the dust under cover of darkness lest the enemy see how much injury he had inflicted, and, thank God, never a member of my company who could not answer to the roll-call.

There were forty-one so seriously wounded that it was necessary a certain force be told off from among the garrison to play the part of nurses, and, when to the number of disabled is added those who were to care for them, it can be seen that St. Leger struck us a severe blow, even though he did not succeed in his purpose.

We buried our comrades in the horn-works, just under the stockade they had defended so gallantly, and threw over the fence of logs fifty-two of Thayendanega's wolves who would take no further part in murder and rapine. It is positive that there must have been many wounded among the Indians, some so severely that it would have been impossible for them to accompany their fellows in the retreat; but yet we found none that had any life in them when we searched among the ghastly evidences of the fight for our own people.

Peter Sitz declared that he had seen one of the wounded savages deliberately kill himself with a knife, when it was seen that the assault had failed, and I doubt not but that several did the same rather than fall into our hands. Then, also, it is possible, in the heat of battle, and remembering what these human wolves had done to the women and children of the settlements which had been attacked, some of our men had sent more than one of the helpless wretches to the Happy Hunting Grounds. I count myself as tender-hearted as any other, and yet it would not have troubled my conscience had I put a few wounded villains out of the world, rather than let them live to commit yet more murders.

On the morning after the assault a white flag was raised over the fort, and when St. Leger sent in hot haste a messenger to learn what we wanted, thinking, most like, we had made up our minds to surrender, he was informed that Colonel Gansevoort was willing to grant an hour's truce that the British and Indian dead might be buried.

This the enemy accepted, and I was surprised to see that never one of Thayendanega's beauties came forward to carry off the slain of his tribe. I had always heard it said that the redskins would brave any danger rather than allow a dead Indian to fall into the hands of an enemy; but certain it is that on this day the rascally Tories dragged away the bodies, with not even a squaw to help them.

Within the time set we were rid of the ghastly evidence of the battle, which might have proven a menace to the health of the garrison had the corpses been allowed to remain unburied while the weather was so warm, and during all the coming night we could hear distinctly cries of lamentation from the Indian camp. It was as if every brave, squaw, and papoose howled his or her loudest in token of sorrow, and three of us within the fort had a very good idea of what would have been our fate had we not been rescued before the assault.

"This would have been our last night on earth, had the Minute Boys not come to the rescue," Peter Sitz said to me, as we stood near the sally-port for an instant, listening to the wild cries, and, strong man though he was, I took note of the fact that his face shone pale in the faint light.

It did not need that I should strain my imagination very much to paint a mental picture of our condition at that time, if we had remained in the power of the savages. Of a verity we would have tested their keenest torture before death came to our relief.

"It would seem as if that company of ours had been formed to some purpose, an' not all of them were children," I said, minded that he who had laughed most heartily at what he was pleased to call our "pretensions," should give credit where it was due.

James Otis

"If I live to see home again, there is never a man in Cherry Valley who shall not hear from me what I owe to you lads!"

"Don't forget that I had no part in the rescue, Master Sitz, for surely I was trussed up as stoutly as either you or Sergeant Corney."

"Yet but for your persistence we would never have thought of enlisting the boys to aid in our defence, therefore must you take your portion of the praise, an' more especially since it is said by Sergeant Corney himself that you have proven yourself a man at every time when danger threatened."

"Sergeant Corney has no idea how my knees shook beneath me when, as he believed, I was stout-hearted," I replied, with a careless laugh that served to cloak the feeling of pride which rose in my bosom when he gave good words to the Minute Boys.

While weeping over our dead, and rejoicing because of having beaten back the enemy when it seemed as if the assault was about to be successful, fear regarding the safety of Colonel Willett and Lieutenant Stockwell lay heavily upon our hearts. It was the belief of nearly all the garrison that the two officers had been captured, and, if such had been the case, there could be no question but that they suffered a terrible death at the stake while the savages were mourning over their loss.

Those among us who felt convinced that the messengers had succeeded in their attempt, and Colonel Gansevoort was one of the hopeful ones, insisted that if the Indians had tortured any prisoners to death, we must have heard yells and shouts of triumph;

yet the night wind had brought to our ears nothing more than the cries of sorrow.

Viewing the situation in the brightest light possible, many days must of a necessity elapse before we could hope for any good results from their brave venture, and if in the meantime the enemy pressed us sharply, we would be in hard straits, more particularly since so much of our ammunition had been expended in defending the fort against that first assault.

When a large number of men are confined in a limited space, and exposed to danger, it needs but the lightest word to make cowards of the more faint-hearted, as we soon had good proof.

On the day following the truce, after the enemy had buried their dead, work on the parallels was continued, and it gave me no little satisfaction to see that the Tories were forced to perform the greater portion of the labor.

As I have already said, these trenches extended within an hundred and fifty yards of the fort by this time, and we knew only too well that it was not within our power to prevent their being advanced as near as the enemy saw fit to carry them.

After a certain time mining would probably be begun, and then, if our supply of ammunition had not been replenished, the end must be near at hand, when St. Leger would have opportunity to carry into execution his threat of allowing Thayendanega's murderers to work their cruel will.

All this was talked over and commented upon by our

people as the days wore on, and the more timid seemed to find delight in picturing what would take place if the fort was captured.

"Why must they keep harpin' on that possibility all the time?" I asked, angrily, of Sergeant Corney, when I had turned away in disgust from a group of men who were painting horrible word-pictures, and the old soldier had followed me to the parade-ground beyond sound of such words.

"It is all as plain as the nose on your face, lad," the old man said, grimly. "Look about, an' you'll see that them as are makin' the howl over what the Injuns may do are the faintest-hearted among us. It's all done for one purpose."

"What can that be?" I asked, in surprise. "How do they suppose any good can come of conjuring up everything horrible?"

"They're of the same kidney that drove General Herkimer into the ambush, an' are tryin' to force the colonel to surrender."

"That can't be possible!" I cried, sharply. "There's never one among them who does not know full well what the result will be if Colonel Gansevoort surrenders the fort! St. Leger's promises would be as the idle wind when Thayendanega's followers wanted victims for the stake!"

"True for you, lad, an' yet these cowards are ready to howl for capitulation rather than fight as men should, in the presence of such an enemy, to the last ditch," the sergeant replied, bitterly.

I could not believe that among the entire garrison might be found one soldier who would willingly consent to a surrender, and said as much to the old man, who replied, grimly:

"I haven't been around here for the past four an' twenty hours with my eyes shut an' my ears filled with moss. Take a turn about the works, listenin' to all that is said, an' you'll find I'm not wrong in my figgerin'. The colonel knows as well as do I what's in the wind, an' I'll agree never to eat sweet-cake agin if he ain't makin' ready for trouble inside the fort as well as outside."

I remained silent a full minute, horrified by the bare possibility, and then asked, in a voice which trembled despite all my efforts to render it steady:

"Think you they can force him against his will, as the militia did General Herkimer?"

"It is my belief that he'd shoot down a round dozen before consentin' to give us all over to death; but there's no knowin' what a man may be forced into when pressure enough has been brought to bear upon him."

At this moment Jacob came up, looking like his old self now that his father was safe, at least, for the time being, and to him I put the matter much as I had had it from the sergeant.

"Within the hour I have heard the same word from my father. He believes there are a full hundred of the garrison who, when they have worked themselves up to just such a pitch, will howl for surrender."

Even then I refused to believe in what was as yet no more than a suspicion, and Sergeant Corney said, impatiently:

"It won't cost you much time to find out for yourself, lad. Take a couple of turns around, an' I'll guarantee you'll agree that Peter Sitz an' I are not tryin' to make mountains out of mole-hills."

"I'll go with you," Jacob said, promptly, and straightway we set out, keeping our ears open whenever we came within speaking distance of a group of men who appeared to be talking earnestly upon some particular subject.

It was not necessary that we should go twice around the inside of the fortification, for before we completed the first circuit I had heard enough to convince me that Sergeant Corney, instead of exaggerating the matter, had not made his statements strong enough by one-half.

As it seemed to me, a full third of the garrison were arguing in favor of surrender, giving as their reasons the scanty supply of powder for the cannon, and the probability that St. Leger's army would constantly increase as the Tories from the Mohawk Valley got wind of what was going on.

I was sick at heart and literally faint with fear when this knowledge was forced in upon me, for I knew only too well how idle would be all the promises of St. Leger if the savages were inclined to massacre the prisoners that were surrendered on promises of fair treatment.

Chapter XIV.

Mutiny

I had thought that we would never again be called upon to witness such a scene as that in General Herkimer's encampment on the morning when those who, later, were the first to show the white feather, literally drove him into a place where he, as a soldier, knew it was not safe to venture until all the arrangements for a sortie from the fort were completed.

Now, however, it seemed to me that we were to be treated to a second dose of mutiny, and this one more serious than the first, for, in case these fools in the fort succeeded in badgering Colonel Gansevoort as the others had the general, then would nearly a thousand men be given over to the savage foe, whom we knew full well would show no mercy.

To me the strange part of it all was that these very simpletons who were howling so loudly for surrender would be among those counted as prisoners, and I failed utterly to understand how they could figure themselves as being better off in the power of Thayendanega's wolves, than in the fort where they had a chance of fighting to the death.

Even to this day it seems so strange that I would not

dare set it down as a fact unless those gentlemen who write history had spoken of it so plainly.

"You can make up your mind that those fellows who are lettin' out the most noise are the ones who've got a cowardly streak in 'em somewhere," Sergeant Corney said, when Jacob and I, having satisfied ourselves that mutiny was rife in the fort, went to him for the purpose of talking the matter over.

"The greater the cowards the less inclined they should be to surrender, as it seems to me," I replied, in perplexity.

"Ay, lad, that's the way it looks to a decent man; but sich fellows as these here who are makin' a row, are the ones who're always lookin' ahead, thinkin' matters may be bettered, an' regardin' not the possibility of their growin' worse. Here they are, like to come on short allowance, an' obleeged to take their turn at bein' shot at now an' then, consequently, not havin' the heart to endure even the lightest sufferin', they say we can't be any worse off, an' ought to surrender."

"But they know the nature of Thayendanega's wolves as well as do you or I."

"Yes, they did know yesterday; but now, because their stomachs are not quite full, they're ready to admit that every redskin is an imitation angel."

"Think you they can badger the colonel?" Jacob asked, thoughtfully, thus repeating my question in different words.

"I will say to you as I did to Noel, that they're like to

get the rough end of it before drivin' him into a mistake. We who are not inclined to be mutinous can help him out a good bit in this matter."

"How?" I asked, in perplexity.

"By standin' out stiffly against their fool talk, though there ain't much chance you can convince 'em with words; but if one, or half a dozen, for that matter, gives me an openin', I'll see if the weight of my fist can't beat some sense into them."

It is not agreeable to set down the details of such a disgraceful scene as we witnessed during the next four and twenty hours, and more than painful to describe how the mutiny was finally checked. It must be done, however, if I would write fairly the part which we Minute Boys of the Mohawk Valley took in the troubles and triumphs round-about Fort Schuyler; but I will give the story in as few words as possible.

It so chanced that during this day the rations dealt out to us were smaller than before, and this gave the fool croakers an opportunity of airing their grievances in fine style.

Those who should have been steadily attentive to their duties, with never a thought in their minds of anything save besting the motley crew that besieged us, began to talk openly of starvation, as if there was no question whatsoever but that we had come nearly to the end of our provisions, and thus, as I believe, they brought over to their way of thinking many who never would have listened to such wild talk, but for the fact that it seemed probable the hour of surrender must be near at hand.

I saw to it that none of the Minute Boys sided with these malcontents, while Sergeant Corney and Peter Sitz moved here and there throughout the day, trying to persuade the men to do only that which was for their own good, but without success.

The longer such talk ran through the garrison the stronger it became, until shortly before sunset the mutiny was so well advanced that the commandant could do no less than take serious notice of it, and it pleased me that he did not delay.

Save for the sentinels on the walls, the entire garrison was called out as for parade, and, having been clumsily formed in a hollow square, Colonel Gansevoort, surrounded by his staff of officers, undertook to still the rising tempest.

He began by saying that it was the opinion of himself and his staff that the men ought to know exactly the condition of affairs, lest they be led astray by idle fears, and to that end he called upon the quartermaster for a detailed statement of the amount of eatables then on hand.

When this had been given, and it required some time to read the entire list, he announced the number of men, women, and children which were inside the walls of the fort, figuring out that by slightly decreasing the size of the rations it would be possible to provide every person with food during three weeks at least.

True it is the supply was not large enough to admit of our gorging ourselves; but I dare venture to say that many there would have lived on much less had they been thrown upon their own resources in their own homes.

Then he told how many times the big guns had been fired during the late assault, and stated that we had two hundred and fifty rounds of ammunition remaining for the cannon. He claimed that it was possible for us to hold the fort even though we did not use the heavy weapons, and showed that we could yet put up as much of a fight as St. Leger's army would be able to stomach.

After all these details, he described to the men what would likely be their fate in event of surrender, declaring that we had every reason and the ability to hold the fort if we were so minded, and urged us to be men rather than cowards.

It was a good speech, and one which should have put heart into the veriest white-livered militiaman that ever pretended to be a soldier; but, to my surprise, I could see on the faces of those who had talked surrender the loudest, an expression telling that the words passed by them as does the wind.

When we were dismissed the contention was greater than before the colonel spoke, and I began to believe it would have been better had he held his peace, for surely it seemed as if they believed his words of cheer were but proof that he shared their fears.

During the evening one of the bolder poltroons declared it was the duty of all the garrison, in order to save their lives, to force Colonel Gansevoort to do as they desired, and while the talk was the hottest Sergeant Corney "broke loose," as he afterward expressed it.

"This lad an' I," he said, laying his hand on my shoulder, after attracting the attention of all within sound of his voice, "have within a short time seen just such scoundrelly curs as you are provin' yourselves to be. We have heard them cry out against a commander who was fitted to lead brave men, and their blood is not yet dry on the banks of the Oriskany. They forced General Herkimer into an ambush against his better judgment, - against his will, - an' at the first volley from Thayendanega's painted wretches they turned tail. Until that time I had thought an Indian was the meanest specimen of humanity on the face of the earth; but I have come to know different, an' am yet gettin' fresh proof. If you talk so boldly of what St. Leger's promises are worth, why don't you put 'em to the test? If you believe death by starvation awaits you here, an' that all the heart of man can desire is to be found among yonder yellin' imps, why don't you make an exchange? The garrison would be the stronger for your absence, an' if it so be any man here wants to consort with the red wolves, I, who pride myself on never yet havin' disobeyed a military order, will stand by an' help him to leave the fort."

For a moment after the old man ceased speaking I fully expected he would be set upon and ill-treated by those whom he had so severely lashed with his tongue.

That no move toward open violence was attempted simply gave proof that they were the cowards he had accused them of being; but I believed it was possible to see in their faces that his ironical advice might bear fruit, and so I told him when the opportunity came.

"More than one of them has had it in his mind to desert an' go over to the enemy," I said, whereupon he replied, as if the possibility gave him great satisfaction:

"I wish they might! It's true I said more than I meant when declarin' my willingness to help 'em get away; but I promise you, Noel Campbell, that my hand never will be raised to stop them, if they try any sich fool trick."

When my lads were together in the barracks once more, and had settled down for the night, none of us having been detailed for guard-duty, the thought of what I fancied I saw on the faces of the mutineers troubled me not a little, and, instead of lying down to sleep with the majority of my comrades, I called Peter Sitz and Sergeant Corney aside, urging that one or the other go to Colonel Gansevoort for the purpose of telling him what it was possible some of the garrison might attempt to do before morning.

Peter Sitz claimed that, since he was not a soldier, he had no right to make what might seem to the commandant like a suggestion, and shoved all the responsibility on the sergeant.

The old man declared, as he had previously, that the men might do as they pleased; that if it was possible to stop them by a single word his lips should remain closed.

Whereupon I suggested that if the men should desert, in however small numbers, they might leave some portion of the fortification unguarded, which would work to the peril of all, and insisted, if the sergeant would not do what he might to prevent the desertion, it was at least our duty to so act that the remainder of the garrison would not be put in jeopardy because of their folly.

Not until I had spoken at some length would the old soldier give any heed, and then, upon a suggestion from Peter Sitz, he said:

"This much I'm willin' to do, an' no more: from now till mornin' I'll make it my business, although clearly I am goin' beyond the bounds of ordinary duty, to move to an' fro around the fort, an' will summon the Minute Boys in case any point is left unguarded."

Both Jacob and I proposed to share the labor with him; but he would have none of it.

"Stay where you are," he said, "for I'm not minded you shall do that which may disgruntle the commandant. When he learns that we took it upon ourselves to look after the safety of the garrison without orders from him, there'll be a good chance for a row. I'll stand the brunt of it alone, without draggin' you lads into the scrape."

I knew from the expression on his face that any attempt at argument with him at the time would be useless, therefore held my peace; but had it in mind that by thus interfering he might be committing an offence such as the commandant would not readily forget.

If any number of men should desert on this night, there could not be any question but that we, having had an inkling of it, might justly be held accountable, but yet I was not pleased at the thought of doing or suffering to be done that which the old soldier had set his face against.

However, as has been said, I could have done nothing to change matters save by going to the commandant, and therefore rema ined in the barracks, mightily uncomfortable in mind, but trying my best at holding conversation with Jacob on indifferent subjects.

The majority of my company had no idea of what might be done that night, therefore they lay down to sleep as usual, Jacob and I seeking the open air after we found it was impossible to take interest in any subject save that which lay, just at that time, nearest our hearts.

We paced to and fro in front of the barracks, taking good care not to disturb the sleepers, until perhaps half an hour before midnight, and then the sergeant came up, looking much like a man who has just settled a very disagreeable question.

"Well, it's done," he said, abruptly, "an' to-morrow at this time I reckon there'll be less fools in the world."

"What do you mean?" I cried, excitedly, for, although expecting to hear that a certain number of men had deserted, I could not but feel astonishment when the suspicions thus became a certainty.

"Five of the cowards have deserted, countin' that St. Leger will receive 'em with open arms. They had a good deal to say about the need of somethin' to fill up their stomachs, an' I reckon that within four an' twenty hours sich a question as that won't give 'em any further trouble."

"How did they go?" Jacob asked, eagerly.

"Out through the horn-works, an' over the stockade."

"How did it happen that only five started?"

"The rest of the mutinous ones were not quite sich fools when it came to the last pinch, an' I'm allowin' we're well rid of those who have gone, save that they can carry information to St. Leger of a kind he'll be glad to receive."

That was a possibility which I had failed to realize until this moment, and immediately the knowledge came I understood clearly that it was our duty to have notified the commandant at once of what we suspected, for, if the enemy learned that we were on short allowance and with a scarcity of ammunition, as he certainly would from these men who were bound to make matters appear as bad as possible, we might expect more than one vigorous assault within a very short time.

"Did you stand quietly by while they went?" Jacob asked, in a tone of reproach.

"I wasn't quite sich a fool as that, lad, even though I did advise 'em to go. I kept my eye on the gang, however, an' was hidden in the horn-works when they made the final plans. Those who had been left behind seemed to be frightened, an' I reckon there'll be less show of mutiny in this 'ere fort to-morrow mornin' than we've seen in the past four an' twenty hours."

Jacob and I would have insisted that the old soldier tell us more regarding the desertion, although it was evident he had imparted all the information at his command; but he, bent on getting some rest before morning, entered the barracks, and we could hardly do better than follow him.

Although it had not seemed possible I would close my eyes in slumber that night, with so much which was disagreeable to keep me awake, I did fall asleep, and that right soon after I lay down by the side of Jacob.

We were astir very early next morning, through some whim of Sergeant Corney's, who insisted that the Minute Boys should be the first to make an appearance, and I left the barracks fully expecting to find a scene of confusion outside.

Matters were much as they had been the night previous, and I came to the conclusion, that as yet the commandant was ignorant of the fact that five of his men had gone over to the enemy.

However that may have been, no signs of disquietude among the officers were apparent until the sun was two hours or more high, and then half a dozen men belonging to the same company as those who had deserted, were summoned to headquarters.

"You might save the commandant a good bit of trouble by telling him what you know," Jacob suggested to Sergeant Corney, and the latter replied, grimly:

"I'm not sich a fool. It's one thing to let a lot of sneaks get away when you think the garrison will be the better off without 'em, an' quite another to own up to your superior officer that you've winked at desertion. I'll keep a close tongue in my head, an' so will them as are my friends."

With this the old man walked away, leaving us gazing at each other in something very like astonishment, for we understood by his tone that he was much the same as threatening us in case we should take it upon ourselves to tell what we knew regarding the matter.

Before ten o'clock all of the garrison were aware that five of the force had deserted, and those men who had been loudest spoken regarding the wisdom of surrendering, were now moving about very uneasily, doubtless fearing they might be called upon to answer for some of the unsoldierly remarks in which they had indulged.

There was no real confusion in the fort, but a general air of disquietude and apprehension, which I thought quite wholesome, since it caused every man to do his duty more promptly and more thoroughly than I had ever seen it done.

When those who had been summoned to headquarters appeared on the parade-ground once more, they were surrounded by eager comrades, all anxious to know what had been said to them; but they could give very little definite information, and were unwilling to talk openly regarding the matter, for the reason, as I fancied, that some of them, being privy to the desertion, had denied such fact to the officers.

Well, by noon it seemed as if the matter had entirely blown over. Everything went along much as on the day previous, save that, according to my idea, there was a more healthy tone among the men, because we no longer heard talk of surrender, and I suggested that perhaps Colonel Gansevoort was as glad to be rid of his mutinous soldiers as Sergeant Corney had been to see them depart.

It goes without saying that all of us, whether on duty or not, kept a sharper lookout over the enemy's encampment than ever before, for there was good reason to expect that St. Leger would order another assault; but not one of us dreamed of that horrible spectacle which was to be presented, much as if Thayendanega's murderers were of a mind to give would-be deserters such a lesson as could never be forgotten.

The afternoon passed quietly and without unusual incident; but when the sun was just about to set we observed the Indians crossing the river from their encampment to the meadow at a point near the creek, where it was possible for us to hold them in plain view, while they were yet beyond range of any except the heavier guns, which could not be brought to bear upon them.

The first movement was made by a party of a dozen or more, who seemed to be carrying heavy burdens on their backs, and this was such an unusual thing for a redskin to do that we were keenly curious.

This first squad was followed by a veritable swarm of the painted murderers, and I said nervously to Sergeant Corney, who was standing near me at the moment:

"The savages are goin' to try their hand at an assault, an' we're like to have warm work before mornin'."

"There's little fear anything of that kind will happen, lad. The painted devil never lived who was willin' to stand up an' fight face to face, man-fashion."

"Then why are they goin' out of their encampment like a swarm of bees?"

"There's some mischief afoot, though what it is I can't rightly make out. Perhaps St. Leger has summoned 'em to another powwow, in order that they may know of our condition, as has been told by the deserters."

In a very few moments it was positive that this guess was not correct, for, instead of crossing the creek to approach the British encampment, the Indians halted when they were about midway between the fort, the camps of the British soldiers, and the quarters of the Tories.

It was at a point where every man on either side could see what was being done, and yet so far away that, save by a sortie, no one could molest them.

I dare venture to say that every man in the garrison, save perhaps the officers, was watching intently the movements of Thayendanega's gang, and it was as if the knowledge of what was about to be done burst upon us all at the same instant.

A low murmur of horror involuntarily came from our lips, and men said in whispers, one to another, the blood suddenly leaving their bronzed faces:

"The Indians are going to torture prisoners!"

By this time we could see that two stout posts had been set firmly in the earth, and around them were heaped piles of light wood, such as the squaws and children were bringing up in great quantities.

Thayendanega's bloodthirsty crew was bent on showing us what would be our fate if we fell into their clutches.

When the first shock of horror had passed away in a measure, there came the question as to who might be the victims, and then those who had talked mutiny and urged their fellows on to rankest insubordination turned pale as death, while many of them walked totteringly away as if unable to control their limbs. We all believed, and with good reason, that those unfortunates who were to suffer death at the hands of the most cruel-minded men God ever made, were none other than the deserters from our ranks.

During the assault not one of the garrison had been taken prisoner, and certain it was that the besiegers had not left the vicinity of the fort for such length of time as would be sufficient to enable them to procure captives elsewhere, therefore did we know beyond a peradventure who the victims would be, but why only two were to suffer was something at which we could not even so much as guess.

I saw Colonel Gansevoort and several of the officers come out from headquarters, having most likely been informed as to what was going on, and, when they stood where it was possible to have an unobstructed view of the horrible preparations, the entire garrison of Fort Schuyler were assembled as spectators.

"Cannot something be done for the poor fellows?" I heard a man behind me ask in a quavering tone, and, turning, I saw one who had declared most vehemently but a few hours previous that if we would surrender the fort we could be assured beyond question of such treatment as civilized people give to prisoners of war.

No one answered his question, and in a whisper I repeated it to Sergeant Corney, whereupon he shook his head decidedly.

"The commander who would make a sortie for the purpose of savin' only two lives would be guilty of criminal folly," the old soldier said, emphatically. "If those who are to suffer were Colonel Gansevoort's nearest friends, still must he remain here idle rather than put in jeopardy all the garrison. As it is, those painted devils are givin' us sich a lesson as will cause every man here to fight until the death, rather than so much as hint that we might trust to the enemy's promises. It's a harsh remedy - the harshest man could imagine; but yet there are an hundred or more lookin' on at this minute who need it."

I cannot make the feeblest attempt at describing the horror which took possession of me as I realized that we could make no effort toward saving the unfortunate men, who were not the less to be pitied because they had brought about their own misery, and, unable longer to gaze at what was so soon to be such a terrible scene, I turned away with a mind to shut myself up in the barracks.

Chapter XV.

The Torture

There was one odd thing I noted while turning away, sick at heart, which was that those friends of the deserters, the men whose voices had been raised highest against Colonel Gansevoort because he would not surrender the fort at St. Leger's bidding, had no word to say now that their friends were in such dire distress, while those who had struggled to quell the mutiny were asking loudly if it were not possible to do something toward saving the lives of the unfortunate men.

Twenty or more of the bolder spirits, among whom was Sergeant Corney, were making ready to ask permission of the commandant to their creeping out of the fort on that side nearest the river, and then trying by a sudden dash to rescue the prisoners.

Even the slight experience which I had had in savage warfare was sufficient to show me that there was nothing which we could do in behalf of the wretched men, and any plan, however promising, could not fail of exposing the entire garrison to the keenest peril.

There could be no question but that the enemy hoped we might be so venturesome as to sally out, and I doubt if there was a man within the fortification who did not feel convinced that St. Leger's troops were ready to swoop down in assault at the first show of our having sent away any portion of our force.

All knew that we inside the fortification were powerless to aid those who had wilfully gone to their doom, and none better than those same brave fellows who were ready to risk their lives in behalf of comrades who would have worked disaster to the entire garrison, yet they could not stand idle without at least a show of willingness to face danger in the hope of saving life.

The one lesson which all of us learned at this time was as to how much dependence might be placed upon the word of the British commander. He had declared that he would protect all who came to him promising to serve the king, and yet, when the five foolish cowards from our garrison presented themselves, they were given over to the merciless savages, much as honest people give play-things to their children.

I had turned away from the scene sick with horror, even though the fiendish work had not yet begun; but as I stood near the barracks, trembling in every limb, the thought came that perhaps our deserters were not the ones for whom the stakes were intended. Of course, it would be equally terrible to see any human being tortured to death; but at the moment it seemed as if the frightfulness of it would in some degree be lessened if it were strangers who suffered, and straightway I went back to the walls, taking station by the side of Jacob, as I strained my eyes to see who the Indians led out.

"Where is the sergeant?" I asked, in a whisper.

"Gone, in company with a dozen others, to ask permission of the commandant to leave the fort for a short time."

"Do they want to compass their own death?" I asked, angrily. "I dare venture to say every Tory in yonder encampment is ready to cut off any who, from motives of mercy and pity, venture beyond the walls."

"Ay, so my father believes. He says that Colonel Gansevoort cannot, in justice to the remainder of the force, allow such a sacrifice of life as would result from a sortie."

"But we are not yet certain that it is our deserters who are to be put to death," I suggested, and at the moment a hoarse cry went up from all that company of heart-sick spectators.

Accompanied by war-songs from the warriors and hoots and yells from the squaws and fiendish children, the unfortunate men were being brought across the river in triumph, and then a deep hush fell upon our garrison, as every person within the walls bent forward anxiously to get a glimpse of those who were being carried to the theatre of a terrible death.

The unfortunate prisoners were yet too far away for me to distinguish their features, when a soldier standing near by, a man whom I recognized as one of those who had howled most loudly for surrender, cried with a groan as of mortal agony:

"There is Seth Morton!"

This was the name of one of the deserters, and there

was no longer any hope but that the savages were ready to show us how our own people could die.

At this moment the party with whom Sergeant Corney had gone to the commandant for permission to attempt a rescue came up, and but one glance at their faces was needed to show that the request had been denied.

"He wouldn't let you go?" I whispered, as the old man stood by my side.

"No, lad, an' we should have had better sense than to ask him. A commandant who would agree to sich a plan has no right to expect his troops can rely upon his showin' good judgment in a tight fix."

"What did he say?"

"He talked like a gentleman who speaks with his friends. Instead of roarin' out that we were all kinds of idjuts, as another commander might have done, he told us exactly what would be the result if any of us attempted to leave the fort, an' wound up by sayin' that if his own brother was in the hands of the red devils, he would not consider it doin' justice by the garrison even to let one man venture forth. He only told us the truth, an' I'm not sorry I went to him, even though nothin' came of it, for it ain't cheerful to stand still without makin' a little bit of a try while sich work as that yonder is goin' on."

When the prisoners had been taken across the stream the savages lost no time in setting about their terrible work, and, although so many years have elapsed since then, I cannot bring myself to set down that which I know was done.

While the poor fellows were being bound to the stakes, Jacob and I ran into the barracks, where we remained, trying to shut out from our ears the yells and whoops which told of what was going on.

"And I would have suffered the same bitter death but for what you did, dear lad!" I said, hardly able to control my voice.

"Don't think of it, Noel," he replied, soothingly, as he pressed my hand. "An', above everything, don't give me the credit. All our company had a part in that rescue."

"Ay, yet they'd never known of our peril but for you, an' it was you alone, when they were arrived, who braved the danger of coming across the encampment to the lodge."

"Talk of somethin' else, Noel Campbell!" Jacob cried, fiercely. "Even though the colonel knows best what should be done, it seems cowardly for us to be sittin' here in safety while those poor fellows are sufferin' all that men can!"

I tried to do as he would have me; but one can readily understand that at such a time it would be well-nigh impossible to think of anything save that which was being done within sight of all the garrison.

It seemed to me like a very long time before the sergeant joined us, and then I knew that the unfortunate men were out of their misery at last.

"They have paid a fearful price for their folly," the old man said, solemnly; "but by thus dyin' they've ensured the holdin' of this fort, for there's not a man within the walls who wouldn't delight in drawin' his last breath at the post of duty rather than take the chances of sich protection as St. Leger has shown he's ready to give. We'll have no more mutiny, an' all hands will be starved to death before the enemy gets possession of the fortification."

"What about the other three men?" Jacob asked, in a whisper, not daring to trust his voice lest it should betray the fear in his heart.

"I reckon their turn will come soon - perhaps to-morrow night. Thayendanega's 'noble red men' can't afford to waste their victims. But, hark ye, lads, it won't do for you to moon over what is enough to turn any man's blood to water. Take a brisk walk up an' down the parade-ground for half an hour, an' then come to bed. I'm thinkin' we may have a bit of work cut out for us within the next four an' twenty hours."

"Of what kind?" I asked, not inclined to follow the old man's advice so far as to venture out while the howling Indians were making night something of which to be afraid.

"It stands to reason that before the deserters were turned over to the painted wolves St. Leger got from them all the information concernin' this fort which they could give. The British general now knows that we haven't any too much ammunition for the cannon, an' it'll be odd if he don't give us a chance to spend a good bit more of it."

This seemed a plausible line of reasoning, and yet I was not in the lightest degree troubled by the possibility; I had known so much of horror during the past few hours that an assault, however desperate, was something to be courted rather than feared.

Sergeant Corney smoked his pipe long and furiously that night as he sat in the barracks, giving no heed as to whether we followed his advice, and we two lads sat side by side with little inclination to indulge in conversation.

One by one our boys, pale-faced and trembling, entered the sleeping-quarters, some even going so far as to lie down, but positive am I that never an eye was closed in slumber during all that night, and every one of us welcomed the first rays of the rising sun as if years had passed since he last showed his face.

Before another six hours passed we had good proof that those who deserted gave all the information at their command to General St. Leger regarding the condition of affairs at the fort, and yet never a word was spoken against them, because of the frightful punishment which followed their treachery.

From what our party of Minute Boys had seen up to this time, the work of the siege was not pushed vigorously by the Britishers, and even the little which was done had been performed by the Tories. It is true that the parallels were run unpleasantly near the fort, yet, had the besiegers so desired, there would have been twice as much to show for their efforts.

On the morning after two of the deserters had been tortured to death, it began to look as if our people would have little time for idleness.

The enemy's trenches were filled with men, - regulars as well as Tories, - all of whom worked with a will, and at different points sharpshooters were stationed to pick off our sentinels.

"Now this is somethin' like business," Sergeant Corney said, as if the sense of additional danger was most pleasing to him. "Barry St. Leger has just found out that there's a chance of takin' this fort by storm, an' from now on we'll have our hands full."

Jacob and I were in the barracks trying to sleep when the old man burst in upon us with the remark I have set down, and as he spoke he began furbishing up his rifle with unusual care.

"Have you any especial work on hand?" I asked, looking curiously at him.

"Ay, lad, that's what I have. This 'ere garrison ain't in any very great danger of runnin' short of ammunition for the small arms, an' we're goin' to give the enemy lead in the place of iron for a spell."

"What do you mean?" I asked, somewhat petulantly, for it seemed as if the old man was making sport of me.

"Only that we've given the enemy's sharpshooters a chance all the forenoon without interferin' to any great extent, an' now we're countin' on takin' our turn. Fifty men have been detailed to pick off as many of St. Leger's force as we can draw a bead on. I reckon workin' in the trenches won't be a healthy job from this time on. Colonel Gansevoort allows to show the Britishers that he can stir his stumps if needs must."

The sergeant left the barracks without giving us further information; but we soon learned that our people were to be kept sharply up to their work, instead of being allowed to spend five hours out of every six in lounging around.

The force of sharpshooters to which Sergeant Corney was assigned had been stationed on the north and east sides of the fort, where they could command a view of the British and Tory encampments and the trenches.

Another company of fifty was told off especially for the horn-works, while we Minute Boys were ordered to keep at least ten of our number constantly on watch over the sally-port, from which point the best view of the Indian encampment could be had.

Yet others of the force were detailed to go from one division to another of those I have named, in order to lend a hand in case it might become necessary, and thus it was we no longer had any loungers on the parade-grounds or near the barracks.

The orders were that every effort be made to pick off such of the enemy as offered themselves for targets, and before the day had come to an end St. Leger's men must have begun to understand that the siege of Fort Schuyler was no longer the one-sided affair which it had been.

My lads could not have been stationed in any other position where they would have been as well satisfied, for thus were they fighting the savages who had threatened to ravage the Mohawk Valley, and every time we made a successful shot it was much as if we struck a blow in defence of our homes.

　　　　James Otis

Thayendanega's so-called braves did not give us very much opportunity to display our skill as marksmen, however. Within five minutes after the curs discovered that we were straining every effort to reduce their number, they hugged the encampment mighty snug, and I am of the opinion that General St. Leger would have found it difficult to make them obey any order which might necessitate their coming within our line of fire.

In addition to this slow method of whipping a large force, I noted the fact that twenty men or more were at work moving one of the guns in the northwest bastion, and was not a little puzzled to make out why such a piece of work should be done at a time when we could not afford to use the cannon any more than was absolutely necessary.

My surprise was not lessened when the laborers with great difficulty transferred the big gun directly to our station, mounting it almost directly over the port, after which six rounds of ammunition were brought from the magazine and placed where it could be got at handily.

"Does the commandant think we lads can handle that cannon properly?" I asked of the corporal who was superintending the work, and he replied, with a laugh of satisfaction:

"I reckon he wasn't thinkin' very much about you when he gave orders to have the gun moved. That's to help out on our surprise-party; it'll carry a ball farther an' with truer aim than any other piece in the fort, as I know, havin' had somewhat to do with all of 'em."

"What do you mean by a surprise-party?" I asked, in perplexity. "An' why should the best gun be brought here?"

"Well, you see, lad, the chances are them bloody sneaks will soon try to work the same deviltry which we had to look at idly last night, for it stands to reason that all who deserted from this fort fell into their clutches. The next time they start in to kill a man by inches, believin' they're out of range, we'll plump a ball into the middle of the gang that'll make em' hop a bit."

I laughed in glee at the prospect of turning the tables on the bloodthirsty wretches, but very shortly came the thought that the unfortunate prisoners would be in as much danger as the savages, and this I suggested to the corporal, whereupon he said, gravely:

"We'll hope the first shot kills as many as are trussed up to the stakes, lad, because a quick death is the only favor we can do for the poor fellows."

It would indeed be a mercy to kill the prisoners, if we could not save their lives; but of a verity we were come to hard lines when it was to be hoped our missiles would slay those who had been our comrades.

I believed all the garrison were better content, now that Colonel Gansevoort was finding work for every man. Certainly there was less chance for searching out bugbears when they were busily engaged, and each of us felt a grim satisfaction at knowing that we inflicted some punishment on the enemy, however slight.

It must not be supposed that our sharpshooters found all the targets they desired, else had we wiped St.

Leger's force out in a twinkling; but there were in the white portion of his army a sufficient number who scorned to show fear of what we might be able to do, and these kept our men so engaged that the reports of the rifles were ringing out almost without intermission.

As I have already said, we Minute Boys had but little opportunity to show our skill after the first hour, because the savages kept so close within their lodges; but now and then we had a crack at a painted figure, and seldom missed our aim.

As the day wore away it became evident that the Indians counted on torturing the remainder of their prisoners as before, and, instead of suffering from the sickness of horror, as I had twenty-four hours previous, there was in my mind a most pleasing anticipation of what would be the result.

Half an hour before sunset they began setting up new posts, a fact which told that St. Leger had indeed turned over to them all the deserters.

Word was passed around the fort that the commandant counted on putting an end to their cruel sport, if perchance the distance was not greater than he had estimated, and by sunset every person inside the walls, save those who were acting as sentinels on the westerly side, had their faces turned in the direction of the Indian encampment.

It was claimed that the corporal with whom I had previously spoken was the best gunner in the command, and to him had been entrusted the work of sighting the cannon.

He had already charged it heavily, and when the savages began setting up new posts he knew the time had come to look for the proper range.

The corporal had no need to call for a crew to aid him. An hundred pairs of hands were out-stretched eagerly whenever he signified the desire to have this thing or that done, and he was more like to suffer from a surplus of helpers than a lack.

It looked much as if Colonel Gansevoort feared that, while our attention was attracted toward the fiendish work of the savages, the British and Tory soldiers might make an assault, for he ordered the number of sentinels doubled and all the spectators to be in line, weapons in hand, that no time might be lost in case it became necessary to move them from one point to another.

Thayendanega's wolves did not count on keeping us waiting very long; but as soon as the sun had set began crossing the river with their unfortunate prisoners, singing and shouting, as if the capture and torturing of these unarmed men was some signal act of bravery.

The corporal told off a certain number of those nearest to act as crew for the gun, explaining to them just how they should set about the task of recharging when once it had been discharged, and then the remainder of the spectators, save we Minute Boys who were entitled to remain at our stations, were forced to fall back that they might not impede the work after it was once begun.

By this time Colonel Gansevoort himself had come up, and thus we understood that he was to direct the firing.

If our cannon could carry a missile to the place of torture, then certain it was the red-skinned brutes would receive a lesson well calculated to surprise those who were left alive after the piece had been discharged.

The commandant did not wait until the horrible work was begun; but, once the stakes were surrounded by the howling, screaming, dancing mob as they placed the prisoners in the desired positions, the corporal got the word for which he had been eagerly waiting.

A puff of dense white smoke, a report which was almost deafening to those of us standing near by rang out.

Then we could follow the flight of the missile in the air until it struck, as it seemed to me, within a dozen paces of those bloodthirsty villains who stood on the outside of the throng, and, rebounding as does a flat stone when a boy drives it along the surface of the water, it plunged into the very midst of the fiendish crew.

I could see that one of the posts had been carried away by the ball, but whether or no the prisoner was killed could not be told from so great a distance and while he was surrounded by such numbers.

It was to be hoped the poor fellow had gone to his final account without pain, as would have been the case had the huge shot struck him.

The gunners did not wait to see the result of their work; but instantly the cannon was discharged every man sprang to the task allotted him, and the savages had not yet recovered from the first surprise before a second shot came hurtling among them, striking down half a score before it rebounded.

I do not believe forty seconds elapsed before the gunners were ready for the third discharge. In order to save time they did not wait to swab out the piece, and the only preparation make by them was to clear the interior of smoke.

To tell it in the fewest possible words, the corporal had for his target nearly the entire number of Indians who had attempted to witness the torture, while we fired four shots, and not until then did the panic-stricken crew get their wits about them sufficiently to beat a retreat.

But the gun was discharged twice more while they were crossing the river, and I know for a certainty that one boat was swamped, while the ground in the vicinity of the posts set up for the prisoners seemed literally strewn with the dead and the dying.

At that moment, while we were making the air ring with our shouts of triumph, I saw a figure emerge from that sinister pile of dead and maimed and come limpingly in the direction of the fort, moving evidently with great effort and slowly.

At first I believed it was a wounded Indian, who was so crazed with pain or fear as not to be aware of the direction in which he was proceeding, and then a cry went up from the soldiers nearabout me:

"Reuben Cox! Reuben Cox!"

"Was he one of the deserters?" I asked of the corporal,

who, his work having been done, was leaning out over the wall to watch the frightened sneaks as they scuttled into their lodges out of sight.

"Ay, that he was," the corporal replied, "an' it looks much as if he stood a chance to gain the fort before those painted beauties dare stick their noses out from cover."

As we watched it was possible to see that the man's arms were tied behind him, while it seemed as if his legs were fettered in some way; yet he was able to take short steps, and in his eagerness to make better speed he fell to the ground again and again, rising only with difficulty.

The fugitive was a deserter from the fort, one who had doubtless given such information to the British general as might work serious harm to all of us; but yet never a cry was heard from our garrison, save such as expressed hope that he might escape the terrible doom from which we had at least temporarily saved him, and all appeared eager for him to gain the fortification.

Even Colonel Gansevoort seemed to lose sight of the fact that if this man came among us once more it would be necessary to treat him as a deserter; but to check, if possible, pursuit from the British and Tory soldiers, he lined the walls with men under command to fire without waiting for the word, upon any of the enemy who might approach within range.

The crews of the guns in the northeastern bastion were sent to their posts of duty, in order that the pieces might be used in case an opportunity presented itself, and, in fact, every possible effort, save the absolute sallying out of a relief party, was made to preserve the life of the man who by all military laws deserved death.

It seemed to me as if I did not breathe while that poor, struggling creature was straining every effort to find a place of refuge among those whom he had wronged. It was as if the distance increased even as he came toward us, and I found it difficult to remain silent while he stumbled, fell, rose, and fell again during his painful flight.

Fifty men or more ran to the sally-port, ready to open the gates if he should draw near, and Colonel Gansevoort made no effort to check them.

I believe at the moment that he entirely lost sight of the fact that this man could no longer claim the right of entrance, having forfeited it when he went over to the enemy. He, and all within the walls, saw before them only a wretched prisoner, striving to escape from those who would torture him to death, and had he been a dear friend no greater anxiety could have been shown for his safety.

Not until he was within fifty yards of the walls of the fort did a shot come from the direction of the Indian encampment, and then the bullet sped wide of its mark.

From the camp of the Tories a squad of men dashed out, as if intent on cutting off the poor fellow even after he was close under the walls, but a gun from the northeastern bastion hurled a shot uncomfortably near, sending them flying back beyond range, and five minutes later Reuben Cox was in our midst, as nearly dead from wounds and fatigue as he ever would be again until his final moment had come.

Chapter XVI.

Short Allowance

Five men had deserted from the fort trusting to the promises made by General St. Leger, and one had returned, after having suffered more than death, rejoicing because he was able to be once again with those whom he had betrayed.

At the moment, however, we had no thought of the deserter, but saw before us only a former comrade who had come out from the very jaws of death to claim protection.

The poor fellow had been cruelly cut on the legs and arms by the savages while they were bringing him across the river, and had lost much blood. His face and hands were covered with huge blisters, and it was not necessary either Sergeant Corney or I should ask how he came by them, for we knew through bitterest experience what the squaws and children would do when a white man was at their mercy.

Not until a full hour had passed could Reuben Cox tell his story, and even then he was in such a sorry plight that it was possible for him to speak only a moment at a time; but before morning came - before we were able to do very much toward relieving his sufferings - we had a fairly good account of all that had occurred from the moment the five foolish men clambered over the stockade until our cannon had done its work of mercy.

It seems that the deserters, after getting outside the fort, decided to make their way as nearly to St. Leger's quarters as might be possible, and to that end made a long detour to the westward. The sun had risen before they came upon a sentinel, and he was, fortunately, as it seemed to them, one of the British regulars.

Their story was soon told; no attempt was made to hide the fact that they had deserted, for all believed that such a statement would ensure their receiving a hearty welcome from the commander.

Much to their surprise, however, the British soldiers treated them with the utmost contempt and no slight degree of harshness. The Tories were the only white men who appeared particularly pleased with what had been done, and they gave the fellows a friendly reception only because, being renegades themselves, it gladdened them to know there were others in the valley who could be so contemptible.

As a matter of course they were soon taken before the commander that he might question them; but even he evidently looked upon them with no slight disgust, for he forced them to remain standing while in his presence, and failed to give any instructions as to how they should be quartered or fed.

Reuben Cox admitted, with many a groan and plea for mercy, that he and his companions had given St. Leger all the information concerning the fort which was in their power, and even made our situation appear more desperate than really was the case; but when they asked for permission to serve the king under his command, he roughly told them to present themselves to Sir John Johnson, declaring that the regulars would not receive them as companions-in-arms.

Just at that moment it was impossible for them to find Sir John, and, more hungry than they had ever been inside Fort Schuyler, they wandered about until arriving face to face with a party of Indians, who had come from their encampment to lounge around near the white soldiers, from whom they begged rum and tobacco.

That meeting sealed their fate, and the poor wretches came to understand what was in store for them, even before St. Leger had agreed that they might be turned over to the tender mercies of his savage allies.

During an hour they did their best to escape, but only to be dragged back with many a kick and blow each time they endeavored to sneak out of the encampment.

As nearly as the unhappy men could understand, there was a long, angry interview between Sir John, Thayen-danega, and some of the British officers before the matter was settled, and then they were delivered up to the Indians, even the Tories shutting their ears to the prayers for mercy.

It was not necessary I should hear what he had to say about the treatment the deserters received in the Indian encampment prior to being led out to the stake. I knew full well what suffering must have been theirs before the hour arrived when all was to be ended. I had had some slight experience as a prisoner in the power of the savages, and even then could not listen to another's story of similar treatment without severe mental pain.

The three who were reserved for the second evening's entertainment suffered nearly all the agonies of death when their comrades were tortured, for the Indians forced them to be present as spectators, and it is little wonder they were half-dead with fear when their turn came to afford amusement for those who found their greatest delight in listening to screams of agony from helpless victims.

The first shot from the fort killed two of the deserters outright and overturned the post to which Cox was being bound. He could not tell very much about the execution done by the balls, for at first he believed it was some new form of torture which the savages had invented; but when the painted crew fled across the river in abject fear, leaving him comparatively at liberty, he began to understand that the comrades whom he had wickedly wronged were doing what they could to aid him.

He declared that there were no less than twenty dead savages lying nearabout the place when he started for the fort, while as many more, badly wounded, were putting forth every effort at escaping beyond range of our gun.

All this was repeated to me by Sergeant Corney, who had heard it from Reuben Cox himself, and when he was come to an end of the recital I asked:

"Now that he is here, an' likely to live, what will be done with him?"

"That's what I can't say, lad, an' I'm of the belief that it puzzles the commandant not a little. Desertion in the face of an enemy is punishable by death the world over, an' rightly, for a soldier can commit no greater crime; but what about shootin' a man who has already suffered a dozen deaths?"

I soon came to know that the question I had asked of the sergeant was being discussed by all the garrison, many of the men declaring that Reuben Cox deserved to be treated as any other deserter, while a large number claimed that the sufferings he had endured should be considered as having atoned for the crime.

The arguments became so warm that it was evident Colonel Gansevoort would be forced to come to some decision regarding the matter, and so he did on this same day when we were called out on the parade-ground, being formed in a hollow square.

Then it was that the commandant laid the affair before us without comment, save as he declared that neither he nor his staff were willing to settle the question themselves, and he had decided to leave it to the garrison, - the men who must suffer because of the information given to St. Leger, if it so chanced that the British commander gained any advantage through it.

"Discuss it thoroughly among yourselves," the colonel said, "and, having made up your minds as to what punishment should be dealt out to Cox, write the verdict on a bit of paper, signing your names thereto, and leave the same at headquarters. Whatsoever the majority of you declare just to all concerned, shall be done."

Then we were dismissed from parade, and on the instant there ensued such a buzzing and humming that one might have thought an hundred swarms of bees had taken possession of the fort, as each man tried to impress upon his neighbor that he had the only correct solution to the painful question.

Our Minute Boys were all of the same mind, and it gave me no little satisfaction to know that my company were of the mind that Cox had been fully punished for his wrong-doing. Without any delay we stated our views in few words at the top of a sheet of paper, and each member signed his name, after which I carried it to headquarters.

It was Colonel Gansevoort himself whom I saw, and he asked, after glancing over the list of names:

"How does it happen that you lads arrived at a decision so quickly? Desertion is a very serious offence, and, because of the lesson which others may receive, should be punished severely."

"True, sir," I made bold to say; "but among those who signed the paper are two who were prisoners among the savages, and, while not havin' been subjected to great torture, they have a fair idea of what Cox must have suffered."

"Are you speaking of yourself and the old soldier?"

"Ay, sir."

"And yet because of what Cox has told St. Leger you may soon be again in the power of the Indians."

"That can never be, sir," I replied, gravely. "We know full well you will not surrender, however sore our plight, therefore the savages must take their prisoners in a fight, an' one need not be captured alive."

"Then you would rather die with a musket in your hands than fall into their clutches?"

"A good many times over, if that could be, sir," and so great was the horror in my heart through simply calling the possibility to mind that the colonel must have understood I spoke no more than the truth.

"Well, my lad, I will tell you this much for the gratification of yourself and friends: When it comes, if it ever does, that I am convinced, because of lack of food, ammunition, or any other contingency, that we cannot hold the fort, I will lead as many of the garrison as choose to follow me in an attempt to cut our way through the enemy's lines. I, like you, prefer to die fighting, rather than at the stake."

These words gave me greatest relief of mind, even though to do as the colonel promised was much like going to certain death, and I asked:

"May I repeat to my comrades what you have said, sir?"

"Ay, that you may, lad, and unless succor comes soon I shall speak quite as plainly to all the garrison, for to-morrow morning the rations are of a necessity to be cut down one-half, which will give our discontented men good chance to talk of starvation."

It would have given me greatest satisfaction to ask him

a few questions concerning our supplies, which, when he made the statement to the garrison, had seemed so plentiful; but, fortunately, I had sense enough to understand that, for a lad like me, to make searching inquiries of the commandant of a fort was something which the most easy-going officer would not tolerate for an instant.

Therefore, thanking him for having given me the assurance which he had, I took my leave, going with all speed to the barracks that I might acquaint Sergeant Corney with what I had heard.

"It's good news, lad, though not much different from what I've come to expect from sich a soldier as the commandant. Now we've nothin' in particular to worry about, seem's there won't be any question of takin' advantage of the Britisher's offer, which would be kept in the case of all hands much as it was when our poor fools deserted. But what is this about short allowance? I thought it was proven to us that we had supplies in plenty for many days to come?"

"I can only tell you what the commandant said."

"I reckon he'll explain matters when he tells us why the rations are short, an' that he'll have to do in order to satisfy some of the imitation soldiers we've got in this 'ere fort."

Then the old man went to his post of duty, and I rejoined the Minute Boys over the sally-port, where every member of my company was aching to get a fair shot at one of Thayendanega's curs.

The Indians were not inclined to show themselves on

this morning after we gave our surprise-party. I fancy they had come to understand it wouldn't be an easy matter to get the best of us, and were having considerably more of fighting than was pleasing.

Never one of the painted snakes came within range of our rifles. At some time during the night they had plucked up courage enough to drag off their wounded, and, if they visited the British or Tory camp that day, it was after making such a detour through the thicket as kept them screened from our view.

In the trenches the white portion of St. Leger's army worked like men who feel the whip behind them, and our people succeeded in sending six to the hospital or their last resting-place, without receiving a scratch.

Such a siege as had been carried on during the past eight and forty hours could not be cheerful amusement, and I began to have an idea that it would not take very much of a reverse to send the Tories flying to some other section of the country. If our people would only follow the example set them by Colonel Gansevoort, it seemed certain we could hold the fort at no greater cost than that of being hungry during a certain length of time!

When another day had come, and the rations were reduced in size as the commandant had said they would be, there was a hum of dissatisfaction all over the fort, even those whom we counted as being the stoutest-hearted doing their full share of grumbling, and wholly because the commandant had so lately told them that we had sufficient of food for many days.

They were not yet done with the business of deciding

what punishment should be dealt out to Cox; but that was entirely lost sight of in face of this apparent change in the situation. It seemed as if the store of provisions must be very low indeed, else the rations would not have been cut down so soon after the statements made by the quartermaster.

It is true that there was no mutinous talk to be heard; the fate of the deserters had taught the grumblers a lesson that would not soon be forgotten, but much was said that did not tend to improve the discipline.

At noon word was passed among the men that the last of the votes on Cox's case must be in the commandant's hands within two hours, and it was generally understood, if not stated as a fact, that at nightfall we would hear the verdict. Then also, so nearly all the members of the garrison believed, Colonel Gansevoort would explain the reason for putting us on short allowance after having stated that we had food in plenty.

Therefore it was the men went about their work as usual, content to wait until night; but the commandant would have been unwise to keep them in ignorance longer.

"The only mistake that has been made in this business was when Colonel Gansevoort condescended to give out any statement while the men were ripe for mutiny," Sergeant Corney stopped to say to me, as I met him on the parade-ground while going to the barracks to summon some of the lads whose time for sentinel-duty had come. "If a dozen or more of the loudest-mouthed had been put under arrest, an' such as the deserters strung up by the thumbs, four lives might have been saved, an' there wouldn't be any foolish talk made now."

I had no time to reply to the old man, for, having thus relieved his mind, he passed on, and I went about my duties.

The Britishers and Tories worked half-heartedly in the trenches, the savages kept well out of sight, and we of the garrison watched eagerly for an opportunity to send home a bullet where it would do the most good, until nightfall, and then came the call for us to fall into line.

The fate of Cox had been decided, and we were to be told about the reduction of rations, therefore nearly every man wore an expression of anxious expectation.

Sergeant Corney was an exception to the general rule; he apparently had no particular interest in either matter, and obeyed the call as if he did so only because it was necessary.

As on the previous occasion, we were drawn up in a hollow square, with Colonel Gansevoort and his staff inside, and without wasting many words in leading up to the subject, the commandant announced that the majority of the men had decided there was no need of further punishment for Reuben Cox; that the penalty which he had already paid was a sufficient lesson for those of us who entertained any idea of trusting to the promises made by the British commander.

Then he spoke of our being put on short allowance, and straightway the men pricked up their ears, listening intently to the end that they might be able to prove the quartermaster had told a deliberate falsehood.

"You were told that we had food sufficient with which to feed all inside the walls for a term of three weeks," he said, speaking slowly that there might be no mistake as to his words. "The statement, under the conditions then existing, was true; but you must bear in mind that since that time General St. Leger has been informed of our situation, so far as the deserters understood it. The result of his learning that the stock of provisions is not as great as it should be has been the increased activity of the foe, which entails much severe labor upon you, and causes him to guard more closely against the succor which may be sent us.

"Therefore my officers and I have believed it wisest to say to ourselves that it is not reasonable to expect aid from the outside can come to us for four or five weeks, even if Colonel Willett and Lieutenant Stockwell finally succeed in finding General Schuyler, because it must arrive in sufficient force to break through the lines St. Leger will throw around us. Now in order that we may safely count on having sufficient food to sustain life during at least five weeks, it has been decided, after due deliberation, to put the entire garrison, the commandant as well as the men, on short allowance."

"And what if General Schuyler has so much on his hands because of Burgoyne that he can't come to our relief?"

"If when we are come to our last two rations we get no definite information that relief is near at hand, we will sally out at night and cut our way through the enemy's lines!" Colonel Gansevoort cried in ringing tones, and straightway Sergeant Corney set about clapping his hands with such vigor that, almost before the men were aware of the fact, they were applauding the commandant heartily.

In the midst of this involuntary token of good-will the officers very wisely went to their quarters, leaving us to stew over the situation in such fashion as best pleased us.

Every man on the parade-ground understood full well that if he would save his life it stood him in hand to get back to his post of duty without unnecessary delay, and in a very few minutes those whose turn it was to go on duty were setting about the regular routine as laid down since the besiegers displayed unusual activity.

That night, when Sergeant Corney should have been sleeping, he came to my post, and the two of us discussed the situation in all its bearings, coming to the conclusion that the garrison was in much better shape than it would have been but for the horrible lesson Thayendanega's villains gave us regarding their treatment of prisoners.

Certain it was that we would hear no more about surrendering, therefore we need not fear another mutiny, and, as the old man said grimly:

"If the men want more to eat, let 'em go outside to get it, for it won't do any good to whine after what has been said."

During the week which followed every man did his full duty, and we heard very little grumbling, although I am sorry to set it down that some of the faint-hearted did wag their tongues more than was seemly; but on the whole the garrison showed themselves to be fairly good soldiers.

Reuben Cox was able to move about on the fourth day after he succeeded in getting inside the fort, and as I saw this man and that, who had formerly been his close comrades, move aside lest he should speak to them, I decided that the man's punishment was far greater than any we could have inflicted upon him. Death, according to my way of thinking, would have been far preferable to being thus scorned.

Cox must have had some such thoughts himself, for, coming full upon the commandant one day, the two being not above twenty paces from where I was stationed, he pleaded piteously to leave the fort in order that he might do what he could toward hurrying forward the relief for which we were hoping.

"You would not live to get two hundred yards away," Colonel Gansevoort replied, speaking not unkindly. "The enemy are doubtless on the alert for some such attempt on our part, since knowing we are not overly burdened with food."

"I would like to make the try, sir," Cox said, in a pleading tone, "an', if it so be that they get hold of me again, it'll be better to die in their hands than stay here where every man looks upon me as somethin' to be despised."

"You can't be surprised, Cox, that the brave fellows, whose plight has been rendered more desperate by what you and your companions did, should be averse to making friendly with you."

"I'm not surprised, sir, an' I'd like to end it all by

showin' that I've still got man enough in me to die tryin' to repair the mischief that's been done."

"The only way to make atonement is by doing whatsoever comes to your hand here in the fort. There's like to be plenty of fighting ahead of us, and you should be able to do more than your share."

"Could it be fixed, sir, so that I might give up nearly all my rations to those who need 'em the most?" the poor fellow asked, in a tone so pitiful and weak that my heart really went out in sympathy to him.

"We will stand or fall on the same footing, my man," the colonel said, as he walked away, and immediately I was relieved of duty I made it my business to repeat the conversation to every man I came across.

We were all so near death just then that it surely seemed as if we should have forgiveness in our hearts for such as Cox, lest we be denied that same boon in the next world.

From that day our people showed less aversion for the repentant deserter, and of a verity he did the work of three men during every four and twenty hours thereafter while we remained in Fort Schuyler.

In just eight days after that assault when the Indians so nearly succeeded in gaining a foothold in the horn-works, another attack was threatened, and this time it was not unexpected.

We had been punishing so severely those who were working in the trenches, and had kept the savages such close prisoners in their own encampment, that it seemed only natural the more soldierly of the men in St. Leger's army should insist on being led against us.

It was possible for us to tell by the shouts and yells that on a certain night Thayendanega's cowards had assembled in the British camp for a powwow, although they had taken good care not to let us see them going there, and Sergeant Corney said to me, as if he had a written programme of the entire proceedings:

"To-morrow we will have redcoats in plenty at which to shoot."

"Why do you say that?" I asked, in surprise.

"I'll eat my head if Barry St. Leger hasn't called Thayendanega's gang together with the idea of stiffenin' their backs so they'll be willin' to make an assault. The regulars have been gettin' mighty uneasy these two days, an' somethin' has got to be done, different from ditch-diggin', to keep 'em in good spirits."

"Won't Cox fight if he gets another show at the beauties who came so near killing him at the stake!" I cried, giving words to the first thought which entered my mind.

"He won't get the chance. The assault will be made before to-morrow night, an' never a feather can be seen."

"Why are you so positive about that?"

"They've much the same as told us. If we hadn't got 'em cowed by sendin' a bullet their way whenever one of the sneaks showed his nose, they'd been cavortin' 'round here this week past tryin' to make it lively for us. I tell you, Noel, we can count the painted murderers out of the game from this on."

"I hope you may be right," I said, with a long-drawn sigh, "for if St. Leger has lost as many of his army as Thayendanega's crowd represents, it won't be such a desperate venture to cut our way through his lines when we've eaten the last ration."

"Don't stop believin' that General Schuyler will contrive to give us a lift. I'm countin' that he's lookin' after the matter now," the sergeant replied, and then he walked away whistling softly, as if the thought of taking part against another assault pleased him mightily.

Before morning came I understood that Sergeant Corney was not the only one in the garrison who believed the enemy would soon show unusual signs of life.

The howling and yelling of the savages at the powwow continued until near to midnight, and the noise had hardly more than died away when the commandant came to where I was stationed, halting a moment to gaze in the direction of the Indian camp before he asked:

"Have you seen any targets in this direction lately?"

"It has been a good many days since any of the crew gave us a chance to show what we could do with a bullet, sir."

"How long are you on duty to-night?"

"Until morning, sir. Jacob Sitz and I have thought best to stay with the sentinels of our company during all the hours of darkness. We catch a cat-nap now and then, so it isn't like doin' extra work."

"Your lads will make good names for themselves among those who love the Cause, if they keep on as they've begun," the colonel said in the most kindly tone, and the praise made me as proud as any peacock, for I had hoped we might be able to show him we could do the work of men.

For the life of me I couldn't get my wits together quickly enough to thank him as I should have done, and immediately he said, as if speaking to one of his officers:

"See that a sharp watch be kept from now on, and do not hesitate to raise an alarm if anything unusual is seen, Captain Campbell."

I am certain my cheeks reddened when he thus recognized my rank, yet I was such a simple that I could only stammer:

"You must have in mind, sir, somethin' the same as has Sergeant Corney. He has lately been here predicting an assault for to-morrow."

"The sergeant uses his ears to some purpose," the colonel said, with a laugh, and then he walked away, leaving me with a determination to keep guard as I had never kept it before.

Chapter XVII.

Perplexing Scenes

Surely if ever a boy had been warned of coming danger I was that one, and the great fear in my mind was lest at the critical moment I fail to do my duty.

It seemed as if the commandant had much the same as told me he was depending upon the Minute Boys to bring him word of the first sign or sound of danger, and I was nervously afraid lest, by some unlucky chance, I might disappoint him.

After having dwelt upon the matter for half an hour or more, giving undue prominence to my own responsibility, I aroused Jacob, who was sleeping in an angle of the wall hard by, and repeated to him the substance of the conversations with Colonel Gansevoort and Sergeant Corney.

"Well, I don't know why we should be in a better position than any other to know what may be goin' on," he said, rubbing his eyes sleepily. "If the sergeant has the rights of it, an' the savages are done with the siege, then we're not likely to see much from this point."

"But we're not certain the old man knows better than any one else; he has figured it out to suit himself, without havin' definite knowledge. The commandant has much the same as praised our company, an' we must see to it that he has no cause to blame."

By this time Jacob was fully awake, and he set out along such portion of the wall as was under our charge, straining his eyes in the direction of the Indian encampment, but without seeing anything whatsoever. Not a camp-fire was burning, and I failed to hear even the howling of a dog, which was something so unusual as to cause us no little surprise.

"Can it be that Thayendanega's gang has deserted General St. Leger?" I asked, in a whisper. "The sergeant will have it that they are done with the siege, in which case it wouldn't be surprisin' if they had sneaked away."

"There's no such good news as that," Jacob said, with a laugh; "but I'm puzzled to make out why they're so quiet."

Had we been left to our own counsels ten minutes longer I believe I might have been tempted to waken the sergeant, which would have given him an opportunity to laugh at us because we had grown nervous over the absence of all danger-signs; but just then Peter Sitz approached, and I whispered to my comrade in a tone of relief that he and I were not the only nervous members of the garrison.

"It seems as if all hands had it in mind that we need lookin' after," Jacob replied, grimly, and then his father asked if we had seen anything unusual since the powwow came to an end.

"It's what we've neither seen nor heard that's puzzlin' us, sir," my comrade said, and then he called his father's attention to the remarkable quiet which reigned where, ordinarily, noises of some kind could be heard during every hour of the night.

Master Sitz appeared decidedly disturbed in mind, yet he made no comment, and, after listening in vain five minutes or more, he walked away without giving heed to us.

It really appeared, before that long night had come to an end, as if every officer in the fort suspected something might be wrong, and, what seemed yet more strange to me, they all came directly to our post, instead of visiting those sentinels who, if the savages had really cut loose from St. Leger, should have been in the best positions to hear or see the first signs of the expected assault.

I have set all this down at considerable length because, in view of what finally occurred, it was much as if our people had a premonition of that which was to come.

The night passed without alarm, and I am willing to take my oath that if any animal as large as a dog had passed within an hundred yards of the sally-port we would have seen it.

The entire garrison, even including women and children, was astir when the first gray light of coming day appeared in the eastern sky, and as each man came out upon the parade-ground I noted the fact that he had all his weapons with him.

Of course these details are of no particular importance,

and yet I have set them down in order to show how strong was the belief of every person in the fort that something unusual was about to happen, although, with the exception of the powwow held in St. Leger's camp the evening previous, we had seen nothing to betoken especial activity on the part of the enemy.

It was early in the morning; the men had not yet broken their fast, when one of the sentinels shouted:

"Here they come! Here they come!"

I expected to see every man spring toward the walls in order to learn for himself what had caused the alarm, and at any other time they would have done so; but so great was the sense of impending danger that instinctively the garrison formed in line ready for orders.

I had not yet been relieved from duty, and therefore remained where it was possible to have a fairly good view of all the encampments occupied by the enemy.

Near the quarters of the British regulars I could see the men drawn up in line as if making ready to advance, and in the Tory camp there was a bustle and confusion such as might have been made by half-baked soldiers, while trying to copy after those who knew their business; but the Indians gave no signs of life, save as their squaws went about the ordinary camp work.

Because everything had been so suspiciously quiet in this last quarter during the night, I more than half expected to discover that they had withdrawn under cover of darkness; but the presence of the women and children told I was mistaken. Unless the entire gang had spent the night with the white men, however, it was positive these exceedingly brave warriors of whom Thayendanega boasted, had no idea of continuing the part of allies during this day at least.

A plentiful supply of ammunition was dealt out to our men, and the big guns were served as if our magazine was filled to overflowing, after which the garrison went to quarters, Reuben Cox being the happiest member of the army, for he believed the time was near at hand when it might be possible for him to wipe out some of the stain which rested upon him.

The Minute Boys were ordered to remain at their post over the sally-port, much to my disappointment, for if the Indians did not take part in the assault, which we had every reason to believe was near at hand, then would our duties be so light that we could not hope to win much credit.

Do not let it be supposed that I had become a swash-buckler of a soldier. The cold chill of fear still crept up and down my spine whenever I thought of taking part in an engagement; but I was becoming so nearly a man as to desire, in case it became necessary to fight, that I might gain some honor for standing stiffly when really my heart was faint.

We remained at quarters a full half-hour, expecting each instant to see the long lines of soldiers emerge from amid the fringe of foliage which partially screened their encampment, and yet the advance was delayed.

"What's the matter?" Jacob asked, nervously, as he pressed close to my side.

"I wish I knew, lad," was my reply, in a voice that was not overly steady. "This waitin' while others are gettin' ready to try to kill a fellow is not to my likin'."

"I had rather have a full hour of hot fightin' than such idleness, when we know that soon the bullets will be whistlin' around our ears," Jacob replied, and just then John Sammons came up, as he said:

"I reckon they're goin' to bring their siege-guns with 'em this time. It looks to me much as if a big crowd was gatherin' in the rear of the line."

Then it was that we could see the Tories running to and fro, each man for himself, and in a twinkling the line of regulars melted away. There was no longer any semblance of military formation to be seen, and yet certain it was that a few moments previous the enemy was nearly ready for an assault.

We lads were not the only ones who felt disturbed because of this strange behavior on the part of the enemy. I could see that Colonel Gansevoort and all his officers were on that portion of the wall nearest the British camp, gazing earnestly toward it, while our men moved about uneasily, as if having forgotten that they had been sent to their several posts of duty.

Strain our eyes as we might, it was impossible to make so much as a guess regarding what could be the cause of the odd proceedings, and it was in my mind to go in search of Sergeant Corney to ask his opinion of the situation, when John Sammons cried, suddenly:

"Look there! The sneaks are comin' out at last! I reckon the Britishers have been waitin' for 'em!"

But one glance was sufficient to show me that John had spoken truly. From the lodges I could see troops of savages pouring forth with every token of excitement, like a swarm of hornets, and that something unusual was afoot might be told by the fact that no effort was made to keep beyond range of our guns, as the befeathered and painted horde went swiftly toward St. Leger's quarters.

I was determined that my company should remain at its post, no matter what might happen, until we got the word that it was no longer needed, there fore neither Jacob nor I could hear the speculations of the men as to what had happened in the enemy's encampment; but after a time Sergeant Corney came along as if looking for us, and, on seeing the Minute Boys standing in rank while all the remainder of the garrison were flitting here and there like flies on the scent of molasses, he said, grimly:

"Here's a sight I never expected to see in this blessed country where private soldiers have the habit of commandin' their superiors! Why ain't you lads huntin' 'round to find out what's goin' on?"

"We were ordered here, an' to be ready for action," I replied, not a little pleased to hear the old soldier's tone of approval. "This company will stay where it is until I have permission to break ranks."

"It don't seem to be the military fashion for Americans to obey a command so strictly, an' I'm afraid you're settin' a bad example to them who demand that a list of the supplies be read to 'em whenever they're feelin' a bit out of sorts. There's a chance I'll grow proud of havin' licked you into shape if you don't change your ways mighty quick."

"I don't fancy you came here just to see why we stayed on duty," Jacob said, with a laugh, which told me he was well pleased with what the old man had said.

"I'm free to admit that I didn't expect to see anythin' quite so soldierly in this 'ere fort, an' that's the fact. I had been detailed to hang 'round headquarters till the scrimmage began, but was given liberty to do as I pleased five minutes ago, consequently I came here to find out why the fight ain't on."

"We're expectin' you to answer that question, sergeant. You've never been backward in findin' fault with the ways of American soldiers, an' now perhaps you can tell what's gone wrong with the Britishers?"

"I wish I knew, lad, an' that's the fact! It looks as if they'd clean forgot we're waitin' for 'em, an' as for them precious babies of Thayendanega's, they've gone out of their heads completely. It's a puzzle all 'round, an' I reckon the commandant is as much in the dark as are the rest of us."

"Can't you make a guess?" Jacob asked, impatiently.

"Not a bit of it, lad; but it's certain there's trouble of some kind at Barry St. Leger's quarters, an' I'm of the mind to find out, if you an' Jacob want to stir yourselves a bit."

"How do you count on doin' it?" I asked in surprise, half-inclined to believe the old man was joking.

"Look at the Indian encampment; do you think there's

anybody nearabout that place who's keepin' an eye on this 'ere fort?"

"Even the squaws have gone over to the British quarters; they've been paddlin' across the river for the last half-hour," Jacob replied, and as a matter of fact I failed to see a living being outside the lodges, search with my eyes as I might.

"An' it's much the same over yonder," Sergeant Corney said, as he pointed to the other encampments. "Every blessed one of us might sneak out an' not attract any attention from them as are supposed to be besiegin' us."

"Well?" I asked, as the old man paused.

"Well, if you an' Jacob feel like havin' a look around, I'll ask the commandant's permission to do a little scoutin' on our own account, agreein', in case we're laid by the heels, not to expect any help from this 'ere garrison."

"Do you mean to go outside the fort?" John Sammons asked, his eyes opening wide in surprise.

"You've guessed it the first time," Sergeant Corney replied, with a laugh, and I said, in a tone of conviction:

"The commandant never will give you permission. I heard him refuse Reuben Cox most emphatically."

"But that was when everythin' seemed to be runnin' smooth, an' Cox only wanted to get himself killed. Now I'll go bail that Colonel Gansevoort is more eager than we to know the meanin' of this queer business, an' will jump at the plan."

"You'll know better after you've asked him," I suggested. "If he gives permission, Jacob an' I are with you."

The old man sauntered away as if he had nothing of importance to do, and with a look on his face which told that he was certain of getting the desired permission without very much difficulty.

The thought was in my mind that he would receive a very decided answer from the commandant without delay, and after a fashion that would not be pleasing to him, for it seemed to me that no sane officer could sanction an attempt to send out scouts across the open plain in the clear light of day, therefore one can imagine somewhat of my surprise when word came for Jacob and me to report at headquarters without delay.

"Can it be possible that Colonel Gansevoort is seriously thinkin' of allowin' the sergeant to leave the fort in the daytime?" I asked of my comrade, as we went rapidly across the parade-ground to obey the summons.

"It looks like it, for a fact, else why should we have been sent for? I'm beginnin' to think, Noel, that you said 'yes' to his wild scheme too quickly. There won't be any child's play in tryin' to get from the fort to where we can find the first show of cover."

"Meanin' that you're not willin' to make the venture?" I asked, quickly, hoping my comrade would flatly refuse to go, for, now that the venture seemed countenanced by Colonel Gansevoort, I was growing mighty weak-kneed.

"I would stick my nose into a good deal of danger before bein' willin' to go back on a promise made to the sergeant," Jacob replied, thoughtfully. "If he has told the commandant that we are minded to go, there's nothin' for it but to tackle the job."

I was decidedly disappointed by the reply, and yet could make no protest, since I was the one who had spoken for us both when the old man broached the subject, and in silence we walked on until having come to the door of the colonel's quarters.

The sentinel on duty there had evidently received orders concerning us, for he announced that we were to go in at once, and I pushed Jacob ahead as we entered the apartment where Sergeant Corney was standing in a soldierly attitude in front of the commandant.

We were not called on to wait many seconds before learning the reason for the summons, since Colonel Gansevoort jumped into the subject by saying:

"So you lads are keen for a hazardous venture, eh?"

I would have given much if at that moment I could have called up sufficient courage to say that I was well content to remain within the walls of the fort; but instead of boldly declaring myself I remained silent until Jacob said, with only a faint show of enthusiasm:

"We told Sergeant Corney that we would go with him to find out what may be the trouble in General St. Leger's camp, if so be you gave permission, sir."

Now was I fully committed to a matter which was by no means to my liking, and, with a certain sense of being ill-treated, I listened to that which followed.

"Under almost any other circumstances I would flatly refuse permission for any man to leave the fort; but now it seems as if it was of the highest importance we should know what is taking place in the enemy's camp. Whatever it may be is of such a serious nature as to attract the attention of the entire encampment so entirely that no attention whatsoever appears to be paid to us. I believe that, by leaving through the horn-works, you can make your way to the rear of the British encampment without incurring any very grave danger, and if it is the desire of you lads to go with the sergeant you have my permission."

It was just what I didn't want, but, under the circumstances, I could do no less than look as if he had granted us the greatest favor possible, and at the same moment it would have done me solid good had I been able to kick the sergeant with sufficient vigor to convince him that he had made an ass of himself.

Then the colonel, after receiving our thanks for permission to run our heads into unnecessary danger, went on to explain what he would have us do in case we lived long enough to get an idea of that which was going on in the enemy's camp.

As he had already said, we were to scale the stockade in the horn-works, and then, making a detour to the westward, gain the cover of such shelter as might be found on the high lands, working well toward the ruins of Fort Newport before trying to strike across to and behind the line of earthworks which St. Leger had caused to be thrown up early in the siege.

He had laid out a long journey for us, and one that might not be performed before nightfall; but it had the merit of being comparatively safe until we were in the vicinity of the British encampment.

The interview was brought to a close within five minutes after it had begun, and then we were at liberty to make our preparations for that which might result in our death by torture, for it was certain that if the Indians laid hands on another man from the fort they would take good care he was neither rescued nor killed until they had worked their cruel will upon him.

Sergeant Corney was inclined to boast of having succeeded when I had declared he must fail, and would have congratulated himself in great shape while we were crossing the parade-ground on our way to the barracks, but that I said, curtly:

"That man who exerts himself to go into danger will one day find himself in a box from which his best friends can't extricate him."

"Which is the same as sayin' that you've changed your mind about goin' out scoutin'?" he cried sharply, looking me squarely in the face. "There is no reason why you should go if the job isn't to your likin'."

"Both Jacob an' I must keep on with you, or write ourselves down as cowards; but at the same time we have the right to think it a foolish venture."

The words had no sooner escaped my lips than I regretted having spoken, and without delay I hastened to make amends by explaining that I was in truth frightened at the idea of venturing into that nest of snakes from which we had once barely gotten away with our lives.

The old man must have understood that I spoke rather from nervousness than because I was really in anger, and immediately he acted as if nothing unpleasant had been said, but began to discuss the question of whether it would be wise to burden ourselves with weapons when, if brought to bay, we could not hope to fight our way through.

Before we had more than gained the barracks half the men in the fortification had some knowledge of our intentions, and we were overwhelmed alike with questions and suggestions.

But very few minutes were needed in which to make ready for the venture, and when we came out of the barracks all three of us had rifles strapped upon our backs in such a manner that they would not interfere with our movements in case it became necessary to trust to the fleetness of our feet. Three rounds of ammunition for each one, sufficient corn bread to make a single meal, and hunting-knives, completed the outfit.

It would have pleased us better had we been allowed to depart unaided; but a full half of the garrison appeared to think it absolutely necessary to go with us to the very limits of the fort, and if good wishes are of any avail at such a time, then were we certain of returning in good condition.

Once on the plain outside the stockaded portion of the

works, Sergeant Corney led the way by going in a southerly direction for a distance of an hundred yards or more, and then striking sharply off toward the west, where was to be found the nearest cover.

Having gained the line of foliage which fringed the high tract of land, it was possible to march off at a smart pace without need of taking particular heed to our steps, and we travelled rapidly until having arrived at a point midway between our starting-place and the ruins of Fort Newport.

"Here's where I allow we'll be wise to change the commandant's plan a bit," the old man said, coming to a halt for the first time since we set out. "We can't gain very much in lengthenin' the journey by three or four miles, an' I'm in favor of strikin' across to the hill from here?"

The statement was made in the form of a question, and I replied that it suited me to do as he thought best, for when Colonel Gansevoort mapped out the route I believed he was sending us on a longer detour than was necessary.

We crossed the Albany road at that point where it bends in toward the hill, walking at our best pace, and, once behind the elevation, were screened from view of the enemy's camp.

While we were going over the open country I kept my eyes fixed upon the British batteries and the redoubts thrown up to cover them, but failed to see any signs of human life. That the enemy had abandoned these posts even for a few moments seemed incredible, and yet it was all of the same piece with what we could see in their camp.

Sergeant Corney led us directly into the redoubts which had made so much trouble for us in the fort, and, had we been disposed, we might have loaded ourselves down with plunder of every description, for the belongings of the men were strewn about as if cast aside in great haste.

It was not safe to remain many moments where we were; in fact, I came near to believing the sergeant had lost his wits when he led us into the British nest, and we hurried out of the works, going directly toward St. Leger's quarters until we were sufficiently near to see men moving about excitedly, when he struck off for the rear of the encampment, where could be found such cover as stout bushes and small fir-trees would afford.

We had advanced boldly on this last stage of the journey, emboldened to do so by the evidences of panic, or something near akin to it, which we saw on every hand, and trusting to the possibility that if seen it would be believed that we belonged to the encampment.

The sun was yet an hour high in the heavens when we found a hiding-place overlooking the camp, and so easy of accomplishment had been our task, with nothing of danger attaching to it, that I was heartily ashamed of having displayed ill-temper in the sergeant's presence.

Neither of us spoke when we were finally come to where we could have a fairly good view of the scene of confusion. The surprise at what we saw, and the perplexity because of it, was so great that we could do no more or no less than stare in bewilderment at this army, every member of which appeared to have suddenly been deprived of his reason.

The foremost scene which met our wondering gaze was a group composed of General St. Leger himself, Sir John Johnson, Thayendanega, and a dozen or more leading sachems of the Six Nations.

These men were too far away to admit of our hearing the spirited conversation which was going on. It appeared to me at times that the commander was pleading for some favor, and, again, that he threatened; but the savages seemed to give little heed to his words.

Then Sir John talked for several moments, apparently appealing to each of his companions in turn, where-upon one of the sachems spoke excitedly, using more gestures than I ever saw one of the scoundrels employ, and when he was come to an end all the savages save Thayendanega stalked off as if in a rage.

Our stupefaction was complete when General St. Leger made a peculiar gesture, and straightway two soldiers led forward a half-grown man whose vacant look proclaimed him to be one of those unfortunates whom God has deprived of wits, and in his wake came three Oneida Indians.

It was enough to make a fellow lose a full year's growth, thus seeing his Majesty's general in such company; but when the Oneidas appeared my surprise gave way to fear.

We had always counted, and with good cause, on these

Indians being friendly to our people who were struggling to throw off the yoke which the king had put upon us, yet the fact that they were in the encampment, apparently on friendly terms with our enemies, seemed to betoken still more trouble and misery for us of the valley.

Jacob gripped my hand tightly as the Oneidas appeared, and I could see the corners of the sergeant's mouth twitching as if he had suddenly lost that feeling of security which had been so strong upon him until this moment.

Then the foolish man began to tell a long story to the general, the Indians added a word now and then, and even Thayendanega began to wear a troubled look.

It was all so strange and unnatural that I pinched my own arm more than once to make certain I was not in a dream.

Chapter XVIII.

Close Quarters

The scenes shifted before us as if they had been painted on bubbles which were blown hither and thither by the wind.

Even as we gazed at the leaders of the army while they stood listening to the foolish man as if believing him to be inspired, a mob of Tories and Indians surged toward that portion of the encampment, and in an instant St. Leger, Thayendanega, and Sir John Johnson were blotted out from our view.

Nothing could have happened to give us who crouched amid the stunted bushes a more vivid idea of the change which had come over the besieging army than this one incident, when the commanders, at whose frowns savages as well as white men cringed, were treated with such utter lack of ceremony.

I fully expected to hear one or the other of these three burst into a towering rage, and order the immediate punishment of those who had offended, whereas the men extricated themselves from the tangle of half-drunken soldiers and savages as best they could, immediately resuming the apparently confidential conversation with the idiot.

I saw Sergeant Corney shrug his shoulders, as if to say that he had given over even trying to guess what might have happened, and then he beckoned for us to follow as he crept straight away from the, to us, perplexing scene.

There was little need for us to give much heed to our movements so far as concerned making a noise, for I dare venture to say that a full company of men might have marched boldly past without raising an alarm, so long as they remained hidden from view.

When we were twenty yards or more from where the commanders stood trying to hold their position against the drunken tide of reds and whites, the sergeant halted and looked at us lads inquiringly:

"Well?" I said, irritably, vexed because of my bewilderment. "If you can't explain the situation there is no need to look at us. It beats anything I ever heard of or dreamed about. Have they all lost their senses?"

"Somethin' is goin' mightily wrong!" Sergeant Corney said, impressively, as if he was imparting valuable information.

"Goin' wrong!" Jacob repeated. "I should say it had already gone wrong with a vengeance. Can't you make some kind of a guess, sergeant?"

"Not a bit of it, lad. This 'ere business lays way over anythin' I ever saw in all my experience as a soldier. There's one thing certain, howsomever, which is that jest now an hundred of our people could walk through the entire encampment without bein' called upon to spill a drop of blood."

"Well?" I asked again, as the old man ceased speaking.

"Colonel Gansevoort must know how mixed up is this 'ere army."

"We can go back an' tell him," Jacob replied, promptly. "I reckon we might walk straight out toward the fort, an' never a man here would give heed to us."

"If we knew exactly what had happened it might be as well for all three to go back to the fort; but there's no knowin' when matters may take a turn, an' we must keep a sharp watch lest through us our people are brought into a trap."

"Why don't you say what you mean, without talkin' all around the subject?" I cried, nervously. "What have you got in your mind?"

"That one of us must go back to the fort, while the others stay here on watch to give the alarm in case this 'ere army suddenly comes to its senses."

It was not my desire to travel back alone to carry the tidings. There was no thought in my mind that any danger might threaten while the enemy was in such a state of confusion; and I was most eager to watch these apparently crazy people, in the hope of being able to come at a solution of the riddle, therefore I asked, sharply:

"Who do you think should go back?"

"Do either of you lads want to tackle the job?" the sergeant asked, and I understood by his tone that he was as loath to leave the place as was I.

Neither of us made reply, and he went on, as if already having had the plan fixed in his mind:

"Then we'll draw lots to see who it shall be. As the matter stands, we know full well that the commandant must be told of what we have seen. It won't require two hours' travelling because there's no call to make a very wide circuit, an', in case these fellows pull themselves together before midnight, them as stays on watch can warn our people."

"Fix the drawin' of lots to suit yourself, an' he who gets the worst of it will set out at once," I said, curtly, and the old man broke off three small twigs, which he held in his closed hand.

"I haven't taken note of which is the shortest; but, in case you might think I had, make your choice, an' the one which is left shall be mine."

"He who gets the shortest goes back, eh?" Jacob asked, and I replied:

"That is understood. Take the first choice, an' let us settle this business as soon as we can, for I am wild to get over yonder where I can see the king's army playin' the fool, if it so be that I'm not forced to turn back."

Jacob drew one of the twigs without stopping to make a selection, I took the second, and Sergeant Corney opened his hand to show the third.

They were all so nearly of a length that we were forced to measure each in order to learn who was the unfortunate, and then it was found that Jacob had been selected to play the part of messenger.

Disappointed though the lad must have been, he did not make any delay, but asked as he rose to his feet:

"What shall I say to the commandant?"

"Tell him what you have seen," the sergeant replied, "an' say that with two hundred men at the most he can capture the whole blessed army. If there should be any change within the next two hours, one or both of us will hurry back, goin' around by way of the hill opposite the batteries, - the same course we came, - therefore, if he sends out a detachment, let it approach by that route."

Immediately the old man ceased speaking Jacob wheeled about, and in a twinkling was lost to our view in the gloom.

By this time night had fully come, and I knew the lad would be in no danger if he made a direct line for the fort, therefore I ceased to think of him as I urged my companion to return with me to where we could overlook the scene of confusion.

We went back at once without giving especial heed to moving noiselessly, and soon were gazing upon the wildest, oddest scene that ever a military encampment presented.

During the short time we were absent the men had built small fires here, there, and everywhere around, and now that which had at first looked like a panic began to present the appearance of an orgy.

We saw directly in front of General St. Leger's camp a dozen or more Indians broaching a cask of rum, and hardly more than twenty feet away were a lot of Tories, drinking from bottles which had evidently been plundered from the commander's private store.

Had the camp been in the possession of an enemy there could not have been greater evidences of lawlessness, and again and again I asked myself what could have happened to bring about such a condition of affairs.

It would be well-nigh impossible to set down all the wild pictures we saw during the hour which followed. Instead of recovering from their panic, insubordination, or whatever it may have been, the men were momentarily growing more disorderly, and that the officers made no effort to preserve even the semblance of order, we knew from seeing them from time to time moving about the encampment with no heed to what was being done.

The three commanders, however, remained beyond our line of vision, and, because no one save the rioting soldiery and the savages entered or came out of the headquarters tent, I began to suspect that the leaders had run away.

As can be supposed, in a comparatively short time the Indians were thoroughly under the influence of the enormous amount of strong drink which had been consumed, and ripe for mischief of any kind.

One of the Tories, a fellow who had been hob-nobbing with the savages, himself drinking until he could stand only with difficulty, was set upon by two of the feathered wolves, murdered and scalped before our eyes, without an alarm being raised.

Then the Indians began a war-dance, waving the bloody scalp in the air with frenzied gestures as they circled around and around the lifeless body, and many of the drunken white men applauded heartily, although it must be set down in extenuation that they were so drunk as not really to understand what had taken place.

"It's a nice kind of a tea-party," Sergeant Corney whispered to me, while the orgy was at its height. "If the rum holds out these villains will settle matters among themselves, so that Colonel Gansevoort won't find any to stand against him when he arrives."

To this I could make no reply. I was literally sickened by the horrible scene, and began to wish most fervently that I had been the one to draw the shortest twig, for it was by no means agreeable to remain there idle while murder was being done, even though it was a bitter enemy who had thus been cowardly done to death.

The savages soon brought their dance to an end as they stumbled into this tent and that, searching for more spirits although the cask was not yet empty, and I was on the point of suggesting to Sergeant Corney that it would be wise to move back among the bushes lest some of the drunkards come upon us by mistake, when a heavy body suddenly fell, or was thrown, directly upon my back, pinning me to the earth.

My first thought was that the rioters had flung some heavy piece of camp equipage into the bushes at random, and then the blood grew cold in my veins as I felt two hands clutching at my throat.

Like a flash of light came the knowledge that one of the drunkards, an Indian as I believed, had stumbled upon me accidentally. I expected each second to hear an alarm raised which would bring the murderous crew to the spot without delay, when there could be no question as to the result, for the sergeant and I could not hold out many moments against such a mob, even though every one of them was intoxicated to a greater or less degree.

That which rendered my situation critical was the fact of my being virtually unarmed. It will be remembered that the rifle was strapped to my back, and even though I had been unhampered, it would have required no slight time in which to unsling it. My knife was quite as useless, because, borne to the earth as I had been, it could not be removed from my belt.

To set all this down in words makes it appear as if I had ample time in which to think over the situation, whereas no more than five seconds could have elapsed before the sinewy fingers were closed so tightly about my throat that I could not breathe.

At almost the same instant that the pressure began to be painful, before a single cry had been uttered by my assailant, a second shock was felt by me, while the weight which pressed me down to the earth was increased, and dimly I understood that the sergeant had leaped upon the back of him who was strangling me.

Why the Indian made no cry for help I cannot understand, except that he was too drunk to realize he had within his grasp an enemy instead of one of his own company.

Certain it is, however, that no alarm was raised even when the sergeant came to my relief, and in silence, save for the rustling of the foliage as we swayed to this side or that, the battle was continued until I felt the cruel fingers about my throat suddenly relax, while a warm liquid of a peculiar, salty odor poured down over my neck and head.

When he who had been striving to kill me rolled from my back, I lay motionless, unable to raise a hand and gasping for breath, until Sergeant Corney lifted me up as he whispered in my ear:

"Are you hurt, lad?"

"Only choked well-nigh to death," I contrived to say, and then tried to struggle to my feet, but found myself yet pinned to the earth by the lifeless body which lay across my legs.

"Let us get out of here," I said, after releasing myself from the sinister weight. "This is worse than such an ambush as we fell into on the Oriskany."

"Ay, lad, I reckon you're right as to that; but it strikes me we're bound by the word I sent the commandant to stay here till we make certain these reptiles don't come to their senses."

While he spoke the sergeant was helping me retreat yet farther among the bushes, for my knees bent beneath me, owing to the horror of it all, as well as the rough handling I had received.

The old man was not willing to move so far away that it would not be possible to have a fairly good view of what might be going on; but we did walk to what I believed was a comparatively safe distance, and then sat down upon the ground on the alert for anything more of the same kind which had come so near to putting me out of the world.

"It was a close shave, lad, an' ought'er be a lesson to sich fools as we've shown ourselves, never to carry good weapons where they can't be got hold of for use at a moment's notice."

"A fellow isn't supposed to be on his guard against drunkards," I replied, curtly, caressing my throat, which was exceeding sore.

"True for you, lad; but I'm free to say that, while we've had considerable experience in the business of fightin', I never run up agin quite sich a mess as this. It actually gives me a pain because I can't make head or tail of it."

I was already weary with trying to solve the problem, for indeed it was puzzling to even make a guess at why an army of near to seventeen hundred men had been thrown into such a state of panic and lawlessness. Then, again, why were the commanders not present with their officers to check these proceedings? Why had they allowed the men to take part in such an orgy, for to my knowledge St. Leger was near at hand when the first cask of rum was broached?

"It is no use to speculate as to how this thing came about," I said; "but it strikes me that you ought to post yourself so far as to be able to tell Colonel Gansevoort, or whoever he sends in command of the detachment, exactly where the blow may best be struck, for just now all we know is regardin' the row close hereabout."

"You never spoke a truer word in your life, lad," the

old man said, excitedly, as he rose to his feet. "I got so mixed up with this 'ere hubbub, tryin' to make out how it came about, as to have clean lost sight of all that a soldier ought to do. Jacob hasn't been gone over an hour, an' we have as much more time to find out how things are in the rest of the encampment, so let's set about it without delay."

The scene immediately before us was so revolting that I had no desire to gaze at it longer, and there was a certain sense of relief in my mind when the sergeant, prompted by me, had thus decided upon a definite course of action.

With so much of confusion and drunkenness everywhere around, it was a simple matter for us to go and come as we pleased, save by chance we might stumble upon those who yet remained sober, for all the men I had thus far seen, except the leaders themselves, were in such a maudlin condition as to be unable to distinguish friend from foe.

We had already learned that the batteries fronting Fort Schuyler on the northeast had been abandoned, and it was only necessary to get a view of the remainder of the British encampment. There was little need to visit the Tory quarters, for, as it seemed to me, all those renegades were present, taking part in the orgy.

With no care as to advancing noiselessly, but keeping a sharp lookout lest we come upon sober men, the sergeant and I moved about at will, finding everywhere the same condition of affairs, and when half an hour had passed it was positive our people might come into the enemy's lines and gather up prisoners by the hundreds without being molested in any way, for I question if their presence would have been suspected.

During all this time of inspection we saw nothing of St. Leger, Sir John, or Thayendanega, and I was of the opinion that they had run away; but Sergeant Corney held to it that most like they were in the Indian encampment, proposing that we cross the river in order to hunt them up, but to this I would not listen.

According to my mind, such of the Indians as remained sober, if there were any, would be in their own lodges, and because we had had such singular success in our scout thus far was no reason why we might not suddenly find ourselves face to face with the gravest danger, if we acted the fools by poking our noses among the camps of the savages.

"Why not go to the fort?" I asked. "There is nothin' more to be learned here. We know to a certainty that the greater portion of all the Tories an' Indians are hereabout, and every one of them so drunk that the army will be harmless, save as to each other, until daybreak. Let us go back by way of the batteries, an' we can reach the fort almost as soon as will Jacob, if perchance he went to the northward of the hill."

The sergeant was not inclined to leave the encampment immediately, although he agreed that we could learn nothing further of importance; it was as if the scene of confusion had a certain fascination for him. He finally agreed, however unwillingly, to my proposition, and we set out leisurely on the return, being forced to pass once more in the rear of all the British camps because of having continued our investigations to the eastern-most line of tents.

We began the return without thought of haste or of danger, and were come midway between headquarters and the most southerly battery, when without warning we arrived face to face with a party of six Tories, who, with their arms around each other's necks, were reeling to and fro in the most convivial fashion on what was probably intended to be a pleasant stroll in the night air.

Just for an instant I was startled, fearing lest we might be discovered and find ourselves in trouble when we believed we were safest; but then, realizing that we had already met many who mistook us for comrades, I would have gone on but that Sergeant Corney halted suddenly, unslung the rifle from his back, and, presenting it full at the drunken renegades, said in a low, stern tone:

"We are prepared to shoot one or all at a moment's notice if you make the slightest resistance. The orders are to gather in every mother's son in this encampment who has been makin' a fool of himself, an' I reckon you come in that class. About face, an' the first who so much as yips gets a bullet through the head."

The fellows must have believed that we were acting under orders from their general, for, with many a laugh and good-natured quip, they obeyed the sergeant's order as promptly as a party of small boys would have done, and, still supporting each other, moved toward the fort, we two following directly in the rear.

I could have laughed aloud at the comical situation. Here were two scouts who had gone out to spy upon an encampment of seventeen hundred men, marching boldly through the entire place, and taking as prisoners six soldiers who made no effort whatsoever to defend themselves.

I question if in the annals of warfare there be found anything that can match such a situation!

"Are you goin' to take them into the fort, sergeant?" I asked, in a whisper, and he replied, speaking with difficulty because of his mirth:

"Why not, lad? It will be a rare lark, an' somethin' to tell about in the days to come, that we took out from almost directly in front of St. Leger's headquarters six men, marchin' 'em into a fort which was supposed to be closely invested."

There could be little danger attending such a performance, save perchance we might come upon some of those who were sober, and that risk I was more than willing to take for the sake, as the sergeant had said, of being able to tell the story in the future.

We marched our prisoners out past the batteries, they giving no heed to the direction we were going, evidently fancying we were taking them to the guard-tent, until arriving midway between the fort and the redoubts.

Then somewhat of the truth seemed to dawn upon them, and this was so startling as to restore a portion of their befuddled senses. The entire party halted as if with one accord, and would have turned to look at us, but that the sergeant said, sharply, emphasizing the words by the click of his rifle-lock as he cocked the weapon:

"Keep a-movin' unless you're achin' to have a bullet put through the back of every blessed one in the gang!"

"But, look here, this is too much of a joke," one of them cried, with a drunken laugh. "We can't go very far on this course without bein' seen by the rebels."

"You've been seen by 'em already, an' that's why we've got you in charge. We count on movin' the whole of St. Leger's force over to the fort in squads, an' you're the first that has been started on the road."

By this time the renegades had a fairly good idea of the situation, and I fully expected they would turn upon us, but each of them was a coward. If they wheeled about suddenly, taking the chances that one might be killed in the squabble, it would have been possible to over-power us, even though they were without firearms; but it was the probability of our doing some considerable execution before knocking under that prevented them from escaping at the favorable moment.

I walked with my rifle cocked and pointed at the man directly in front of me, prodding him with the muzzle now and then that he might know I was ready for action, and Sergeant Corney kept the whole party moving at a good smart pace, for we had no assurance that there were not sober men enough in the enemy's camp to play the mischief with our bold plan.

Before we were hailed by the sentinels I came to believe that every member of the besieging army was more or less incapacitated for duty through having drank too much rum, for we heard nothing whatsoever from any one in the enemy's camp, although we were in fairly good view of them for no less than half an hour.

When the sentinel hailed we were yet half a musket-shot distant, and my companion answered it by shouting:

"Report to the officer of the day that Captain Campbell, of the Minute Boys, an' Sergeant Braun, unattached, are come with a few prisoners as sample of what may be had for the takin'."

This reply caused some mystification among the sentinels, as we could understand by the hum of conversation which followed; but the old man did not call a halt, and we continued straight on toward the sally-port, I feeling more than a bit nervous lest the sergeant's loud words might have been heard by such of the enemy as were able to come in pursuit.

When we had come near the gate, the Tories now well sobered by fright, Colonel Gansevoort himself hailed, and again the sergeant replied, but this time in a respectful tone, after which we heard the command to open the port.

A throng of curious, laughing men crowded around as we marched in, and not until the uniforms of our prisoners could be seen did they believe we had really made a capture.

It was a squad of Johnson Greens which we had run across so fortunately and accidentally, and none of St. Leger's force could have been more welcome to our lads than they, for that organization was made up wholly of renegades from the Mohawk Valley, who needed such a lesson as we were now in position to give them.

With such proof as we had with us, Colonel Gansevoort could no longer doubt the report which had already been brought in by Jacob. He had not thought it possible the entire force of the enemy could be in a helpless condition, and it is hardly to be wondered at that he was incredulous.

The prisoners were speedily cared for in such a fashion that there could be no possibility of their escaping, and then the commandant summoned all three of us who had visited the British encampment, to his head-quarters, that we might tell the story to himself and the officers.

No one could even make a guess as to what had happened within the enemy's lines; but there was not a man present who did not believe that now had come our time to raise the siege in such a manner that the fort would not be invested again for many days to come.

"When your messenger came in with his report, he admitted that you had seen but a small portion of the encampment, therefore I hesitated to accept it as a fact regarding the entire army; but now, after you have made a tour of the works, it would be worse than folly to delay," the commandant said to the sergeant. "If you who have so lately returned want to join in the sortie, it will be necessary to make your preparations quickly."

And the old man replied, grimly:

"The advance can't be made any too soon to please us, sir."

Chapter XIX.

The Pursuit

No more than three hundred men were sent out to take advantage of the singular state of affairs which we, the scouts, had reported as existing in the British camp, and when I expressed surprise because of the small number ordered on duty, Sergeant Corney replied, contentedly:

"If you an' I told the truth, lad, as we know we did, then a detachment of three hundred is way off more than enough to take care of all St. Leger's army in its present condition; but if we made a mistake, or if in some way it turned out to be a big trick intended for our undoin', - though I don't see how it *can* be, - then have men in plenty been taken from the garrison here."

"All of which means that you're entirely satisfied with everything this night?" I said, with a laugh, for the capture of the Tories had pleased me so thoroughly that my mouth was stretched in a grin nearly all the time.

"That's about the size of it, lad, though in this case I couldn't find anythin' to be disgruntled with, however soreheaded I might be. The colonel is sendin' out men in plenty."

It was Captain Jackman who led the force, and I knew full well that if it was possible to punish the Britishers he was the one above all others to tackle the job, for a braver, more cool-headed man I have never seen.

It is well that I make the story short, so far as our own movements were concerned, for what we said or did before visiting the enemy's camp in force is of very little importance.

We set off within an hour after Sergeant Corney and I brought in the prisoners, and were marched boldly across the plain on a bee-line for the batteries without hearing a single note of alarm. It seemed to me that even the noises of the orgy had died away.

Arriving at the batteries, Captain Jackman ordered thirty of his force to take possession of the guns and hold them until the last possible moment, in case the enemy rallied sufficiently to do anything toward caring for their own safety.

A few yards farther on, at the redoubts covering the batteries, thirty more men were left, and, since there was an ample supply of ammunition for the big guns as well as the small arms, we who were entering the encampment would have a fine support in case of trouble.

All these precautions were proper, and the captain would have been a poor soldier indeed had he failed to take them; but, as was soon shown, they were needless.

When we arrived near General St. Leger's quarters we saw the last of the army fleeing as if panic-stricken in the direction of Oneida Lake, no longer preserving any semblance of military formation, but each man for himself, and, what was yet more puzzling, their Indian allies were in close pursuit, striking down laggards whenever the opportunity offered.

These so-called warriors of whom Thayendanega had been so proud, were taking Tory and British scalps as if they had been summoned for no other purpose, and during two or three minutes all our people stood as if suddenly turned into graven images, so much of astonishment and bewilderment was caused by the wonderful change in affairs.

Captain Jackman's first act, after understanding that the enemy was actually in retreat, with their former allies harassing the fleeing men to the best of their ability, was to send a messenger in hot haste to the fort with the word that he counted on taking his entire force, save those left to hold the batteries and redoubts, in pursuit, and advising that nearly all the British equipment could be seized upon without fear of interruption.

Then we began the pursuit, and this, like the panic in the camp, was the oddest ever known. British regulars and Tories running helter-skelter, casting aside their weapons and accoutrements lest they be impeded in the unreasoning flight, and close at their heels the savages, who fell upon every unarmed man they saw, sometimes killing him outright, but, in many cases which came under my personal observation, disabling and then scalping the poor wretch, leaving him to a lingering death.

More than once did the frightened soldiers flee toward us for protection, and again and again we lent them weapons with which to defend themselves against their late friends.

It is almost impossible to give any details of that pursuit, which was not brought to an end until we were close upon the shore of Oneida Lake, because it was all so confusing - more like the wildest kind of a foot-race, wherein each man was trying to gain the lead, and the hindermost frantic with fear.

It would have been strange indeed had our people been able to hold anything like a military formation. Captain Jackman yelled himself hoarse trying to keep us together, and, when it seemed as if he was on the point of succeeding, some one would set off at a mad pace to save the life of a British soldier who had fallen at the mercy of a savage.

At first we turned our attention to taking prisoners; but before having left the main encampment a mile in the rear the Indians, eager for scalps, began to grow careless of what we might do, and then we paid off many an old score, although all could not have been settled had we slaughtered every last one of them.

During that time of pursuit we saw nothing of the leaders, and I had come to believe that they were among the first to flee, when suddenly the sergeant, in whose company Jacob and I had remained, pointed out amid the bushes what appeared to be a large portmanteau which had evidently been cast aside by some of the fugitives.

In the excitement of the chase either Jacob or I would have passed it by as being of no particular value when there were so many things to be picked up; but the old

James Otis

man was too good and experienced a soldier not to realize the possibilities of the find, and, heedless of all the wild scenes around him, he seized upon it, breaking the lock with a rock.

Then it was we learned that the apparently valueless case was none other than the writing-desk, or official portfolio, belonging to General St. Leger himself, and in it were not only private letters and documents, but all his correspondence and papers relating to the campaign, such as afterward served to show that the king's officers had actually hired the Indians to murder those whom they called "rebels."

"I reckon we've captured the prize of the day," the sergeant said, gleefully, after making certain as to the contents of the case. "This is of more value than a score of prisoners, although there's far less satisfaction in seizin' it."

A moment later the old man began to understand that if he held on to the prize he would be left far behind in the chase by our people, because it was far too cumbersome to be carried at a rapid pace, and then he regretted having found it.

I believe that for a moment he had it in his mind to throw the heavy portfolio away, willing to lose what he believed to be the most valuable of all the plunder that might be found, rather than miss the excitement of the chase; but, fortunately, just then John Sammons came limping back with a wound in the leg which had been inflicted by a savage whom he afterward succeeded in killing.

"It's the toughest kind of ill-fortune to be crippled just

when the fun is the hottest," he said, after explaining how the wound had been received. "I can't go on, an' I don't want to miss the show when the crazy Britishers an' Tories arrive at the shore of the lake."

"It looks pretty bad," Sergeant Corney said, when he had made the most careless examination of the wound, and I was surprised to hear him speak in such a tone, for it was not his custom to make much ado over any injury, however severe. "I reckon you'd better hobble back to the fort without delay, an', once there, look well to it that you wash an' bandage the leg well."

"I s'pose I'll have to go," Sammons replied, with a sigh, and the sergeant made haste to add:

"Of course you will, lad, an' I've got here that which will ensure you a warm reception by Colonel Gansevoort. Take this case to him, an' you'll be glad you had to go back."

Then it was that I understood why the old man was so solicitous regarding John's injury.

Sammons took up the bulky portfolio and limped back in the direction of the fort, the sergeant saying with a peculiar twinkle of the eyes as the lad passed beyond earshot:

"Now I reckon there's nothin' to prevent us from goin' on so long as do the others. Strike out lively, lads; we've wasted too much time already!"

Then we tailed on behind the crowd of our people who howled and yelled as if at a fair, shooting at every bunch of feathers we saw amid the foliage, but making no effort to capture the fugitives lest we find ourselves so hampered that further advance would be out of the question.

There were many of our people who thought much as we did on that day, otherwise Fort Schuyler might have been crowded with prisoners before morning.

When we had finally come within sight of the lake, it was to find the foremost of our party drawn up in something approaching military order. Captain Jack-man had succeeded in bringing them to a halt while yet half a mile from the shore, and this was done because the British and Tories had made a stand while their boats, which had been left at that point when they marched to the investment of Fort Schuyler, could be put in sailing trim.

We of the American army were far too few in numbers to risk an action by pressing on, for, no matter how demoralized the enemy had become during the flight, it was more than probable they would fight with desperation now safety was within view.

More than one of our party cried out in anger because the captain displayed too much caution according to their ideas; but the cooler-headed, among whom was Sergeant Corney, declared that it would be the height of folly for us to throw ourselves upon at least a thousand men when no great good could come from such a venture, and much of disaster to the Cause might result.

The savages had no such reason for lagging, however, nor did they intend to fall upon their late friends in a manner which could involve them in a pitched battle;

but yet they did a large amount of mischief without putting their precious bodies in danger.

Wherever a squad of the fugitives was withdrawn from the main body, making ready a boat, the painted fiends would swoop down upon it, performing their murderous work and getting away with a fresh supply of scalps before the victims' friends could rush to their assistance.

I saw a boat laden with men, the greater number of whom were unarmed because of having thrown away their weapons during the flight, push off in company with several others; but the oarsmen of this particular craft were clumsy, and she drifted down the shore until beyond range of the remainder of the force.

Then it was that the feather-bedecked wolves began shooting at the helpless men until a full half of the crew were wounded, after which Thayendanega's beauties swam out to her, killing and scalping all on board.

This is but a single instance of what the savages did during that mad retreat. More than once had my rifle been emptied in behalf of some sore-beset soldier, and I even went so far in my sympathy for the white men that I saved the life of a Tory who would have been killed had we not come up in the nick of time. After rescuing him, however, we turned the fellow over to a squad who were guarding twenty or more prisoners, thus making certain he would not be left at liberty to work mischief among our people.

The following brief account of the retreat was written and printed by one who took every care to learn all the truth regarding the affair, and I set it down here that he who reads may know I have not exaggerated the story for the purpose of shaming the enemy:

"The Indians, it is said, made merry at the precipitate flight of the whites, who threw away their arms and knapsacks, so that nothing should impede their progress. The savages also gratified their passion for murder and plunder by killing many of the retreating allies on the borders of the lake, and stripping them of every article of value. They also plundered them of their boats, and, according to St. Leger, 'became more formidable than the enemy they had to expect.'"

It was late in the afternoon before Captain Jackman gave us the word to turn back. He would have returned sooner, but our men pleaded for permission to watch the fugitives until they had embarked, and he could hardly do otherwise than remain.

A happy, light-hearted company it was that marched back to what had been the British encampment, there to find many of those we had left in the fort busily engaged hauling in the plunder abandoned by his Majesty's valiant army, to the fortification.

Now we had ammunition in plenty, both for our own guns and those we brought in from the batteries, while there was such a store of provisions that the wagons were kept busy during the entire night transporting it.

We feasted from sunset until sunrise, much after the fashion of the savages, for it made a fellow feel good to know from actual test that there was no longer any need of saving every scrap of food against that day when it might be necessary to fight and fast at the same time.

Even though we had not thus made merry, I question if there was a man among us, from the highest to the lowest, who could have closed his eyes in slumber. The relief of mind was so great, and the wonderment because of what had happened so overpowering, that we were able to do nothing save discuss the matter again and again, but without coming to any satisfactory solution of the riddle.

The Tory encampment, which was a long distance westward from St. Leger's quarters, presented the same scene of confusion and evidences of hasty departure as had the British, and from there we got a large quantity of plunder; but in the Indian camp was nothing left but the lodges, and these we carted into the fort, although they would be of little value to us. It was satisfying to despoil Thayendanega's snakes, even though only to a slight extent.

When another day had come Colonel Gansevoort brought all us merrymakers up with a sharp turn, by forcing us to perform military duty once more. The stores of the British and Tories had all been brought in, and then we were called upon to level the earthworks which had been thrown up at the beginning of the siege, lest General Burgoyne, who had been reported as possibly coming our way, might be able to turn them to his own advantage and our discomfiture.

It was downright hard work to handle shovel and pick hour after hour under the burning rays of the summer sun; but no fellow cared to show himself indolent after having had such rare good fortune, and we petitioned the commandant to let us continue the labor throughout the night, to the end that it might the sooner be performed.

Within six and thirty hours after we had returned from the pursuit matters were so far straightened that we had nothing save ordinary garrison duty to perform, and we lounged around discussing the exciting and mysterious events which we had witnessed, until I dare venture to say that every man was absolutely weary with so much tongue-wagging.

Messengers had been sent on the road toward Stillwater to learn, if possible, what had caused such a panic among the enemy, and Sergeant Corney said to Jacob and me while we were waiting with whatsoever of patience we could command for some definite information to be brought in:

"We must get out of this, lads, within four an' twenty hours after the matter has been made plain, an' we know somewhat concernin' the movements of our friends on the outside."

"How surprised the people of Cherry Valley will be when they hear all that we can tell them!" Jacob said, as if speaking to himself.

"An' is it in your mind, lad, that we're to go back there rather than anywhere else?"

"Where else could we go?" I asked, in surprise.

"I've been thinkin' that we might do our people at home more good by marchin' the Minute Boys to where they could be of real service, than goin' back to let 'em loaf 'round the settlement."

At that moment the old soldier was called away to attend to some duty, and Jacob and I had ample food for thought as we turned over in mind what he had said.

Before the day had come to an end we had reinforcements - when we no longer needed them - in plenty. Company after company of soldiers marched in from the direction of Stillwater, and through the earliest arrivals we learned that twelve hundred men, under General Benedict Arnold, had been sent to our relief.

To our great joy, they could give valuable information regarding the strange behavior of St. Leger's army, and by putting together this and that bit of news we had a fairly good solution to the puzzle before the arrival of General Arnold, who came with a small force twenty hours behind the main body.

And this is the story as we heard it from one source and another until there could be no question but that we had all the facts with no embellishments:

Colonel Willett and Lieutenant Stockwell succeeded in getting past the several encampments without being discovered, and made their way to German Flats. There they procured horses, and rode at full speed until arriving at the headquarters of General Schuyler at Stillwater.

Now it must be understood that when General Washington heard the news of the fall of Ticonderoga, he sent General Benedict Arnold with as many troops as could be gathered, to strengthen the northern army. General Arnold arrived at Stillwater nearabout three weeks before Colonel Willett rode into that place with the request that assistance be sent as soon as possible to Fort Schuyler.

Now it seems, as I have heard it said by those who knew, and, later, have seen it printed, that immediately the messengers from the besieged fort stated the purpose of their coming, General Schuyler, eager to send Colonel Gansevoort all the succor he might, called a council of war to decide upon what should be done, when, greatly to his surprise, he found that the members of his staff were bitterly opposed to weakening the force then at Stillwater by sending any away, even on so important a mission as that of aiding the beleaguered garrison.

Here is what I have seen printed regarding the matter, and I will copy it lest any one think I may have imagined some portion of this contention, which, as we look at the situation now, seems so improbable, for one can hardly believe that any officer in the patriot army would have refused at such a time to aid those who were so sorely pressed as were Gansevoort's troops:

[Footnote: Fiske's "American Revolution."] "General Schuyler understood the importance of rescuing the stronghold and its brave garrison, and called a council of war; but he was bitterly opposed by his officers, one of whom presently said to another, in an audible whisper:

"'He only wants to weaken the army!'

"At this vile accusation the indignant general set his teeth so hard as to bite through the stem of the pipe he was smoking, which fell on the floor and was smashed.

"'Enough!' he cried. 'I assume the whole responsibility. Where is the brigadier who will go?'

"The brigadiers all sat in sullen silence, and Arnold, who had been brooding over his private grievances, suddenly jumped up.

"'Here!' said he. 'Washington sent me here to make myself useful. I will go.'

"The commander gratefully seized him by the hand, and the drum beat for volunteers. Arnold's unpopularity in New England was mainly with the politicians. It did not extend to the common soldiers, who admired his impulsive bravery and had unbounded faith in his resources as a leader. Accordingly twelve hundred Massachusetts men were easily enlisted in the course of the next forenoon, and the expedition started up the Mohawk Valley.

"Arnold pushed on with characteristic energy, but the natural difficulties of the road were such that after a week of hard work he had only reached the German Flats, where he was still more than twenty miles from Fort Schuyler. Believing that no time should be lost, and that everything should be done to encourage the garrison and dishearten the enemy, he had recourse to a stratagem, which succeeded beyond his utmost anticipation.

"A party of Tory spies had just been arrested in the neighborhood, and among them was a certain Yan Yost Cuyler, a queer, half-witted fellow not devoid of cunning, whom the Indians regarded with that mysterious awe with which fools and lunatics are wont to inspire them, as creatures possessed with a devil.

"Yan Yost was summarily condemned to death, and his brother and gipsy-like mother, in wild alarm, hastened to the camp to plead for his life. Arnold for awhile was inexorable, but presently offered to pardon the culprit on condition that he should go and spread a panic in the camp of St. Leger.

"Yan Yost joyfully consented, and started off forthwith, while his brother was detained as a hostage, to be hanged in case of his failure. To make the matter still surer, some friendly Oneidas were sent along to keep an eye upon him and act in concert with him.

"Next day St. Leger's scouts, as they stole through the forest, began to hear rumors that Burgoyne had been totally defeated, and that a great American army was coming up the valley of the Mohawk. They carried back these rumors to the camp, and, while officers and soldiers were standing about in anxious consultation, Yan Yost came running in, with a dozen bullet-holes in his coat and terror in his face, and said that he had barely escaped with his life from the resistless American host which was close at hand.

"As many knew him for a Tory, his tale found ready belief, and, when interrogated as to the numbers of the advancing host, he gave a warning frown and pointed significantly to the countless leaves that fluttered on the branches overhead."

[Footnote: Lossing's "Field Book American Revolution."] "The Indians were greatly agitated. They had been decoyed into their present situation, and had been moody and uneasy since the battle of Oriskany. At the moment of Yan Yost's arrival they were engaged in a religious observance, - a consultation, through their prophet, of the Great Spirit, to supplicate his guidance and protection.

"The council of chiefs at the powwow at once resolved upon flight, and told St. Leger so. He sent for and questioned Yan Yost, who told him that Arnold, with two thousand men, would be upon him in twenty-four hours.

"At that moment, according to arrangements, the friendly Oneida who had taken a circuitous route approached the camp from another direction with a belt. On his way he met two or three straggling Indians of his tribe, who joined him, and they all confirmed the story of Yan Yost. They pretended that a bird had brought them the news that the valley below was swarming with warriors.

"One said that the army of Burgoyne was cut in pieces, and another told St. Leger that Arnold had three thousand men near at hand. They shook their heads mysteriously when questioned about the numbers of the enemy, and pointed, like Yan Yost, upward to the leaves.

"The savages, now thoroughly alarmed, prepared to flee. St. Leger tried every means, by offers of bribes and promises, to induce them to remain, but the panic and suspicion of foul play had determined them to go. He tried to make them drunk, but they refused to drink. He then besought them to take the rear of his army in retreating; this they refused, and indignantly said:

"'You mean to sacrifice us. When you marched down, you said there would be no fighting for us Indians; we might go down and smoke our pipes; whereas numbers of our warriors have been killed, and you mean to sacrifice us also.'

"Nothing more was needed to complete the panic. It was in vain that Sir John and St. Leger coaxed and threatened the savages. They were already filled with fear, and while a certain number deliberately ran away, taking their squaws with them, others drank rum until they were drunk, and began to assault the officers."

That is the story as has been set down by others, and I have already told what we ourselves saw. All which seemed so unaccountable to us at that time, would have been as plain as the sun at noon-day had we possessed the key to the seeming riddle.

Chapter XX

Enlisted Men

On the morning after General Arnold's arrival, when we learned that the reinforcements which had been sent to us at Fort Schuyler were to be marched directly back to the main army then at Stillwater, the Minute Boys held a conference to decide what should be done, for it was in my mind that each member of the company had a right to discuss freely the question that must be settled without delay.

We knew that Peter Sitz was to return to Cherry Valley as soon as he could make ready for the journey, and I was of the belief that Jacob desired to accompany his father; but never a word had passed between us on the subject.

From all we could hear concerning affairs in the Mohawk Valley, it seemed much as if the senseless panic among St. Leger's force had resulted in breaking up the combination between the British and the Indians, in which case Thayendanega would not be able to ravage the country nearabout Cherry Valley, as he had doubtless counted on.

When I considered the matter, with a sickness for home in my heart, it seemed much as if my proper place was with my parents, and there, if trouble should come, I would be able to strike a blow in defence of those I loved; but while listening to the conversation of the soldiers, and being brought to understand how sorely the colonists needed the aid which should come from their midst, I said to myself that strong, hulking lads like our Minute Boys ought to be ashamed to do other than remain in the service, doing their part in showing the king that we would have no more of his misrule.

It seemed to me that Sergeant Corney was averse to talking with any of us concerning the future, for, as soon as it was known that we must decide at once upon some course, he kept aloof whenever he heard two or three discussing the question of what we Minute Boys ought to do, now that we were no longer needed at Fort Schuyler.

I have thus set down that which was in my mind at the time, not that it is of any especial importance, but to the end that he who reads may understand how undecided I was as to what my company had best do at such a time; and I believe every person will realize that a lad's love for country must be great when it prompts him to turn his back on home and loved ones after having passed through as many dangers as had our boys from Cherry Valley.

During the evening previous I had notified all the members of the company that we would meet in the barracks at eight o'clock in the morning to decide what course should be pursued, and considerably before the time set every lad was in waiting; but Sergeant Corney did not put in an appearance.

We had come to consider him as the head and front of the Minute Boys, and his absence at such an important time seemed odd, to say the least.

"I believe he has it in mind to join General Arnold's force," John Sammons said, when the hour for the conference had come and passed without the sergeant's having shown himself, and the idea of such a possibility brought a strange sensation of loneliness to my heart.

Then Jacob suggested that the old man might have been detained against his will at headquarters, and I proposed that the lad go at once to learn if such was the case.

He did not absolutely refuse to obey what might have been considered as an order from the captain, but tried to shift the duty by saying:

"It would be of more avail for you to go, Noel, if so be the old man really has it in mind to enlist under General Arnold. You have ever been a favorite of his, whereas I am little more than an outsider, who has caused you an' he much trouble an' sufferin'."

The lad did not really believe his own statements, but made them simply to shift the duty to my shoulders, for it was a bold and might be considered an impertinent act for us to presume to advise or urge one of so much and so varied experience as Sergeant Corney.

I set off without further parley, and to my great surprise found the old man on the parade-ground talking idly with Peter Sitz.

"Had you forgotten that the company was called together at eight o'clock this mornin'?" I asked, as if in surprise.

"Not a bit of it, lad."

"Then why didn't you come to the barracks?"

"I knew you lads had somewhat of importance to decide, an' wasn't countin' on goin' where I might be said to have influenced you."

"But don't you reckon yourself as belongin' any longer to the company?"

"I didn't count on bein' able to pass myself off for a boy, even among blind men," the old soldier said, with a laugh, and I cried, hotly:

"That isn't answerin' my question, sergeant. Is there any good reason why you should stand stiffly here while we're tryin' to make up our minds what to do?"

"Yes, lad, I believe there is."

"What may it be, if you're willin' to tell us?"

"It shouldn't be hard to guess. All my life long I've followed soldierin' as another man follows a trade, an' I'm not the one who ought to speak when lads are makin' up their minds as to the future, lest I say that which pleases me, an' may not be the best thing for them."

"Answer me one question squarely, Sergeant Corney, without beatin' about the bush. Do you think we're too young to enlist as soldiers, if it so be the lads decide that the Minute Boys ought to do all they can for the Cause?"

"Not a bit of it; it strikes me your company has shown that it may be of value in any army, an' I'll go bail Colonel Gansevoort will agree with me. What say you, Peter Sitz?"

"Speakin' for my Jacob, he's shown that his services are not to be despised in sich warfare as we're like to have in the valley; but it must be for him to say what he'll do, without word or look from me."

Now it was that I began to understand what these two were driving at. They were minded that we of the company should decide the question before us without aid from them, and it was not difficult to guess that, in their opinion, the Minute Boys ought to remain where they could do the best service for the colony.

However, I was determined that they should be present while we discussed the matter, and by dint of much coaxing finally succeeded in my purpose.

When we were all together I put the matter before the lads to the best of my ability, asking each to say if he was minded to go home at once, or whether he would be willing to regularly enlist in the American army, and before any other could speak John Sammons made a suggestion which showed him to be a lad of rare good sense.

"It seems to me that it would be a good idea to first learn whether we're wanted in the army. There's hardly one among us of an age to be taken as a recruit, an' if they won't let us enlist as a full company, allowin' our own officers to remain in command, I for my part would rather go home."

There could be no question but that very many of us shared John's ideas, and then came the question as to how we might learn what we wanted to know.

This we could not determine upon until Peter Sitz said, quietly:

"Most likely Colonel Gansevoort can tell you in short order; but, if he can't, he won't be long in findin' out from General Arnold."

This was just the suggestion we needed, and then came the question as to who would go to the commandant. I flatly refused, because it would look too much as if I was eager to hold my rank as captain, and after considerable tongue-wagging it was decided that Jacob should tackle the job, his father agreeing to go with him to headquarters.

While these two were absent we talked much among ourselves, and I soon learned that every member of the company was willing to remain in service if it could be done as regularly enlisted men, holding together as a separate company.

Sergeant Corney would take no part in the discussion. He flatly refused to give an opinion until after the matter had been fully decided; but I knew full well the old man would remain with us, even though we were only a company of boys.

Then Jacob and his father returned, and there was no

need of further talk.

"The commandant says that we have only to present ourselves before General Schuyler in order to be enlisted as we desire," Jacob reported. "He promises to write a letter to the general at once, telling him of how much service we have been here in the fort, an' agrees to provide us with provisions for the march, with two baggage-wagons to haul the stores. We're to have from the plunder gotten out of St. Leger's camp all we may need in way of an outfit, so that we'll really show up before the commander equipped for service without cost to the colonies."

Thus the matter was settled. With such a generous offer from the commandant never a member of the company could have hung back had he so desired; but I am proud to say that each and every one of them was eager to join the army, since it might be done as regular soldiers.

Then it was that Sergeant Corney had his say, and he was by no means niggardly with words.

First he congratulated us on having performed such good service that the commander under whom we served was pleased to do all in his power to give us a good send-off, and then declared that he had rather enlist with us than in any regiment of the army. If we had decided to go to Cherry Valley, it was his purpose to join General Arnold's force; but now that he could remain with the Minute Boys he was content.

We were proud lads that day, for it seemed as if every officer and soldier in the fort was eager to give us some word of praise, and those with whom we had served watched jealously when our equipment was being selected from the plunder of the British camp, lest we might not get the best of everything.

We had our hands full of business making ready for the march, when Reuben Cox came shyly up to where Sergeant Corney and I were looking after the stowage of goods in the wagons, and said to me in a half-whisper, as if fearing others might hear him:

"I don't reckon your company is any place for a man who has shown himself sich a sneak as I am, eh?"

"Would you like to go with us?" I asked, in surprise, and pitying from the bottom of my heart the man who was so deeply repentant.

"That I would, Captain Campbell. It may be in time I can live down my record, providin' there be any one who'll look to what I may do, instead of always thinkin' of what I have done."

"But the men in the fort have been kind to you of late, Cox?" I said, questioningly.

"Ay, that they have, considerin' what I've done, an' how nearly I came to workin' the worst of harm to all hands here; but I can see by their eyes that they're always thinkin' I may play the same dirty game agin, though God knows I'd stand at the stake with never a whimper till the life was burned out of me rather than do one of them another wrong."

Had I felt at liberty to decide the matter then and there, Cox would have been a member of the Minute Boys without further parley; but it was only right I should consult the others, therefore I told him to come again within an hour, when I would give him an answer.

He thanked me humbly, and was about to go away, when Sergeant Corney took him by the hand as he said:

"What's in the past can't be brought back for the fixin'; but we've got in our own keepin' the shapin' of the to-morrows. I'm thinkin' you won't go astray agin, Reuben Cox, an' whenever I see a chance to speak a good word for you it shall be said."

The man's face lighted up wonderfully, and in my heart I thanked the old sergeant over and over for having been thus kind to one who, having committed the worst crime possible for a soldier, stood ready to give up his life cheerfully to the end that he might atone.

I called the lads together without loss of time, repeating to them what Cox had said, and again was I made glad when they agreed without hesitation to take him among us.

John Sammons was sent to bring up the new member of the company, and Sergeant Corney said, grimly, as he tried without avail to pucker his wrinkled face into a frown:

"At this rate you'll soon lose the right to call yourselves Minute *Boys*, because this 'ere company is fast becomin' a refuge for the aged and outcast."

There was to be mourning as well as gladness among us on this the last day we were to spend in Fort Schuyler.

Toward noon a messenger from the general commanding came in, bringing with him the sad news that General Herkimer was dead of his wounds, or, perhaps I should say, because of his wounds.

As we were told, the general was safely taken to his home after the battle, being carried on a litter the entire distance. The weather was very warm, and soon the wound became gangrenous. Nine days after his arrival, a young French surgeon who had been with General Arnold's force visited the house, and claimed that the injured limb should be cut off without delay, as the only means of saving the sufferer's life.

The family doctor objected very strongly; but the general's family had faith in the Frenchman, although it is claimed he had evidently been drinking heavily, and the leg was cut off. The operation was performed so unskilfully that it was impossible to entirely check the flow of blood, and the Frenchman, indulging in more wine, became so badly intoxicated that, even had he known how, it would have been beyond his power to take the proper measures.

There was no other surgeon to be had, and toward the close of the day, when the brave old general came to understand that his end was very near, he asked for the Bible, from which he read aloud the thirty-eighth psalm, immediately afterward sinking back upon the pillow dead.

"Murdered if ever a man was!" Sergeant Corney cried, when the sad story had been brought to an end, and I was of the same opinion.

There are several forms of mutiny, and some of them

are called by other names, but all as dangerous as they are wicked. Because many of those who badgered the brave old soldier to his death paid the full penalty of their crime in the ravine under the hatchet or knife of the savages, it may not be well to say harsh words concerning them; but so long as I live there will always be anger in my heart whenever I hear their names mentioned.

During that evening, after everything had been made ready for the march at an early hour next morning, we lads gave to Peter Sitz messages for the loved ones at Cherry Valley, promising that we would never bring disgrace upon the settlement, and so burdening his mind with this matter and the other that, if the poor man remembered but the half of all the words we entrusted him with, he must have had a most prodigious memory.

Right proud was I when I marched out of the fort next morning at the head of my company, followed by the two baggage-wagons; but yet there was a sorrow in my heart because it seemed, in a certain degree, at least, as if by becoming regularly enlisted men we gave up our claim to the name of Minute Boys of the Mohawk Valley.

Those under whom we served did not view the matter in the same light I did, however, for we kept the title we liked best during all the time we served in the army.

It would please me to set down here an account of the adventures which were ours after becoming enlisted men, but it must not be done, else I might never bring the tale to a close, for we saw very much during the time our people were convincing the king, and surely did our duty at Bemis Heights, otherwise our company would never have been mentioned in the flattering terms it then was.

It causes me most profound sorrow to say that our company was far away, fighting for the Cause to the best of our ability, when our homes at Cherry Valley were destroyed and many of our loved ones massacred by the fiendish savages, and there is always in my heart a cruel joy that we lads who had been trained by Sergeant Corney avenged that dastardly act of Thayendanega's in such manly fashion that he must have remembered the reprisals to his dying day.

Then it was we showed ourselves to be Minute Boys of the Mohawk Valley in good truth, however we may have been spoken of elsewhere, and if it so be the good God spares my life sufficiently long I propose to set down the story of that vengeance, when more than one of us, sorely wounded, continued the chase, upheld even when exhausted nigh unto death by the thoughts of what our loved ones had been made to suffer by that wolf in human shape - Joseph Brant.

www.ingramcontent.com/pod-product-compliance
Lightning Source LLC
Chambersburg PA
CBHW031059260626
47172CB00001B/132